One

THE ANTHOLOGY

One

THE ANTHOLOGY

Edited by Robert Yeo

Marshall Cavendish Editions

© 2012 Marshall Cavendish International (Asia) Private Limited

Designed by Bernard Go Kwang Meng

Published by Marshall Cavendish Editions
An imprint of Marshall Cavendish International
1 New Industrial Road, Singapore 536196

All rights reserved

No part of this publication may be reproduced, stored in a retrieval system or transmitted, in any form or by any means, electronic, mechanical, photocopying, recording or otherwise, without the prior permission of the copyright owner. Request for permission should be addressed to the Publisher, Marshall Cavendish International (Asia) Private Limited, 1 New Industrial Road, Singapore 536196. Tel: (65) 6213 9300, Fax: (65) 6285 4871. E-mail: genref@sg.marshallcavendish.com. Website: www.marshallcavendish.com/genref

The publisher makes no representation or warranties with respect to the contents of this book, and specifically disclaims any implied warranties or merchantability or fitness for any particular purpose, and shall in no events be liable for any loss of profit or any other commercial damage, including but not limited to special, incidental, consequential, or other damages.

Other Marshall Cavendish Offices:
Marshall Cavendish International. PO Box 65829 London EC1P 1NY, UK • Marshall Cavendish Corporation. 99 White Plains Road, Tarrytown NY 10591-9001, USA • Marshall Cavendish International (Thailand) Co Ltd. 253 Asoke, 12th Flr, Sukhumvit 21 Road, Klongtoey Nua, Wattana, Bangkok 10110, Thailand • Marshall Cavendish (Malaysia) Sdn Bhd, Times Subang, Lot 46, Subang Hi-Tech Industrial Park, Batu Tiga, 40000 Shah Alam, Selangor Darul Ehsan, Malaysia.

Marshall Cavendish is a trademark of Times Publishing Limited

National Library Board Singapore Cataloguing in Publication Data
One : the anthology / edited by Robert Yeo. – Singapore : Marshall Cavendish Editions, c2012.
p. cm.
ISBN : 978-981-4346-39-9

1. Short stories, Singaporean (English)   I. Yeo, Robert.

PR9570.S52
S823 — dc22   OCN768385132

Printed by Fabulous Printers Pte Ltd

To Catherine Lim

CONTENTS

INTRODUCTION 9

The Terrorist	12	S Rajaratnam
The Expatriate	24	Lim Thean Soo
The Shoes Of My Sensei	36	Goh Sin Tub
The Leg Glance	41	Gopal Baratham
Interrogating Photographs	48	Robert Yeo
A Beginning and a Middle Without an Ending	55	Arthur Yap
Lee Geok Chan	59	Catherine Lim
Amarjit's Whiskey Goes Awry	64	Kirpal Singh
Gloria	70	Suchen Christine Lim
Birds of Paradise	89	Minfong Ho
Everyday Will Be Sunday	105	Don Bosco

The Phenwick Phenomenon	111	Simon Tay
Painting the Tiger	133	Philip Jeyaretnam
Crossing Distance	139	Tan Mei Ching
Hell Hath No Fury	156	Claire Tham
Poisson Ivy	170	Colin Cheong
The First Day	184	David Leo
The Borrowed Boy	194	Alfian Sa'at
Bards By Numbers: The Fundamentals	209	Jeffery Lim
Turning a Blind Eye	216	O Thiam Chin
It's a Wonderful Lie	224	Felix Cheong

ABOUT THE AUTHORS AND THEIR STORIES 228

INTRODUCTION
Robert Yeo

This selection continues the work of anthologising the Singaporean short story that began with *Singapore Short Story Volumes I and II*, back in 1978 and *Singular Stories* in 1993. When I started my research in the mid-seventies, short story writing was in its infancy. I noted that Catherine Lim was the first to appear with a single volume of stories entitled *Little Ironies* in 1978. This year, as I write, the prolific and indefatigible Lim has nearly a dozen short story collections to her credit. Others have followed in her productive wake, publishing works after 1978, though a few of them, like Lim Thean Soo, Goh Sin Tub and Gopal Baratham were born before her.

The last sentence may suggest that this present selection has a historical basis. Yes, it has, to a certain extent. It begins with a story published as far back as the mid-forties, by S. Raja Ratnam, in London in a book edited by Denys Val Baker called *Modern International Short Stories*. Raja Ratnam was listed in the page of contents as having come from India but in fact he was none other than S. Rajaratnam, who was later to become Singapore's first Minister for Culture in self-governing Singapore in 1959 and the first Foreign Minister after independence in 1965. Irene Ng's pioneering biography of him reveals, especially in Chapter 5 of *Rajaratnam: The Singapore Lion,* his activities as a crusading writer of short fiction in London in the years 1941 to 1948.

Researching for the 1978 collection, I had come across Rajaratnam's stories in T. Wignesan's *Bunga Emas* (1964). In fact, the two volumes began with a Rajaratnam story called *The Tiger*. It is appropriate, in this sort of summing-up selection, to again begin with him.

The historical trajectory continues with stories by pioneers who have passed on: Lim Thean Soo, Goh Sin Tub and Gopal Baratham. That all three, as well as Rajaratnam, have left and will not, obviously write any more stories, increases the sense of this collection observing a chronology.

Rajaratnam's story, *The Terrorist*, has a contemporary relevance. The next two stories reflect, conveniently, Singapore's post-war history - British colonial retreat and the Japanese Occupation of Singapore. After that, the chronology observes the date of birth of those who come after the first four and who are still actively writing, namely, Catherine Lim and myself. This is a merely convenient means of organising this anthology and does not necessarily observe the year of publication.

I have called these stories *One* because I wanted to make a dramatic point. Select one story from each author as the best, according to me.

This one story per author is not intended to be representative of the author's total output. I have a few criteria for selection and one of them is a remark from a 1983 book *The Short Story: A Critical Introduction* by Valerie Shaw. She wrote, "There are so many kinds of short story that the genre as a whole seems constantly to resist universal definition..."

The stories in this book are largely realistic and the narration is driven by character in crisis resulting in incidents leading or not leading to an end. The great Indian novelist and short story writer R. K. Narayan, wrote in *Malgudi Days* (1982), "Speaking for myself, I discover a story when a personality passes through a crisis of spirit or circumstances." I have found this sentence of his to be a good guide to my selection.

Departures from the practice mentioned above are few. It is another way of saying that the Singaporean short story, considered as a whole, is not experimental. In my introduction to *Singular Stories*, I cited Catherine Lim's *O Singapore! Stories in Celebration* as veering from her usual practice of writing naturalistic stories in linear form. Others have followed, but not in a big way. Simon Tay, in *Stand Alone* (1991) and Jeffrey Lim in

Faith Lies (1999). I have included one of Jeffery Lim's stories, one of mine, and one from Arthur Yap as examples of writing different from the conventionally-narrated stories in this anthology. Stories have been chosen from books rather than from print or online magazines. This is done in the belief that in this way, it is possible to trace a line of writing resulting from sustained effort, over several books and years. Many of the authors represented here have at least one or more collections to his/her credit and demonstrate preoccupation with the short story genre.

I may be wrong in emphasising my selection from books rather than magazines and am aware that good stories have been published in journals like *Singa,* which had a long life or the e-journal *Quarterly Literary Review of Singapore.*

With rare exceptions, I have included stories that have not been anthologised before. This selection may surprise some but I hope careful reading will show the extent to which the short story in Singapore has developed over the years, commencing in the late eighties.

There is no attempt to suggest that the writing in this genre was a connected enterprise with writers keeping an eye on each other's latest publication and contributing to a developing, continuous practice. But the number of writers publishing short stories do point to a common preoccupation that could be part of a developing canon in the Singaporean short story scene.

I see no need to apologise for canon formation. As a new country with a formative literature, it is good, every now and then, to make a statement such as this, and say, these are the twenty-one stories that should stand out and be counted.

December 2011
Singapore

THE TERRORIST
S. Rajaratnam

"Got a cigarette?"

His voice betrayed his nervous restlessness. "Yes," said his companion, his thick, ponderous lips twisting into an assuring grin, "I should have a few somewhere. That's right. Calm yourself. Steady your nerves. I know how it feels."

The Khan fumbled in his shirt pockets, and brought out a crumpled packet of cigarettes. He extracted one carefully. "Here you are, comrade," said the Khan. The cigarette was brilliantly white against the black fingers. Strong, dangerous fingers, thought Sen dully. The fingers of a killer.

"Thanks!", he said in a flat tone.

"Light?"

There was a hiss between the cupped hands of the Khan. Sen bent forward. Hands like a pair of hooded cobras, he reflected. As Sen drew, the flame spluttered and trembled. His cigarette lit, he straightened up, but his gaze was still fixed upon the Khan's hands. The Khan let the match burn on, watching the flames steal towards his fingers. Then deliberately he seized the blackened head with his free hand, and turned the stick upright. The flame climbed up shuddering as if in the last throes of death. Then it was gone, suddenly and silently. All that remained of it was a deformed black worm.

The Khan studied it intently. Smouldering, piggish eyes sunk in folds of fat.

"Thus, comrade, it must be," he said. "His end, like the last flash of a flame. Quick and silent."

Sen shrugged his shoulders. Ever since he had got into the train that evening, he was oppressed by a feeling that he had stumbled into an unreal world—a fantastic dream in somebody else's mind, in which he himself was a bloodless puppet dancing to the dreamer's desire. The Khan beside him, big and ugly, was a monster spun out in such a dream. And yet...

Slowly he thrust his hands into his pocket, and his fingers touched the cold hard metal of a gun. This was real. Caged in its steel belly was a terrible power. He shivered.

The compartment was dimly lit. The electric bulbs lolled like gouged, jaundiced eyes. Through a still, heavy curtain of smoke he discerned the blurred shapes of a few passengers. At the far end of the carriage a woman bared her big swollen breast to the whimpering mouth of her shrivelled up child. A man seated opposite her, a shadowy gnome, caressed her with his glances. He had seen such a picture in one of the cheaper magazines. How long ago? Yesterday? The day before? Last week? Last year?

Faces and forms swum before his eyes, melting, whirling and breaking apart as in a trick film. The atmosphere was hot and sticky, and he was choked by the pungent odor of unclean, half naked bodies. He sat up and struggled with the catch of the window, but it held fast. His fingers were weak and numbed. His hands caressed the smooth, cold surface of the thick plate of glass, with a strange pleasure. Eagerly he pressed his hot cheeks against it. His tired burning eyes were soothed by the rich blackness of the night outside which encompassed the train like an ocean of black oil. Occasionally a spray of sparks from the engine traced jagged lines of fire. Staring through the plate glass he became conscious of the transparent reflection of his own features. He studied it a little curiously. So this was him! This thin, formless shadow, with two black holes for eye sockets! A young revolutionary who but a year ago had studied for his arts degree. The principal of the college, Dr Mukerjee, had said, "You have talents, my boy. Our country needs men like you." The ghostly lips that trembled in the plate glass curved bitterly. Poor Dr Mukerjee! If you could only see me now! Yesterday another voice had spoken to him. A cold steely voice. "Comrade Sen, you have drawn the blank card. I am glad, comrade, for I know I can trust you to carry out our purpose. You are one of our best men. With more men like you, comrade, we can win great things for our country."

Sen had said, "Thank you, comrade. I shall do my best." He remembered now the thin, shadowed face under the hanging oil lamp. It had smiled and nodded.

When Sen open his eyes there was a twinkle of lights outside. Pale green trees rose out of the darkness and vanished. Underneath the street lamps a road wriggled like a hurrying snake. Vacant-faced houses and open-mouthed huts flitted past. As the train hurried on the lights grew thicker and more confused reminding him of a swarm of bees with their wings on fire. Here and there he caught sight of a few people. Once a woman under a street lamp lifted her face and looked up, her black, liquid eyes mocking at him. Then she was gone. Who was she, I wonder? She looked so young and so lonely under the yellow light.

"What place was that we passed?" he asked the Khan.

"I couldn't tell you," he answered, yawning. "Some village hole, perhaps. Why?"

"I just asked. Thought you might know."

They were silent for awhile.

"How long is it before the train gets to Midnapore?" asked Sen suddenly.

"There is enough time, comrade. You mustn't be impatient."

"I am not impatient. I only asked. Musn't I ask?" His voice was sharp.

"Quiet, comrade. You want everybody awake?" There was a pause. "What time is it?" asked the Khan.

Sen looked at his watch. "Eleven," he said.

"*Ummm*... The train gets to Midnapore at five. That's where we have taken our tickets to. But we get off at Jaleswar instead of going all the way to Midnapore."

"Yes, yes. I know all that," said Sen impatiently. "We have gone through that over and over again."

He is afraid that I might bungle up everything, thought Sen. But what is there to bungle? Everything had been planned to the very minute. Even the ticket to Midnapore instead of Jaleswar was the Khan's idea. The Khan was clever. "The booking-clerk or somebody may remember us. If they search for us they would comb Midnapore…" the Khan had said chuckling.

"You are sure he is alone," asked Sen. "He hasn't his secretary with him or anything?"

"Oh! He is alone all right," said the Khan, "I had a good peep into his private compartment. Well, this is Sir Lal Chand's last journey, eh? There will be one less swine in our country."

The Khan spat out Sir Lal Chand's name as if it were some abomination.

But to-night Sir Lal Chand evoked in Sen no profound emotions. He could not feel the hatred and contempt he felt towards Sir Lal Chand only yesterday. Sir Lal Chand was a traitor and an enemy of his country. Three weeks ago two of the comrades had fallen riddled with bullets from the guns of Sir Lal Chand's special police. The next day Sir Lal Chand had told the press, "We shall hunt down these hot-heads as though they were mad dogs. As mad dogs we will shoot them on sight."

Sir Lal Chand had set out his task energetically and ruthlessly. Many comrades had been arrested; a few shot. He was no fool. He was dangerous. "We must crush him like a dirty beetle before he crushes us," one comrade has said at the meeting.

But now Sir Lal Chand was no more than another ghost in this mad, mad dream. Caged within these walls of glass and varnished wood like actors they had their prescribed parts to play. Within a few hours he would kill a man in cold blood, according to a plan worked out with the precision of a watch. All his actions had been rehearsed over and over again, so that without thinking each action dovetailed into the next. If he could only *feel* some hatred towards his victim now. Oh! But it didn't matter what he felt… he was the instrument of the Cause… useless to struggle… the watch was ticking… tick… tock… tick…

Kill… kill… kill.

The sharp, quick rhythm of the train reached a higher pitch. How fast the train shot through space! Fifty… sixty… seventy miles an hour.

Fifty… sixty… seventy.

Fifty… sixty… seventy.

It reverberated like the mad frenzy of jungle drums.

Around him heads lolled as though their necks were broken.

I must think. Useless to think. I must. There must be no slip up. The plan… the plan. I remember… The Khan would go first, and then I must follow him. Into the compartment… the Khan outside on guard… shoot into the face of the sleeping man. Into the face, remember. Don't you worry, the gun has a silencer… That's all. Then back to the seat. No. No. NO. Recollect. Oh! Yes! I must get rid of the gun through the lavatory window, and wash any stains. The hands, especially Of course, there was bound to be some blood. We get off at Jaleswar, but not together remember. You don't know one another. We meet again, said the Khan, at the Circus… Circus… Circus…

Who was the Khan? What was his real name? But then everyone in the party had false names. It was the rule that members were not to find out anything about one another. Not even where they lived. It was safer. But the Khan was an old hand at this game. This is not the first time the Khan had travelled on such a mission. What was the Khan?

Out of the grey mist the Khan's face floated towards him. It was bigger and uglier than ever. The small, black eyes darted like a cobra's. The thick lips spilt apart, and he heard the crunch of gold teeth. The hot, moist breath from the Khan's mouth suffocated him. Then a strong black hand materialised out of the swirling vapour. The fingers were fat as slugs, filled with blood. The Khan slashed him across the face. He felt the blood spatter in his face, and run down his cheeks. He cried out in terror….

"Quiet, comrade. Quiet…" a voice hissed into his ear. His arms were held as if in a vice.

"Pull yourself together," whispered the Khan. "You must do it now."

"Now?" he echoed vaguely.

"Wake up, comrade. That's better. I have just come back from his compartment. He is fast asleep. You are ready?"

Sen nodded. His face was bathed in perspiration.

"Good," said the Khan, "I shall go first."

He saw the Khan vanish through the door. The carriage was dimmer, and colder. Upon the plate glass droplets of water shone like pearls. It had rained.

Sen got up and walked towards the floor. He could feel the floor throbbing underneath his feet. Treading softly and carefully along the shaking train he reached the door and opened it. The cold air hit him like a wave, washing away the last traces of sleep. The roar of the train was like the crash of cymbals.

As he moved into the next carriage his senses suddenly became alert. His being tingled with the watchfulness of an animal on the hunt, He moved along the narrow, ill-lit corridor, swaying, crouching. Nothing else functioned except his muscles and instincts. He was startled to see the bulky figure of the Khan at the end of the corridor. The Khan nodded reassuringly.

"In there," whispered the Khan, thumb indicating the compartment door. "Good luck, comrade."

The Khan left him.

Sen's eyes were riveted to the door. Behind the glass the blinds were drawn. His right hand slid into his pocket, reached for the handle of the door. Its brass knob was icy cold. He drew it slowly, and the door slid back, noiselessly, effortlessly. He entered and shut the door after him. It was dark within. He stood there with tensed muscles, his eyes striving to tear aside the veil of darkness. Underneath him the grinding wheels shrieked louder, louder...

So this was it! Within the next few seconds he would kill this man whom as yet he could not see. His gun was out, finger at ready round the trigger. Damn it, if only I can only see his face! I dare not move.

Then he became aware of small phosphorescent spots at the far end of the corridor... Of course that was a clock. Eyeing it intently he discerned its faint outlines. The black mist lifted gradually. Besides the clock he now saw a dark blob against the grey of the pillow, and then the figure of the sleeping man.

Sir Lal Chand. Traitor, enemy, swine...!

But these words meant nothing to him now. Even if he were a friend he would have to shoot him. Have to? Why? But his mind denied him the comfort of thought. He felt that he was in the grip of a weird spell as he moved forward slowly, the gun pointing downwards. As he bent forward he could hear the sound of breathing fill the compartment. His muscles were flexed so taut they ached. The huddled form was still, containing within it all its unrealised hopes and ambitions. What plan of action was embedded in that head which lay so still. Sen started at the dim face.

A warning bell rang in his brain. Stop thinking. Act… act… do it now.

What happened after that touched him with a terrible terror. The sleeping man's eyelids parted, and he saw the furtive glints of his eyes. Instantly the face became a blurr…

He fired.

The crash of the gun echoed and re-echoed in his ears. Each was like an explosion that shook the train from end to end. He waited, fists clenched in fear, expecting the mad rush of people into his compartment, the piercing shrieks of terror…

But all he head was the rhythmic beat of the train.

Clangity, clangity, clang.

Clangity, clangity, clang.

He was weak, and he felt the trickle of sweat run down his face. Gradually the intensity of his sensations subsided, and slowly his mind began to tick.

The compartment was filled with the acrid smell of gunpowder. He blinked his eyes and stared at the relaxed body. The right hand which hung over the sides of the bed swung with the motion of the train. In his mind the words formed slowly: *He's dead.*

He heard the pounding of his own heart. He's dead. I must get out of here. At once.

Sen backed towards the door, his eyes still glued to the dangling arm. He fumbled for the door handle, and felt its cold surface. As the door slid back a narrow streak of light fell across the bed. It widened gradually. The pillow was a sparkling crimson. But it was the face lying upon it which made him stiffen. The wide open eyes were flowering at him, glinting like hot charcoals.

He shut the door quickly. He shuddered and something cold crawled over his skin. Panting with this new upsurge of terror, he looked frantically about him. The corridor was deserted and ghostlike. I must get back to my seat. Quickly. The corridor seemed endless. He would never reach the end of it. If somebody should come down the corridor he would scream. The swaying train flung him form side to side. Where am I going? God, the corridor was long! What was that? There was a sharp click of metal against the glass. What was it he was holding in his hand? The gun! He had to get rid of the gun. Where was he going? The lavatory! God, he nearly forgot it! I am going to explode. I am loosing my head.

To the left of him, at the end of the corridor, was the lavatory door. He jerked it open, blinked at the white blur within. He shut the door and fastened the bolt. He leant against the door. Slowly his body relaxed, his head drooping forward, eyes closed. His breathing became more and more regular.

When he opened his eyes he saw his face reflected in the mirror opposite. Whose face was that? Haggard, eyes large and staring. A stranger's face. Whose? *A murderer's!* He laughed, but it was more like a snarl.

First the gun. He opened the lavatory door, and with the cold air there rushed in the roar of the train. The patch of light writhed, rose and fell outside. He wiped the gun carefully, and flung it away.

Now he examined himself. His right hand fingers were red and sticky with blood, and lower down his shirt a large blood stain.

He washed his hands carefully, and then he attended to the stain upon his shirt, but he could not get it off as easily. He swore. But he found that if he buttoned his coat it could not be seen. He would remember to get rid of the shirt at the first opportunity.

When he returned to his seat the Khan was waiting for him.

"All right?" whispered the Khan.

"Yes. All right."

A pause.

"You let him have it in the face?"

"Yes. The face."

"You are sure? You looked?"

"Yes."

"Good. And the gun?"

"What do you think?" Sen was irritated. He wished the Khan would shut up.

"I am sorry, comrade," said the Khan, "I know how you feel. You will feel better tomorrow. But I have to make sure that nothing has been overlooked."

"Of course, that's your job. Anything else you would like to know?"

"Yes, what time is it?"

"Ten to three."

"In fifteen minutes the train will reach Jaleswar. You know what we must do."

"Yes," said Sen. "We must leave separately and then we meet at the Circus. Tell me if I am wrong."

The Khan shot a quick glance at him.

"You are tired, comrade. Just relax. I shall be glad when this is all over."

Sen sank back in his seat, his eyes closed. Was this all a dream? Would he wake up suddenly out of this nightmare and find himself in his own room…?

He felt the Khan's hands upon his shoulder.

"We are there, comrade," said the Khan. "I am getting off the next carriage. Don't forget. The Circus."

"I won't."

The Khan smiled at him. Then the Khan's bulky form slid through the carriage, and vanished. The Khan reminded him of a python wriggling its way though a jungle.

Through the window Sen noticed the dance of lights outside. The train was slowing down. A signal box almost scraped the window. Innumerable steel rails glistened. Sharp clicks of metal as the wheels slid over the points. Pale coloured hoardings glided past the window, slowly. The train drew to a standstill. The sound of rebounding couplings passed and re-passed in waves. A long drawn out hiss of escaping steam, and the train stopped.

Sen got up. The passengers eyed him sleepily. He smiled at the woman with the child.

As he got off the train he sighed. The station was a small building of red bricks. A porter or two rushed about shouting at the top of their voices. As he stood on the gravel platform his eyes travelled the length of the train until they rested upon the dark window frame of the next carriage. He had an irresistible desire to walk up to the window and look inside. But suppose those amber eyes turned to meet his with pain and pleading…?

He hurried towards the exit, already jostling with passengers. He saw the Khan at the head of the queue. Then he stiffened, for beside the ticket collector stood a policeman. Lazily glancing at each passenger who passed through the barrier.

He saw the Khan hand over the ticket. As the Khan was about to walk away the policeman caught him by the arm. Sen felt limp. Had something gone wrong?

He could see the Khan talking, waving his hands energetically. Every gesture of the Khan's told of his rising indignation. Sen envied the Khan his smooth powers of rhetoric. The policeman let go of the Khan's arm with a shrug of his shoulders. As the Khan walked away Sen suddenly wished the Khan were beside him. The Khan was capable, and cool in an emergency. Well, whatever it was the Khan had argued about, it could not have been serious. Perhaps the police were doing a routine check-up. And yet as he moved nearer the barrier his lips went dry. His steps faltered, but he felt a gentle pressure from the man behind him. There grew upon him that feeling of impending disaster. He felt now as he did an hour ago in the dark corridor of the train.

The shrill blast of a whistle bore into his consciousness like a drill. He stopped, his whole frame going rigid. He turned his head slightly. The train was moving out. The polished frames of glass slid past, flashing light. The red coaches crawled like a centipede which had been cut in many places. He heard the slow clang of wheels, and the hiss of steam. And in his mind rose the picture of a dangling arm rocking with new life…

"Ticket! Ticket! Hey, what's the matter with you? Ticket!"

Sen started. He found him looking into the sullen, inquiring face of the ticket collector. The policeman was gazing intently at him.

Sen fumbled in his pockets.

Calm. Must keep calm. I can feel the perspiration upon my forehead.

"Sorry. I have it here. Just a minute…" said Sen.

The clipper clicked impatiently.

Tick, tick, tick…

"Here it is!" he cried, almost with joy, as he handed the green ticket.

The collector snatched it, grunting. Sen made as if to pass through the barrier. The man's hands shot out suddenly, barring his way.

"What another one? Here, what's going on?"

"Going on?" Sen almost screamed. "What do you mean?"

"What's the idea getting off here? This ticket is for Midnapore."

Sen's mind was like a quiet pool whose surface had been suddenly rippled. Think. Think. Keep calm.

"I know. I know. But I am getting off here."

"But why?" asked the quieter voice of the policeman, standing close by him.

"Why? Why? Can't I get off here if I want to?"

"You are the second to get off this station with a ticket for Midnapore," said the policeman, menacingly. "Was that a friend of yours?"

"What friend? I don't know what are you talking about."

"Don't be excited. Look here, are you suspecting me of something. If not I will leave now." My voice. Must control my voice.

"Where to?"

Be careful. Be careful. The only place I know is the Circus… Be indignant like the Khan.

"That's my business. I can go where I like. I am not a criminal. Take your hands off me." My voice is giving me away.

The policeman's grip tightened round his arm.

"I'll have to search you," he said. "Maybe you are all right, but we have had a few robberies in the trains recently. We have orders to keep a sharp look out."

The policeman led him into the waiting room. In the dingy atmosphere his eyes picking out the vague shadows of waiting passengers. Yet Sen was relived that it was only a search. He was glad he got rid of the gun. The policeman searched him systematically though his pockets. On a bench a little pile of odd articles grew.

"Hello!" he heard the policeman exclaim. "Come nearer the light. What's this? Blood stains…"

"Aaa… ah!" It was a gurgle in his throat. "I don't know… It's nothing. A smudge… Nothing… nothing…"

But he knew that the disaster that had hung over him like a thunder cloud all evening had at last broken. It was all over. The dream had come to an end.

He swayed toward the bench, and sank into it. When he felt the cold steel handcuffs around his wrists, its final click told him that the struggle was over.

Around him there was the vague hum of voices.

"I'll phone at once. Could get them before it gets to Midnapore. Let you know the moment I get through…"

"Murder… Midnapore… I wonder who he killed?…"

Everything spun before him. Like the big shining wheels of the train, faster, faster… Oh, stop it! It's too fast…

Whispers hissing like steam, rising like smoke.

Through the mist he saw the face of a woman, the mocking smile of the woman he had seen under the street light. He reached out eagerly, desperately. To touch it, to feel its utter loneliness.

The face drew back in horror. Stand back! Murderer! Murderer!

A black curtain descended over his eyes.

THE EXPATRIATE
Lim Thean Soo

Exiting from the Boeing jumbo, the elderly European walked through the passageway and descended the steps into the arrival hall of the Singapore International Airport. It did not take him long to be checked out. He had nothing but approbation for the system: the expeditious clearance of passengers, the efficient retrieval of their baggage and the facility with which they could purchase duty-free goods. He himself firmly believed in public service of the highest order—his own experience affirmed that. No procrastination, no excuses. No lack of dedication. Always an awareness of duty discharged with due diligence and an acute sense of responsibility.

It was already dark outside when he queued up for the taxi. So orderly, he commented to himself. Soon his turn came up.

A smiling, aged Chinese cabby put his only suitcase into the boot of the taxi. When he was comfortably seated, the man inquired solicitously, "Had a pleasant trip, sir?"

"Yes, thanks."

"Where to, sir?"

"Raffles Hotel."

The cab moved off.

"You are a tourist, sir?"

"You may call me that."

"Where did you come from?"

"London." He unzipped his clutch-bag to check his documents.

From the mirror of the front window screen the cabby saw him doing that and stopped his conversation. As soon as he had secured his bag, the cabby began, "Why do you choose Raffles, sir? There are other classy hotels in the city."

"I once lodged there. It has a quaint charm of its own."

The taxi emerged from the bend into a wide road.

"This is the expressway, sir."

"Really."

"And I take you across Benjamin Sheares Bridge."

"Will do. Who's Benjamin Sheares?"

"Well, he's our former president."

His passenger caught a tinge of patriotic pride in the reply.

"Look at the trees on the left, sir. They are on land reclaimed from the sea."

"Interesting!" No wonder he could not make out the old shoreline.

"From here you can see the tall buildings of the city ahead in the distance."

"There were only two when I was last here."

"Indeed, sir? That must be a long time ago."

"In the fifties."

"Were you on a visit then?"

"No, I was on my way home. They lodged me at Raffles while I awaited the arrival of the liner."

The cabby looked a bit perplexed. "Home, sir?"

"I had done my job. I had to give way to those coming up." He did not amplify on that.

He was a former colonial civil servant, a member of the elite Malayan Civil Service, comprising administrators other than the professionals like doctors, engineers and lawyers. He was one of the specially handpicked few appointed by the Colonial Office to that service. After a brief posting as a cadet to one of the Settlements in Malaya, he was sent to Kulangsu, an island off Amoy to learn Hokkien. Returning to Malaya, he was rotated in a variety of appointments including that of an Assistant District Officer. In his early career he learned that a MCS officer's success lay as much in his ability to get along with the local leaders of trade and industry as in his efficient work performance. And there was no question about the importance of incorruptibility as well as the need to project a public image of integrity and fairness.

After twenty-six years' impeccable service in the course of which he was awarded a medal, he was Malayanised, Malayanisation being the process after the war to compulsorily retire the British civil servants on a munificent pay-off which was described then as "the golden handshake." The local university graduates were taking over. At that time he had nine years' service to go before normal retirement. Nevertheless, the agreed compensation for premature retirement was regarded as extremely generous. So he accepted it. Now he realised that, as far as he was concerned, it was not so, considering that he was not as lucky as some of his colleagues in getting alternative appointments in another colony.

The cabby pointed to a tall structure which he could just make out in the semi-darkness. "That, sir, is the memorial built by the local Chinese in remembrance of their war dead. You know, thousands of us were massacred in the early months of 1942…Where were you during the war, sir?"

The question struck his sensitive nerve chord. What should he tell the garrulous cabby. How was he to reply?

During the war he was attached to a uniformed group operating in Malaya. The campaign went badly for the defenders. Then all was lost. And he was subsequently interned in Changi Prison and later transferred to the Sime Road Camp. How he hated the war. And for a long time he blamed it for the train of troubles it had brought to him.

He observed the cabby's inquiring look on the mirror of the front window screen. So he said offhandedly, "I was with friends at a place waiting for the war to end."

"Me, too! The Occupation was a nightmare. I prayed for the war to be over, for the British to return." Suddenly he looked wistful. "When they did, things weren't like before. But I can't complain."

"You speak good English."

"Well, sir, pre-war we had British teachers in school. I passed my Senior Cambridge in 1937."

The taxi veered into Beach Road. The cabby drew his passenger's attention to the dimly-lit SAFRA, the Singapore Armed Forces Reservist Club. "My grandson underwent national service. He used to buy beer from there."

His passenger recognised the building which once housed the post-war Brittania Club. To his left he could see that the Raffles Institution was no longer there. Soon Raffles Hotel, with its façade graced by travelers palms, loomed before him. And his taxi came to a stop.

He paid the fare, adding to it a tip, which the cabby returned to him, saying, "No tips in our country, sir." Then the taxi drove off. He stood there pleasantly impressed that the cabby regarded the island as his country. It would not have been so in the fifties.

He checked in. The décor of his room had not changed much since he last lodged here. He saw new faces among the staff. Just before he took his dinner, he went for a stroll round the building.

There was no doubt that the hotel retained its old ambience. Except for minor structural alterations and redecoration, it looked the same as when he was last here. The very place seemed to reverberate with ghostly echoes of a colonial past when life was leisurely and resistant to change.

The hotel, he reminded himself, had links with past British culture. Before the war writers like Maugham and Coward had stayed in it. Famous British artistes and top war correspondents had enjoyed its hospitality. And he remembered the popular tea dances to the strains of Victor Sylvester's ballroom music participated in only by Europeans. Now it was different. The dancers were a mix of Europeans and local people. And they did not have to be in formal attire.

The next day found him sauntering to the office of a long-serving member of the staff. He deliberately did not knock at the door. Just flung it open.

"Hey, Teddy! Busy as ever? How are you, old chappy?"

"You speak good English."

"Well, sir, pre-war we had British teachers in school. I passed my Senior Cambridge in 1937."

The taxi veered into Beach Road. The cabby drew his passenger's attention to the dimly-lit SAFRA, the Singapore Armed Forces Reservist Club. "My grandson underwent national service. He used to buy beer from there."

His passenger recognised the building which once housed the post-war Brittania Club. To his left he could see that the Raffles Institution was no longer there. Soon Raffles Hotel, with its façade graced by travelers palms, loomed before him. And his taxi came to a stop.

He paid the fare, adding to it a tip, which the cabby returned to him, saying, "No tips in our country, sir." Then the taxi drove off. He stood there pleasantly impressed that the cabby regarded the island as his country. It would not have been so in the fifties.

He checked in. The décor of his room had not changed much since he last lodged here. He saw new faces among the staff. Just before he took his dinner, he went for a stroll round the building.

There was no doubt that the hotel retained its old ambience. Except for minor structural alterations and redecoration, it looked the same as when he was last here. The very place seemed to reverberate with ghostly echoes of a colonial past when life was leisurely and resistant to change.

The hotel, he reminded himself, had links with past British culture. Before the war writers like Maugham and Coward had stayed in it. Famous British artistes and top war correspondents had enjoyed its hospitality. And he remembered the popular tea dances to the strains of Victor Sylvester's ballroom music participated in only by Europeans. Now it was different. The dancers were a mix of Europeans and local people. And they did not have to be in formal attire.

The next day found him sauntering to the office of a long-serving member of the staff. He deliberately did not knock at the door. Just flung it open.

"Hey, Teddy! Busy as ever? How are you, old chappy?"

The man was momentarily taken aback. Then he brightened. There was only one guest in the many years who called him by that nickname. He got up and hugged his visitor.

"Jim, why didn't you tell me in advance you're coming?"

"Well, it was all so sudden."

"Coffee?"

"No, thanks. I just had a lovely breakfast."

"Is Sylvia with you?"

"No, Teddy. She passed away three years ago."

"Sorry to hear that, Jim."

There was a silence, as Jim brushed aside the sadness evoked by his wife's demise.

"You're on a tour?"

"Not exactly. I came on a whim. You see, Teddy, I can't get away from the past, especially the war. I felt that I had to see Changi Jail once again. But only from the outside. You know I was interned there for three years. And I was so bitter about it."

"Then why go to see it, Jim?"

"One has to come to terms with one's past. There's no point in my carrying the rancour to the grave. The world's changed so much. The hate engendered by the war is out of context today."

"That's wise of you. I too suffered tremendously during the Occupation. But I've been able, more or less, to leave behind the ghosts of my past."

"One thing the old-fashioned Chinese have taught me is to resign oneself to fate. Teddy, when I last lodged here, I was in a depressed mood."

"I urged you to get out of it."

"I tried but failed. After Malayanisation I had no place to go back to. I didn't want to return to Surrey. My parents were dead. And I had no more friends there. I feared that I wouldn't be able to get a job that commensurated with my position. Besides, Sylvia refused to go home for good."

"I understand."

"After being a colonial administrator, I would feel strange to accept a lowly-paid job at home and be at the beck and call of those post-war

"Then I'll drive you there this afternoon."

"Don't trouble yourself. I can get a taxi. Besides, I want to see a bit of the city."

"I'll hire a motor car for you. I can get a good discount for you."

Jim told Teddy not to bother himself—to no avail. It was settled that the car would fetch him after tiffin, which Teddy insisted he must have with him for old times' sake.

The tour of the city gave Jim a good insight into the progress made by Singapore. What he had read and been told was true. Well-dressed, healthy-looking people crowded the walkways. No more were the local Chinese girls skinny and of sallow complexion as in the thirties when most of them wore the *samfoo*. To his mind the pre-war colonial government had been too exploitative to consider the local people's housing needs as well as social and educational facilities for them. While the necessity for exploitation was less cogent after the war, it had by then run out of time to ameliorate the situation for them. Decolonisation had set in.

The Colonial government could have had a longer stretch of borrowed time. But just after the war the results of the British Parliamentary elections made that impossible. The new home government decided to give India independence and that started a landslide.

Soon the hired car took the route to the eastern sector of the island. He could see block after block of new condominiums and well-designed luxury apartments. Across the highway was a long stretch of what appeared to be a public park.

He was now close to his destination. In a moment he saw the forbidding grey walls of Changi Prison. And he felt a lump in his throat. The driver, a reticent Indian, parked the car a distance away.

Approaching the building not without a bit of trepidation, he was emotionally overwhelmed for a while. Painful memories raked his mind. He spotted the huge front door through which he and a chosen group of internees were occasionally allowed to go out to perform some heavy task. On one side was a piece of land where the war prisoners cultivated vegetables under the watchful eye of the cruel Japanese guards.

He imagined hearing the clanking of the iron door to a prison cell where for a totally absurd reason he was kept in solitary confinement for a month. He was subjected to frequent interrogation as to whether he had engaged in espionage activities and repeatedly tortured. He was always in a continual state of pain, in a semi-coma of hunger. There was only one pail of dirty water nearby. They cell stank. The electric bulb had been deliberately removed. Cockroaches kept him company. Strangely enough, their presence helped to maintain his sanity. And he was sometimes amused by their antics.

The Japanese sergeant in charge was fond of mocking him and his fellow prisoners. "Japanese soldiers no surrender. They fight to the end." An on another occasion, "You like go back *Engeerand*. War end soon." The man was temperamental, sadistic, and vindictive. For the slightest transgression by the internees, he would fall into a rage and beat them. To some of the perspicacious internees the man could be regarded as an object of pity. Far away from his homeland, consigned to a boring job, himself bullied by his superior officers, he vented his frustration on the inmates. The more so as the war dragged on year after year with the prospect of victory diminishing.

After his deliverance, Jim rationalised the whole situation—the war, his internment, the terrible trauma that he underwent: there were times in history when the world went mad. And people enmeshed in the global maelstrom suffered extremely. The violent clash of the neo-feudal and the modern way of life was bound to have agonizing repercussions. When the world went berserk, people descended to the level of the beast. They ignored civil decencies and human rights. They ruthlessly baited, hunted down, and killed their enemies. And it required a world war of unprecedented ferocity to snuff out the madness.

Over forty years had elapsed since all that happened. Even the aftermath of the war saw no peace. He recalled the danger to his life during the Malayan Emergency when he acted for a District Officer who went on furlough. Now going round the prison building, he experienced a catharsis. He was laying to rest the gruesome ghosts of the past. And he did not now feel so sorry for himself. Many had suffered worse than he;

others perished. His internment was a tragic waste of his life. But there was nothing he could do about it and there was no point brooding over it anymore.

For some time he had sought solace in religion. He remembered during his internment of making a point to attend the chapel service whenever he could. It was the light that would lead him out of the dark, tortuous tunnel. His prayer for release from incarceration was in due course answered. Now, more than forty years after the event, he only wanted to seek absolution for the wrongs meted to him by his keepers. He was already reaching seventy years.

It was time to get back. The driver took him back to the hotel. As he stepped into his room, he experienced the exhilaration of having undergone an emotional uplift—he felt no longer at variance with his past. A few days more he would return from where he had come purged of all war recrimination. He hoped that from now he would be able to view the war and its aftermath from a detached perspective—it should thereafter be a closed chapter of his life.

It was Saturday evening. The Long Bar was well patronised when Jim entered. He managed to find an unoccupied chair. And ordered a Singapore Sling, following it up with a whisky soda. The live band played music of the thirties, evoking nostalgia in him.

While gazing at his drink, he sensed a figure approaching him. Then a loud, "Stony!"

The voice bridged him to its owner forty-seven years back—it was jarring. A tall, elderly European was looking at him with a disconcerting smirk.

"I didn't expect to meet you after all these years." Jim wished he had not come to the bar. Then he would not have met this fractious apparition from the past.

"Of course, you didn't." The tone of his voice was unmistakenly sarcastic. "As for me, I fervently hoped to meet you some day. And I have."

The man snapped his fingers at a waitress who dragged an empty chair to the table.

"Won't you treat me to a drink, Stony? For old times' sake."

"Why, y-yes. What would you have?"

"Whiskey soda."

Jim beckoned the same waitress and made the order.

"I've a little score to settle with you, Stony."

He had expected that. But the repeated use of the nickname irked Jim. It was given to him by his volunteer colleagues two years before the Pacific War because he had a serious disposition which was reflected in his solemn mien.

"For heaven's sake, stop calling me Stony! I detest it, Jack!"

"Ah, you still remember my name. Since you don't want me to call you Stony, I'll stop doing it."

"What do you want?"

"An explanation, and also an apology."

"Damn it, what for?"

"Remember the war in Malaya?"

"I'd rather forget it. I've reconciled to the traumatic events of yesterday."

He would not disclose to Jack about his trip to Changi Jail.

"Remember after the battle for Slim both of us were on shore patrol duty about thirty miles south of Slim?"

"Of course, I do. The enemy advanced so rapidly that our patrol was dispersed."

"That's right. You and I remained as one unit. You a corporal and I a private."

Jim recalled that vividly. Jack was an assistant manager in a rubber plantation, and he had volunteered to join the Local Defense Corps. On the eve of the war they were mobilized. Their coastal patrol had been assigned the duty of relaying information by mobile couriers to the War Headquarters then at Kuala Lumpur. Headquarters wanted to know whether the Japanese would attempt landings south of Slim to cut off the main British force.

However, right from the beginning everything seemed to have gone wrong for his patrol which was not supplied with a wireless set. In the confusion of the hasty retreat he and Jack took the coastal route.

The rest of the patrol under a sergeant were forced inland by advancing enemy tanks and had to take cover in the jungle. The two of them found the mangrove swamp inhospitable. It afforded poor camouflage—they imagined the enemy planes flying overhead to the south narrowly missed spotting them. During the day the place stank; at night the mosquitoes terrorises them. And they were in constant fear of being ambushed.

Jack continued relentlessly, "I had money with me. That afternoon I asked a Malay fisherman to row me to Sumatra. He agreed to accept one hundred dollars. I persuaded you to join me. But you ordered me not to desert on pain of being court-martialed. Remember?"

"I was then discharging my duty as your superior officer. I regarded your intention to flee as a disgraceful act of disloyalty and cowardice."

"You should have been aware by then that all was lost after the sinking of the *Prince of Wales* and the Slim battle."

"I never gave up hope until the Japanese landed in Singapore."

"You frustrated my only chance to escape. By your straitlaced attitude, you prevented me from leaving."

Jack was quaking with fury. Onlookers from nearby tables stared at him and Jim. They wondered how the altercation would end.

Jim raised his voice. "Why the recrimination after all these years? You should know that I was interned here. And I suffered immensely for that."

"What about me? They sent me to the Death Railway in Siam."

"Even if I had allowed you to proceed to Sumatra, you wouldn't have made it to Ceylon from there. Those who fled there were captured by the Japanese."

"At least I would have had my chance. And you blew it for me."

"You can't undo what has happened."

"No. But I demand an apology from you. At least it would give me satisfaction."

"I won't apologise. And there is nothing you can do about it."

The onlookers listened avidly. Although it was none of their business, they knew the argument had come to a head.

Jack looked grim. "Think carefully. I want you to admit your error which eventually caused me untold suffering. Over the past years I couldn't get it off my chest… You must know that we then belonged to a volunteer unit. We were not soldiers in the real sense. You need not have been so unyielding."

"You could have disobeyed my order."

"I nearly wanted to. I was silly not to have done it… Now, will you apologise to me?"

Jim had recovered his composure. He had made his trip to Singapore for only one purpose. And he must not negate it. If he must come to terms with the horrendous past clean, there was only one way out of the unexpected confrontation. Deep in him he felt that he had acted correctly, considering all the circumstances prevailing then. But there was no harm telling the blighter that he apologised for hindering his chance to escape. He knew he had to sacrifice personal integrity for a higher morality. Moreover, the importance of social flexibility in a crisis was not lost to him as a former administrator.

"Well, Jack, I apologise to you for having prevented you from escaping to Sumatra after the Slim battle. I didn't give you the chance you wanted."

The onlookers were disappointed at the outcome of the fracas—it had paled into an anti-climax.

Jim abruptly go up from his chair and walked away without looking back. Went to the counter to pay for the drinks. Headed for his room where he immediately packed his suitcase. Telephoned the airline to book a seat on the next morning flight. Fortunately one was available.

By the time he boarded the aircraft, he had completely forgotten about Jack.

THE SHOES OF MY SENSEI
Goh Sin Tub

I was glad to hear from my Japanese teacher but his letter also worried me. It was 1945, the British had just returned to Singapore, Sensei and the other Japanese had been interned as POWs, and young Singaporeans (including teenagers like me) were anxious, confused, feeling our way about under colonial rule—phasing from one subjugation to another.

I was surprised that Sensei had not yet been repatriated to Japan, but happy to learn that he was well treated, as he was classified as civilian, not armed forces, or possible war crime suspect. My worry was for myself: I had received a letter from the enemy openly posted to me! Although the enemy was detained, still the letter could have attracted the attention of our new rulers—in particular some clandestine police department responsible for keeping dossiers on subject people in their colony? I could be marked down, barred from education and jobs… Surely they were now watching me—to see how I would respond to Sensei's letter? Indeed the envelope looked as though it had been opened and resealed.

Sensei's letter mentioned a pair of shoes that he had given me. The last time I saw him was at his home in Cavanagh Road (that seemingly long-ago time when Singapore was still *Syonanto*!) He had said, "Take these shoes. They're new. They look too big for you but you're still growing and some day they'll fit. I don't mind going into the POW camp in these old shoes."

I felt sorry for him. He had been good to us. He was an understanding man and had taught his students values at a time when the whole world had gone mad. Through songs he introduced us to character—the old Japanese way, the true Japanese spirit: *Nippon Seishin*.

He had been quietly teaching school back home when the Japanese Imperial Army conscripted him, and shipped him out to teach the Japanese language to the conquered peoples of South-East Asia. We soon found him different from those arrogant and sadistic *heitai-san*, soldiers who treated us like dirt.

Sensei sponsored his students for precious food rations, and more importantly to get jobs. He stuck his neck out to help people. He even took the grave risk of speaking up for students and their relatives who had somehow displeased the notorious *Kempeitai*, the all-powerful Japanese Military Police.

For example, Fong's old father, who was detained by the *Kempeitai* when he got drunk and kicked a Japanese flag. Fong went to Sensei for help. Sensei was not sure he could help. In his shoes I might have chickened out. But Sensei went to the *Kempeitai*, and he got Fong's father released although the old man came out haggard, white hair all straggly, hobbling on sticks and dragging one useless foot along. After that incident Sensei was a hero in our eyes.

He must be feeling desperately low in his detention camp. I owed it to him to visit him. Returning his shoes was no problem. There were too big for me and I was planning to sell them. (My family was short of money—who wasn't then?) But would I get blacklisted if I went to visit the enemy? There would be a register to sign—a record of my visit. What future use might they make of that?

Of course, my fears were groundless, but to a teenager grown up in a *Kempeitai* world, they were very real. Particularly as stories of wartime atrocities were now being widely circulated and the general feeling was that vengeance was about to be exacted on the Japanese and all who had collaborated with them in any way whatsoever.

"Why go? Why take the risk?" My close friends whom I consulted were firm, "Look at the terrible things those Japanese did!" That sounded convincing—fully justifying not going. After all, he was a Japanese too, wasn't he?

Was he? A small voice in me kept reminding me: He was Sensei, an understanding man, in fact our one-time hero, whose shoes I cold never hope to fill, one who had been truly good to us in bad times…

I switched off that voice. I just could not risk going to him. I wrote him a pack of lies: his shoes had been sold off, I had no time as I was studying hard for my exams, I had no transport to get to his camp, I did not even know how to get there—a hundred cowardly excuses.

For weeks after I mailed the letter, I agonised in remorse over what I had done. And then one day I saw in the streets of Chinatown a total stranger—an old man, haggard, white hair all straggly, hobbling on sticks, dragging one useless foot along …

And I remembered a hero, someone whose feet needed shoes, shoes too big for me anyway. I knew then I had to go to him.

I cycled to the camp with those shoes. Outside the camp gates I had cold feet—but I thought of Sensei. As I stood before the British soldiers on gate duty, I sweated cold sweat—but I thought of Sensei.

So I bowed to the soldiers, as I did to the *Kempeitai*. I showed them Sensei's letter. "This is it; I'm putting my neck in a noose," I thought as I signed my personal particulars into their formidable book. "My future's as good as gone!"

And as they escorted me in, I actually wondered if I would be let out at all! I hugged my teacher's shoes tight—somehow the bigness of them gave me courage.

The camp guards took me to the canteen to wait. There were about a dozen other people around—visitors and prisoners. I almost cried when I saw Sensei. He had grown thin and pale but the worst thing was he looked depressed and withdrawn. At first he did not recognise me—or did not want to. He did not look at me in the eye. When he finally spoke he was polite but not warm, speaking only brief words. I handed his shoes to him. He did not take them. I left them on the table before us. I confessed I was scared. I had not been truthful to him in my letter. He said nothing.

I realised it: my letter had hurt him grievously. Perhaps he was not sure whether I had now come as a friend, or out of reluctant duty, or even pity. His *Nippon Seishin* would not accept anything short of true friendship.

I talked and talked. I could not get through to him—and time was running out, for they limited the visiting hours. Finally, I just came right out and said with desperation in my voice, "Sensei, I know I shouldn't have written you those lies… How can I make up for it? Don't stay angry with me. This could be our last time together. Can we not part as friends? We may never meet again…"

A torrent from me. From him: only silence. Still no eye contact.

Then I was inspired. Yes, there was one way I might reach him: the way he passed on *Nippon Seishin* to us. I decided to do it—even though I could be making a fool of myself, even though those guards (and possible British *Kempeitai* agents?) could be watching me…

There, in the midst of those visitors and POWs, I stood up erect before my teacher. And putting my heart into its moving lyrics, I began to sing the *Aogeba*, the song Sensei had taught me, the farewell Japanese students sing to their teachers upon graduation:

"Aogeba to-toshi
Waga-shi no on"

A silence fell on the crowd around us… And then, one by one, people started to stand up and join me in my singing, just as solemnly:

"Oshie no niwa nimo
Hayaiku tose"

And then, to my ecstatic joy, I heard Sensei's voice—weak but singing too:

"Omoeba itotoshi
kono toshi tsuki"

Ima Koso wakareme
Iza saraba…"

"Yes, now is the time we part. We part as friends," Sensei said, quoting the last words of the song. Eyes glistening but looking straight into mine.

And he handed me back this shoes, saying with a smile, "Keep these. They've issued me new ones."

I took them back—no longer to sell. I was growing. I could feel it. I might still be able to fit into Sensei's shoes.

THE LEG GLANCE
Gopal Baratham

My father was an old-fashioned doctor, old fashioned enough to believe that human life was sacred and the confidentiality of patients inviolable. He was comfortable with notions like honour and truth and did not collapse into laughter when he heard words like courage and duty. Try as I might I could not persuade him that these qualities did not originate in England, nor in the game of cricket.

"Cricket," he was fond of repeating, "is a game that depends not on muscular ability but on the very foundations of the human spirit."

I never thought to ask exactly what this meant. I was grateful though an only child. I was a girl and not called upon to play the wretched game. My sex did not, however, excuse me from listening to father talk about it. Often for hours on end. All his heroes seemed to be dead or at least, in retirement. Present day cricketers he looked upon with contempt.

"Where is courage tested," he asked, "when players wear steel helmets on their heads, pads on their bodies and grills across their faces?" Then came the ultimate condemnation. "They might as well be playing what the Americans call football."

"But Pa," I would protest, "they are only trying to protect themselves from injury."

"And thereby denying themselves the possibility of understanding courage."

The men father admired had, bruised and battered, bloodied and broken-boned, gone on batting, bowling, fielding or keeping wicket. Indomitable was a word he often used to describe his guts-'n-glory brigade, most of whom were English. His favourite cricketeer was, strangely enough, not an Englishman but an Indian called K. S. Ranjitsinghji. 'Ranji', as he was popularly known, was a prince who appeared to have spent most of his time playing cricket in Victorian England instead of minding affairs of state in his home country. His greatest contribution to the game was a stroke called the leg glance.

"The leg glance is not just a way of scoring runs. It embodies a whole attitude to life, an attitude which, regrettably, no longer prevails."

I knew well enough what the leg glance was. In playing the stroke, feet and bat were kept close together. Ranji always met the ball with the full face of his bat but at the last minute, with what must have been wrists of steel, flicked it just wide of the wicket keeper but not wide enough for it to be of interest to the deep leg field. It was most effective against fast bowlers and when the ball was pitched well up and in line with the stumps. It was, of course, an unnecessarily dangerous stroke to play. One did not go out and strike the ball but simply waited, at the mercy of all the vagaries of a ball in flight, to redirect it. There was the risk of being bowled, falling leg before or getting caught behind the stumps.

"Isn't it easier and safer to go forward and drive the well-pitched ball down the leg side, or if it is slightly short, hook it back of square?" I had, very early in life, mastered both the technicalities of the game and its terminology.

"Ease and safety were never cardinal considerations in Ranji's game; grace and elegance were." He paused, wondered whether he should continue, then did. "The stroke has to be played flawlessly and when it succeeds it produces more than runs and applause. It proves that one can defy the world, demand the perfect solution and, with flair and courage, get it."

I knew father wouldn't like the question but asked it nevertheless. "What if the stroke is not played perfectly?"

"If played badly, the leg glance is a disaster." He spoke moodily, then brightened. "Which is what makes it the greatest stroke in cricket."

As with most things, father's attitude to abortions was affected by what he saw as the ideals of the game. He didn't think it 'cricket' to attack something as helpless as a blob of jelly clinging to its mother's womb. If the foetus could bite the gynaecologist or infect him with some deadly disease, I am sure father would have been happier about recommending that his patients had their pregnancies terminated. It wasn't that he was a bigot or didn't feel for the woman who was unhappy about her pregnancy.

"No one has the right to ask a woman to allow her body to be used as an incubator for a creature that has invaded her and will, in the course of its exit, literally tear her apart," he said often enough, emphasising the dilemma in which each request for an abortion placed him. And the anguish he suffered was no less real for being self-inflicted. He couldn't discuss the subject with mother, who was an inflexible Catholic, and so turned to me.

"You will, dear Lia, being of the same sex as this unfortunate, understand her predicament much better than I can ever hope to."

I was thirteen at the time and, having been brought up in the protected environment of a middle-class Singaporean girl, knew little, and only in theory, of how girls got pregnant, and nothing about how women felt at having their bodies invaded. I didn't like to let father down, however, and managed to make friendly noises while he agonised over his problems.

Most of the cases that he brought up would not be considered problems to anyone other than a starry-eyed, cricket-playing, old-fashioned family doctor. It was clear even to an inexperienced teenager like me that his patients regarded pregnancy as a disease they were unfortunate enough to contract. They looked to their doctor to cure them of their affliction and didn't really care how he went about this. They regarded father's detailed inquiries into their motives for wishing their pregnancies terminated as unjustifiable nosiness.

"You will understand, Lia, that it is impossible for me to recommend an abortion unless I am myself convinced that this child is being denied life not for economic reasons or those concerning the stigma of illegitimacy."

Very early on I realised it was impossible to convince father that inconvenience, shortage of funds and embarrassment at being an unmarried mother were valid reasons for abortion. I would therefore, in as surreptitious a manner as possible, persuade him that the woman in question hated the father of her child, viewed her state with disgust, and would be irreparably damaged if made to continue with the pregnancy. Most times, this was easy enough. My advice was accepted without question till the case of Mrs X came up. I was nineteen at the time and in my third year of business studies at the university.

"I need your help more than ever with this one, Lia." I stopped staring at the spreadsheet on my computer screen and looked up at him. "I know all the people concerned and am not sure of the impartiality of my judgement."

"Do I know them, pa?"

He smiled slowly. "You know I'm not going to say whether you do or whether you don't. The lady in question will remain Mrs X to you and I will avail myself of your objective judgment."

"Shoot, Pa," I said, turning off the machine before which I had been sitting all evening.

"Mrs X was... still is, a happily married woman with a ten-year-old daughter. She is pregnant but the child is not her husband's. And she wants this child... badly."

"She doesn't need to tell him, does she? She just goes ahead and has the child."

"Ah, but her husband and she practise contraception."

"Then she's for the high jump whatever happens. How can she explain to the dear cuckold the need for an abortion even if she's got the poor sap believing he is the only man in her life?"

"Contraceptive techniques are not perfect, as you know, Lia." I hoped to God that they were but said nothing.

"I have told her to tell him this. Even offered to tell him so myself."

"If your Mrs X gets away with that, her husband will need to have his head examined, but we will no longer have a problem."

"Unfortunately, there's more to it than that." I waited and he continued, "I have to tell you that the X's are English and the good lady's lover is Chinese."

"That doesn't give dear Mrs X much of an option, does it?"

"I don't know." He hummed and hawed for a bit. "She's very much in love with this Chinese gentleman and wants his child more than anything else in the world."

"But not enough to have the whole thing out in the open, divorce her husband and marry this bloke."

"Her lover is a rather well-known ladies' man and a bit of a cad, I'm afraid. Not the sort who would marry her even if she did divorce her husband."

I knew how father was thinking. If the woman didn't want the child, he could persuade himself to arrange an abortion, but a child that was loved before it was born had to be protected at all cost. "What does the high-minded Mrs X suggest?"

"She has posed the problem to her doctor and left him to find a solution."

Charming, I thought, but asked, "And what are you going to advise, Pa?"

"I'm not too sure yet." He suddenly seemed to notice the computer in front of me and said, "I'm sorry. You have exams and things coming up, Lia. So don't worry your pretty little head about the problems an old doctor encounters in the course of a day's work."

I forgot about Mrs X and her problems almost as soon as father stopped talking. I had my exams to pass and was seriously in love with the man I married shortly after graduating.

Five years later, my husband Jer and I were posted to London.

Father decided to visit us while we were there. A few days after his arrival, he suggested that we drop in on some old friends of his. Maria and Stephen Edmonds. They had come to know each other, apparently quite well, when the British army had posted Stephen to Singapore. The Edmonds lived out in Brentwood, in Essex. We took the day off and Jer drove us through what father insisted on calling the remains of 'England's green and pleasant land'.

Maria and Stephen Edmonds seemed near enough the typical couple living in a semi in suburban England. They were in their early forties.

Their daughter Jane had just completed her 'A' levels and was waiting for admission to a secretarial college. Like her parents she remembered Singapore with the kind of nostalgia that is unreal and irritating to us who actually live in that steel-and-plastic high-tech metropolis. I couldn't wait for lunch to be over, and as soon as it was, suggested that we should be making our way back to London.

"Oh, you can't go till you have seen our David," said Maria. "Especially you, doctor," she added, looking steadily at father.

"We won't let you go till you have met my pride and joy," said Stephen. Noticing my impatience, he continued, "Why don't you, Lia, come with me to pick David up from school. I walk him home whenever I can."

We arrived at the school just as the children were released.

"There he is," said Stephen, pointing to a group of five-year-olds huddled together. David, seeing his father, broke free of them and rushed towards us. For a full minute I was ignored while father and son exchanged embraces, kisses and the day's news. It was difficult to believe that they had been apart for a little more than seven hours. I was beginning to feel an intruder when Stephen said, "Say hello to Lia, David. She's come all the way from Singapore where we were before you were born."

The boy did so, but clearly had no time for me. Stephen carried him on his shoulders and the child chattered to his father all the way home.

Maria served tea as soon as we got back but this did little to interrupt the dialogue between father and son.

Jer is one of those people who blurt out things as they cross his mind. He had been staring at David since we came in, and now suddenly said, "It's a funny thing but at certain angles little David looks very Chinese."

He had no sooner finished saying this when he screamed.

Father, who was standing behind him and had just helped himself to his second cup of tea, seemed suddenly to lose control of his hands and hot tea cascaded down the back of Jer's shirt. Maria jumped up to wipe the scalding liquid off my husband's back while father, who seemed to have completely regained his composure, apologised for being a shaky old man.

When we were done with tidying things up, Stephen said, "Yes. I, too, think David looks Chinese. But that's not surprising because many people say that I look slightly Chinese." As he said this, he pulled back the corners of his eyes with his thumbs and turned in the direction of his son.

David smiled at his father and nodded several times. You had to be blind not to be dazzled by the love that shone from his eyes.

INTERROGATING PHOTOGRAPHS
Robert Yeo

I acquired this photograph from my maternal third aunt, or 'Sar Ee' in Hokkien, during one of my New Year visits in the late 1990s. She knew of my interest in old photographs that reveal family history and I asked to see as many of them as she had. She was a little hesitant, fearing, I suppose, that I would stumble on photographs that would divulge more than she was prepared for: aspects of the family she came from, of which she is the third daughter, or bits of her own family history (she, her husband and their four children) which are best concealed from a curious nephew, especially a nephew who she vaguely knew was some sort of writer.

She brought out two albums containing about fifty photographs, all in black and white or sepia. The one that immediately caught my attention is the one I am now interrogating.

She is the one sixth from the left and her name is Oon Geok Lian. Left to right, she is the only daughter standing of the four daughters of the matriarch, who is my maternal grandmother. And there are two men standing behind. Left to right are my other aunts, Tua Ee (eldest aunt), Ee Chik (youngest aunt), their mother, Sar Ee and my mother, the second daughter. And the man on the right I recognise as their brother, my uncle therefore, an only son that the Japanese took.

But the man standing next to him was not known to me.

Who is he? I asked.

"Eh?" Sar Ee said, in surpise. Obviously she had not set eyes on this photo for some time. "Who is he?" she repeated my question. She turned to her husband and asked him. He looked and could not tell.

She peered again and then it came to her. "Oh yes, he is, what's his name, K____ B____."

"But who is this K____ B____?" I asked.

"Oh," she said slowly, in the grip of difficult recall, "he was the person who was interested in your Tua Ee but..."

"What happened?" I persisted.

"But she found out that he had a mistress and she dropped him," she said.

"They must have been on very good terms for him to appear in an intimate family portrait," I said.

"Yes, they were," she replied, "And after that, your aunt was very sad and disappointed, she pined and you know what happened."

Back to the picture. It is a photo of the family of Oon Ee Thiam, my maternal grandfather who lived for many years in Haig Road, but he is absent. His wife, though, is not, and her maiden name is Tan Guat Kee,

On the extreme left is their eldest daughter, Joon Lian, more commonly known as Daisy, next Poh Lian, the fourth and youngest daughter who goes by the name Diana ('Bongsu' to the family), then K____ B____ whose family name is C____, Tan Guat Kee, Hock Ann whose English name was Victor, Geok Lian the third daughter who only has her Chinese name but is 'Molek' to the family, and finally Kim Lian, Nancy, the second daughter.

Nancy is my mother.

"You know what happened," my Sar Ee had said earlier. As I write now, 5 November 2004 at 7.00 PM, the three sisters Nancy, Geok Lian and Diana, are still very much around, In their eighties, the sisters have longevity on their side—except for Aunty Daisy. What happened was that, after the romantic disappointment with K____ B____, she was involved with another man. He was an intellectually brilliant person, a scholar who studied in England and was noticed by Tan Cheng Lock, Tan Guat Kee's eldest brother and Daisy's uncle.

Yes, none other than the great man of Malacca, Dato Sir Tan Cheng Lock and my mother's uncle. I will return to him.

As my mother remembers, and her story is corroborated by her sisters, this bright scholar was taken into one of the companies owned by Dato Tan on the understanding that he was eventually to marry Daisy. Apparently, he had a mind of his own, refused the order that went with the job, quit and left Daisy romantically bereft. To this day, the three sisters maintain that this second disappointment led to the depression which set in and led eventually to her developing breast cancer and dying from it when she was only forty.

Aunty Daisy was well-educated, had a good job as a senior clerk in Quantas, was patrician and independent minded. That she was the first born, had the equivalent of 'O' levels and secure employment, contributed to her independence. It may also have led to her rejection of K____ B____. In the photo, she is seen as tall and slim, physical attributes which are accentuated by the long cheongsam she wears, her ramrod-straight sitting posture and the length of the cheongsam almost covering her legs. The long collar hides her neck and there is an austere beauty on her face, an austereness that is less apparent in the portrait photo of her. Very likely, the latter picture was taken earlier and the collar of her long cheongsam covers her partially to set off a slightly sharp chin. The formality of Daisy's cheongsam contrasts with the *samfoo* of her sisters.

In the family photo, Diana, ten years younger, sits next to her on a double sofa seat with both hands on the side of the antique chair where her mother sits. To the right of the photo stands Geok Lian, also with her hands on the side of the chairs and Nancy sits on a single sofa chair. They make up the front row with their mother. It is worth noticing that their bodies are slightly tilted and they look at the camera at a slight angle, unlike the men, who make up the second row behind them and who face the camera directly.

The Japanese conquered Singapore on 15 February 1942 and surrendered on 12 September 1945. My uncle Victor was killed during that period, and as I was born on 27 January 1940, I might have glimpsed him as a baby but do not remember him at all. A member of the Singapore Volunteer Corps he was among the first to be rounded up by the Japanese. Aunty Diana remembers that he was given three days, along with other volunteers, to report to the Japanese, and he chose to go on third day and never returned. Some who went on the first and second days survived but not those who went on the third day. My mother's cousin, Lee Kip Lee, President of the Peranakan Association, who lived on Amber Road, was a great friend of Victor's.

The brutality of the Japanese, who occupied Singapore for three and a half years, dealt a double blow to the Oon family of Haig Road by removing not only a member of the family but one who was also an only son.

For years, I have wondered how the survivors felt, especially the parents. Did it contribute to the deterioration of the relationship of Grandpa and Grandma? My memory of him was that of a loving, cheerful man but I also heard stories of his infidelity, which were legendary. It is said that he learnt his Cantonese horizontally. He apparently had a succession of mistresses, mostly Cantonese.

Aunty Diana told me a story of how she was once dragged by her mother to a house when her father had stayed with one of his many women. Grandma brought the empty *tengkat* which had originally contained food her husband's mistress had sent to her, went to the gate of the offending mistress, yelled at her and her own husband, pointing repeatedly to their youngest daughter, "Can you see, you spineless husband and your prostitute woman, what you are doing? You can see me here, with our daughter, pity her. Who is taking care of us? Not you, you useless lump, all you know is to take care of your shameless women instead of your own family. You only have one family but how many worthless whores do you have? And who is feeding your family? Tell your slut here is the empty *tengkat*. I cursed the food and threw it away. Tell her I don't need this kind of kindness. I can take care of myself. And if your *sundal* female ever becomes a mother, she can learn what it's like to cook for her husband while he fiddles."

And with that she left the tiered tray of food on the ground while the commotion brought the neighbours out to see what the trouble was about.

Grandpa smoked opium too and one of my earliest surviving memory of him was of him holding me tight like a bolster while he smoked. It must have been in one of the dens in the row of terrace houses opposite the old Roxy cinema in East Coast Road. My second brother Andrew was his favourite bolster.

He was unawed by relationship or reputation. That he had married one of the daughters of perhaps the most prominent Baba Chinese family did not impress him.

Nor the fact that his brother-in-law, Tan Cheng Lock, was a man of growing political importance and a leader, later to he President of the Malayan Chinese Association.

Tan Cheng Lock provided him with a job in Sime Darby which involved handling company money. But his appetites led him to embezzle money for which he was prosecuted and imprisoned for several years. His family visited him in Outram Prison and my mother remembers that even there, he asked for his opium supply. Presumably the prison authorities were lenient enough to allow him his indulgence.

Roland Barthes, in *Camera Lucida Reflections on Photography* (1981) writes, "I might put this differently: what founds the nature of Photography is the pose. The physical duration of this pose is of little consequence; even in the interval of a millionth of a second (Edgerton's drop of milk) there has been a pose. For the pose is not here, the attitude of the target or even a technique of the Operator, but the term of an 'intention' of reading: looking at a photograph, I inevitably include in my scrutiny the thought of that instant, however brief, in which a real thing happened to be motionless in front of the eye. I project the present photograph's immobility upon the past shot, and it is this arrest which constitutes the pose."

This is obviously a studio shot. I am not able to put a date to it nor identify the studio. This pose, this arrangement of the sitting and standing positions with the women in front and the men behind, points to a simplicity of symmetry in a relatively uncluttered interior with a floral carpet, European armchairs and a curtain behind. The seven persons are dressed in three ways, Nyonya, Chinese and Western. At the center is the mother in *sarong kebaya*, with a set of three *kerosang* to pin down her *baju* and give her a slim appearance tapering down to her *kasut manek* slippers. Of her daughters, Daisy wears a formal cheongsam while the three daughters wear *samfoo*.

There is another difference. Why is Daisy's hair permed but not her sisters? The men sport Western suits, presumably white or light-coloured, with ties.

Except for K____ B____, who is on the verge of a smile, the rest are all unsmiling. It calls for an explanation and I think it may have to do with the absent father. He was supposed to come for this important family event but was either called away or had a row with his wife the previous night or the same day and decided to stay away. If this is true, it would account for the unsmiling faces, and together with his absence, cloud what could have been the perfect family portrait.

Perhaps absence, with all its connotations, may sum up an aspect of the life of my grandmother, the second sister of Tan Cheng Lock. In a loving biography of her father, the late Alice Scott-Ross writes about him and his sisters:

> Of course, his duty which was expected of him by his parents was to get his sisters married off before he could ever envisage

his own marriage. The eldest, of the three girls, who was radiantly lovely was married through a matchmaker to a salaried clerk in a British firm called 'Brinkmann & Co. Ltd' in Singapore. My father was not quite yet established in his rubber producing industry. Consequently, his first sister's marriage was the best that could be arranged at the time. At that period, to be married into a well-to-do family, both parties must be equally financially well-established. Subsequently, followed the marriage of his second sister. But the third sister was the luckiest of the three as she married well, into a wealthy family in Singapore, because by that time my father had been better established, and he was looked upon with more esteem.

Alice Scott-Ross
Tun Dato Sir Cheng Lock Tan, 1990

What else could she have added about the 'second sister', her maternal aunt? That she did not marry well, did not marry money. Undoubtedly, Scott-Ross's bare statement, "Subsequently, followed the marriage of the second sister" sharply contrasts with the detailed approval of the marriages of her two sisters. It tells us as much about the author as it does of her subject; and maybe, she knew of the scandalous ways of her second aunt's husband and did not want to say any more. One more conclusion may be drawn from this account and that is the undeniable filial responsibility showed by Cheng Lock towards his sisters. This quality in private life, together with his public, political life, is a shining testimony to the greatness of the man. I know that the Haig Road house in which my grandma stayed belonged to him and she stayed there with her family all her life, until her death. In historical Malacca, a major road is named after him, Jalan Tun Tan Cheng Lock, and in that road is preserved in mint condition the house he inhabited with his family, including his son the former long-standing Malaysian Minister for Finance Tan Siew Sin. The house is a family shrine and a beacon to the enduring legacy of the Peranakan Chinese in Malacca and Singapore.

A BEGINNING AND A MIDDLE WITHOUT AN ENDING
Arthur Yap

When it got to about ten o'clock, the incessant chatter started to peter off. Leng Eng turned to Elaine and asked if her sister would sing a song. Even in asking, Leng Eng was not herself convinced that it was a good idea. It was a dull gathering, a gaggle of girls who, like herself, had completed school a few years back. They met infrequently and never brought their boyfriends along. Similarly, if Jimmy were free, why would Leng Eng be with them?

Hurry up! Elaine's tone, while not as sharp as when rapping out orders at home, was commanding enough. Betty got up and walked to the centre of the room. She showed no awkwardness or embarrassment at being thus singled out. At twelve, she showed a resilience beyond her years. There was something rather vacuous about her face.

What's going on?

My sister's going to sing a song. You don't mind?

What's there to mind? Sing what?

Betty started singing a song in Mandarin. She had heard that song often enough to have learnt it. When she first heard it performed by a Taiwanese singer, she there and then decided it was a song she would sing forever. That Taiwanese singer had been sensational. At every performance, she ended the song with tears hosing down her face. To Betty, it was not only moving. It was like having access to an entire vista of human understanding that had so far eluded her.

Her earnest strong voice and impassive face struck the listeners as comic. But she sang in obedience to the mannerly deployment of her heart. Her voice soared and, when she came to the end and had hit the last note, she fell onto the floor in a heap.

Bring a towel. Quick! Also some water. Leng Eng screamed, more in anger.

Elaine, bent over her sister, suddenly straightened herself.

Betty stood up. And Elaine, who had heard her practising the song so often quickly understood what it was all about. Betty had wanted to extend the Taiwanese's presentation. In place of tears, Betty had chosen the faint, the dramatic crumble. A sense of admiration, shame and anger welled up; Elaine got up and slapped Betty.

The dull gathering ended on a merry note for nearly everyone.

And Betty—who could tell what she felt? Leng Eng started praising Betty; the suppressed snigger and muffled laughter around her was ambient support. You must come more often.

Can't hide all that talent you know. Elaine, must enter her for the talentime. Whether she wins or not, sure to floor the judges. Leng Eng was stacking glasses and plates on a tray.

Want some more coffee or not? Better say quickly, if not no time to make later.

Later, thirty-five years later, Betty was the executive director of a modelling school.

Excuse me, Miss Wong, got two more enrolled this morning. Want to accept or not?

The new secretary did not last long.

You have to speak correctly. Above everything else, you must have poise. In talking to you, the participants, the photographers, whoever they are, must feel as if you are confiding in them. Betty Wong, in her advice to the secretary being interviewed, was herself confidential and highly poised. Her string of pearls secreted the wisdom of the deep sea. There is so much unhappiness in the world. If I could educate every woman to be elegant and charming, half the troubles of the world would be gone. You must understand, such education is the most difficult to instil in people. We have to work very hard. We have to make sacrifices.

Betty Wong levitated from her chair and, in crossing the room in regular, heart-felt steps, thought fleetingly of a song she could no longer fully remember.

Oh, hello Vicki! Your show was fantastic. Such classical lines!

Such poetry of motion!

Vicki reached for the elegant white telephone, her hand a nubile technological extension. Ah, right, right! It doesn't matter.

I'll call again. Hey Betty, do you know what? Bermy's organising a show in Manila next month.

Who's financing it? I see, I see, and all expenses paid. What!

Twenty-five percent guaranteed sales. Betty Wong inclined her head a little and both her hands described quarter-circles of beatitude. It isn't so much the financial success. Just imagine what Benny can and must do. What an educational experience it must be.

Betty Wong returned to her office. In the eggshell splendour, a secondary thought raced through her mind. I must send Elaine some money. She is, after all, my sister. Should I send her a thousand? She wrote out a cheque for two hundred, lit a cigarette, buzzed the intercom, tore up the cheque and, when the secretary came in, she was frowning over a letter like an octopus that had organized its tentacles over a sheet of seaweed. She did not look up immediately and, when she abruptly did, the secretary's obedient eyes suddenly rolled away. Betty Wong smiled an interior smile, a little inner zip had been pulled. An old trick, she thought, but how effective. The secretary was very brand new.

It wasn't cent meditation I dictated. It was Zen. Z for Zip.

You have been very remiss.

> re: Miss Zatika
> I regret to inform that the nominee you proposed for our course on Inner Poise and Zen Meditation has been unsuccessful.

Miss Zatika, prior to nomination, had been Au Lin Soo, a healthy fresh-face. Why would spring lamb want to pass off as meditative mutton? Such a thought was not in Betty Wong's ideational agenda.

But if she likes, she could try again. Her letter to the director of a lesser-known modelling school was one she had sent off hundreds of times. The difference each time was that the name was different. The name of the course was also different. Last week, she had regretted the rejection of a participant for The Externalization of Inner Light.

Betty Wong felt tired. All these trivial details. There is absolutely no one one can depend on. She had wanted, every single day, to plan and map out her Beauty Edification Project. A nearby file carried the inscription:

BEP/II/16 A
Physiognometrics—Within & Without
Beauty, the Art & the Science & the Philosophy of

Apart from the inscription, the file was empty, without.

An ending must be found. Without it, Betty Wong could only go on rejecting the Zatikas. The Zatikas are abundant. Somewhere in between the rejection and the realization that the Zatikas were being rejected for nothing, for things that weren't there; somehow, in between the chuckle and the choke, Betty Wong drew a conclusion. It was the collapse before the song started. And poor Elaine; the face, the recollection of the face that could not launch Betty Wong's hand.

LEE GEOK CHAN
Catherine Lim

Lee Geok Chan was one of my students in pre-university. One of the many for whom long hours of study ensured, at most, a scraping through the examinations. She was a pale, small-sized, earnest-looking girl, always seen with a book or a sheaf of notes in her hand. Her father was a tailor, her mother a washerwoman; there were three brothers and two sisters. Geok Chan was the second in the family and the eldest girl.

Her desire to pass the examination, get a job and help the family put her in a constant state of nervous effort, so that she was to be found at all times blinking anxiously as she took down a teacher's lecture verbatim, copying notes from the blackboard with extreme diligence, or writing an essay with a concentration all the more remarkable for the noise and complete abandon of those around her in the classroom.

I always found it painful to have to tell Geok Chan, in response to her timid inquiry of how she could improve in her written expression, that her English was rather weak, her use of words frequently inappropriate, and that she often strayed off the point in her essay. She would nod in docile agreement, but at the same time the disappointment showed visibly on her face. Additional lessons did not seem to have helped and each week it became a special pain for me to hand back a piece of work, to see it snatched up eagerly and checked for its grade, and then to see the crestfallen look on the thin, pale face.

Like so many others, Geok Chan was preparing for the 'A' level examinations at the end of the year. In the last month before the examination, she often came up to me with a quick nervous smile and handed me a sheaf of essays to mark.

One of the essays caught my attention. It was better than the others; in fact, it was the best she had ever written, and there was hope yet, for her, if she could produce something like that in the examination. I forget the exact words of the essay topic she had picked from somewhere, but it was about happiness. Geok Chan had written simply and with conviction about her concept of happiness; some parts of the essay were, I thought, beautifully lyrical. I suddenly realised that, freed from the constraints of conventional essay topics, she wrote with ease and obvious pleasure.

I called her up and commented favourably on her essay. She glowed with pride. "If I write like that in the General Paper, will I get a credit?" she wanted to know. I had to warn her, rather sadly, that the essay topics in the General Paper were not of the kind that permitted this spontaneity. I encouraged her, though, to go on expressing her innermost feelings.

"They're in me all the time. I couldn't express them before, now I think I can," she said, blinking not with nervousness but, instead, with a kind of feverish joy.

On the morning of the essay paper, Geok Chan was killed in a road accident. She was walking along the pavement just outside the school and was about to enter the school gates when a lorry came racing along, crazily jumped the road divider and crashed into her. She died instantly. It was the most cruel death I had ever known; my colleagues and I wept long for this earnest, good girl who had always tried her best and whose only ambition was to earn enough to support her family.

The essay on happiness that had astonished me by its power and lyricism lay, among a pile of unmarked papers on my desk, almost like a keepsake, for she had collected all the other essays, and had somehow left this one with me. When I went to see her parents, who were too grieved to say anything, I brought this composition with me and handed it to her eldest brother, who just put it aside with her other school things heaped on a little wooden table in the small two-room HDB flat.

The recollection of that small body under sheets of newspapers on the road disturbed me for many days afterwards. The blood had flowed copiously; it was a moment's glance before I turned away and quickly walked back to the staff room from where we had been summoned by the frantic cries of those students who had witnessed the dreadful accident. But the scene stayed in my mind for days, and it was inevitable that some of us would have had dreams about Lee Geok Chan in our sleep.

I dreamt that she approached me with a poem on sorrow or something like that and asked me to grade it. Another colleague dreamt of her exactly as she was that day, under the newspapers on a wet road just in front of the school gate.

In the bustle of a new school year when new eager faces crowded the school corridors, Lee Geok Chan was soon forgotten. Occasionally, however, something or other cropped up to remind us of her and then we recollected that terrible day in December.

One occasion was the release of the examination results in March. Students started coming to the school very early in the morning, as soon as they had learnt from the newspaper that the Ministry of Education would be releasing the results that day. The computer print-out with Geok Chan's name showed the grades for these subjects: History, Chinese Language and the General Paper. She had obtained a credit in Chinese Language, but had failed for History and the General Paper.

There had to be a mistake regarding the General Paper—how could there have been a grade for that subject? Geok Chan was killed before she could sit for the paper. Her death was in the morning; the paper was at two in the afternoon.

It was a very low grade, in fact the lowest on the scale. If a computer had to make a mistake about one who was already dead, some of us laughed uneasily, surely it could have erred on the side of generosity?

Geok Chan's elder brother came to collect the results slip, which he did desultorily, without a glance at the statements on the slip, and was gone almost immediately.

I first of all ascertained from the Minister of Education that there had been no mistake in the printout; then I wrote a very polite letter to the

Cambridge Syndicate of Examiners, asking them to explain why the essay of the candidate Lee Geok Chan had obtained such a low grade. It was a laborious process involving excessive red tape, for there were certain formalities to be gone through, including the payment of a stipulated sum of money.

It took Cambridge a month to reply. I received a plain official statement on how the candidate had gone entirely out of point in the essay section, for she had written a piece on happiness when there was no essay topic even remotely resembling this. The statement added that by itself the essay was commendable for its expressiveness and strength of feeling, but since it was written in total disregard of the given examination topics, it could not be awarded any marks.

The mounting sensation of excitement and terror that gripped me as I read the statement was something I had never experienced before. It was impossible to contain the thoughts that were now crowding my mind, and I soon found myself in urgent consultation with my colleagues. It cannot be, it cannot be, we said again and again. And yet again and again, no matter how hard we tried, no matter how many theories we tested, there was no accounting for the fact that the essay which had been sent to Cambridge together with thousands of other essays, and which had been marked and given a grade, was the essay of a dead student.

Unable to let things lie, I wrote to Cambridge again and requested, urgently, to have the essay script of candidate Lee Geok Chan returned. I added that I was prepared to pay any amount of money that the authorities might deem reasonable to compensate them for their pains.

Probably fearing that a move of this kind could set the precedent for anxious parents or teachers intending to fine-tooth comb a marked script and argue for a better grade, the Cambridge Syndicate turned down the request. It had never been and would never be their policy to return marked scripts to candidates. All they were prepared to do was furnish a statement about the script, and they had already done this.

But this is no ordinary script, a dead person wrote it, I wanted to cry out in exasperation when I read the reply. Then I realised how nearly impossible it would be to give this explanation in the circumscribed language of formal correspondence. I tried, though, so eager was I to get to the bottom of it all, but after a while Cambridge chose not to reply to my requests, probably dismissing me as a crank.

I almost pleaded with them to send me a typewritten copy of the candidate's essay, so that the marking and grading of the script could remain confidential, but they must have misinterpreted the tone of the letter and taken offence, for they finally wrote back to say that they would no longer entertain any correspondence on the subject.

I tried to enlist the help of Geok Chan's family, but it was to no avail. The elder brother had been posted to some other town; the younger brothers and sisters did not seem able to understand me and the parents spoke only a dialect I could not comprehend. In any case, they were still too sorrowful to do much beyond shaking their heads mournfully or raising their voices to curse the driver of the lorry that had killed their daughter.

It is now more than ten years since Lee Geok Chan died. I am not satisfied with the explanation that my colleagues finally settled on. A coincidence, they said, somebody's essay was mistaken for Geok Chan's; after all, there were thousands of essays to be graded and confusions of this kind were not at all surprising.

But the topic was so specific. It was on happiness, I protested, the very same topic she wrote on just before the accident. And the qualities of freshness and expressiveness were precisely those I had noted in that last essay she showed me. That could not have been a coincidence; there must have been a mistake then, said some of my colleagues. A coincidence, a mistake—the words threw a blanket over all that remains, to this day, a mystery.

AMARJIT'S WHISKY GONE AWRY
Kirpal Singh

"You know, the best thing about Ava Gardner, my gawd, you should see her inner thigh—simply creamy, just inviting, waiting for your caress."

"How would you know? You talk as if you had her."

"But I did *yaar*, I did."

"*Yiah*—I am sure—in your dreams."

"Yes."

It is now more than seven years since that dialogue took place. We were all a little pissed, on Fifth Avenue New York, hearing the wails of sirens and the catcalls of those who thought we were truly aliens. There were four of us—Amarjit, a newly graduated engineer from Purdue University come to the east to seek a better fortune; Sarjit, the lawyer whose job was mainly to frame everything for his colleagues in Smith and Smith but not appear in court himself; Harvinder, Amarjit's brother who had come from Malaysia to entice his brother to return home because their parents were getting old and missing their firstborn, and me, yes me—I had newly arrived in New York from Singapore to be interviewed for a possible appointment at Columbia—me of the great universities of the world, where I was hoping to become an agent of real change so the university could truly usher in the new millennium with flourish. And, oh yes, I must not forget Jenny. Jenny was Sarjit's white American girlfriend. Jenny was a painter, an artist whose own parents had written her off.

Poor Amarjit. He really loved the US of A. His parents had spent tens of thousands to get him educated at what everyone considered one of the best engineering schools in the world. And he had done very well, scoring top grades in every examination. Upon graduation, he got a job immediately, in a small firm in Indiana. But he was unhappy because, as he told us, there really had been no future in the small firm. And he had been advised to come East or go East for better prospects. And so, now in New York, Amarjit was drinking his life away, refusing if, return home to Malaysia and refusing to acknowledge, like Sarjit, that life for aliens like him was going to be tough: The blacks-or Afro-Americans as they were increasingly being labelled—didn't welcome the likes of Amarjit for reasons which still remain unfathomable, in spite of numerous theories of competition being put forward by various sociologists. The Hispanics, who were a growing number, just didn't want anyone whose command of English was better—and almost everyone's was! And the whites, *aaahh* yes, the whites, they always said the best of things but did little to actually help Amarjit get a good job. Jenny's explanation for this was, "we whites have a super love-hate thing for you guys—we actually admire you for your hard work, commitment and dedication, but are not sure if you are going to make us brown by marrying our girls." And then she would laugh, ironically, sardonically, sadly. I knew that her relationship with Sarjit was a real contributing factor to her parents' indifference to what she was so desperately trying to achieve as an artist.

"You know what though," said Amarjit, more thoughtfully, "she was simply adorable in *On the Beach*. Any of you saw that beautiful film? Based on the novel by Nevil Shute? Hey, you (pointing to me), surely you must have seen it, after all, aren't you into books and all that?"

Yes. I was into books except that for my immediate purpose, I was not into the kind of books which Columbia for all its talk of openness was really keen on. But yes, I had read Shute's novel and seen the film. It was science fiction to me. And very Australian. And yes, I remembered Ava Gardner's role—stunning, not quite vampish but highly sexual. But we were in America. And Ava Gardner had died a sad, lingering death and never, I thought, found lasting joy in any of her marriages or relationships. For me it was *The Night if the Iguana* which was her best film. I remembered watching that as quite a young boy but I never forgot the tied iguana. Later as I grew up I realised that the iguana was such an apt symbol for so many of us—yearning to be free but trapped in our own prisons. Even here, in New York, I could see how apt the symbolism was. Amarjit was in a prison.

"Yes, of course Amarjit, but I still prefer the novel—I think Ava Gardner should have suicided like the character she portrays in Shute's novel. Would have made it a much better film."

"Maybe," said Amarjit, "but you know Ava Gardner—she was not made for death, she was made for life. For giving life vitality, especially the vitality of sex which keeps us all alive."

"Speak for yourself," said Sarjit.

"Is there nothing you guys talk about but sex?" intervened Jenny. "You know we white girls may be attracted to you guys but we are not dumb. And we are not your sex slaves."

"Of course not honey," said a meek Sarjit.

I felt for Jenny. I almost knew by instinct she was finding the four of us Sikhs a little tiresome; our sense of humour was not exactly her's, though because of her love for Sarjit (Amarjit though was convinced it was not love but pity) she tolerated our ranting and raving and carrying on.

Fifth Avenue New York was enchanting—I had heard so much about it that being there now, physically, was for me almost out-of-this-world. I saw drunks lying around, I saw couples hugging and kissing, I saw executives hurrying and hurrying, I saw old people being told to get out of the way by indifferent young people. I saw wonderful stores selling expensive, branded clothing and goods, I saw some superlative cars making their presences felt as the traffic crawled, I saw people with aimlessness in their eyes just—strolling, staring, stopping, window-shopping. Was this, seriously, the place I wanted to be if Columbia did offer me a job? My reverie was interrupted—or rather, I was supposed to be part of Amarjit's rave.

"You see, even you have come here from your blighted Singapore to seek greener pastures. This is what America is all about. Living your dream. This is the land of the brave and free, people, brave and free. Hey, you again, you man of books, what is that book, that book about; the American dream etc? You know the one I mean; by Fitzgerald."

"I think you mean *The Great Gatsby.*"

"That's the one. Correct. Ava Gardner would have made a brilliant Daisy—the woman whose allure is simply irresistible. The woman all men fall for. Oh man, if only I could have one Ava Gardner in my life. You Sarjit are a bloody lucky bugger man—you have Jenny."

This was a little too close to the bone. Among Sikh men it was not proper to refer to a friend's partner, even in jest. In fact, especially in jest.

"Are you flattering me?" asked Jenny, whose eyes lit up as she queried Amarjit.

"No my dear; I am telling Sarjit what a lucky bastard he is having got you. He should forget about what they call him and just marry you. After all a towel-head who wins the hands of a beautiful white girl can't be that bad!"

Amarjit had crossed the line. He had spoken the unspeakable. Racism was not a subject any of us were comfortable about. I had been warned about discrimination by my colleagues but my answer to them had been it exists everywhere. The difference was in degree.

Sarjit was not going to let this go. Amarjit's remarks were not only hurtful but an affront. Sarjit had been suffering snobbery ever since he made up his mind to live in New York and work at Smith and Smith. Jenny was his consolation. In her and her paintings he found the much-needed transcendence he, as a lawyer, did not always find in the law books. But Amarjit's utterance had made the inner truth the outer stigma come alive.

I remember Sarjit hitting Amarjit hard on the head and Amarjit stumbling, Jenny was shocked and clasped Harvinder tight. For his part, Harvinder was speechless for he was not succeeding in persuading Amarjit to return. I, well I, the man of books, I pushed Sarjit to one side of the pavement and held him there. It was obvious to me that Fifth Avenue New York was not going to sympathise with our sorry state except to savour the fact that we aliens were yet another source for their merriment;

for with the corner of my eye I saw a group of boys laughing at what they had just witnessed.

"Ok, ok, I'm sorry," said Amarjit. "It's the beer you fed me just now."

"*Teri mah dhi*," said Sarjit.

"What did Sarjit just say?" asked Jenny.

"Nothing. Don't worry."

Thoughout the shenanigans I tried to maintain my cool. I was an obvious outsider, except, perhaps, for Harvinder who clearly was even more determined that the time had truly come for his brother to return to Malaysia and be with the family.

We walked on after the incident. Surely the night was not going to end this way, with a fight and the ensuing sullenness. I decided to speak up.

"Hey Amarjit, you know all that you said about Ava Gardner? Well, I think we have our very own Ava Gardners. Many of them vying for the same titles, trying their luck in the same film yards, craving for the same glories. But ours dare not take the risks. And for me the real Ava Gardner is that near tragic woman who took risks, with everything. Like Jenny here who has risked a lot to pursue her passion for art. Maybe this is where we should all stop and reconsider our lives. Do we want to stay safe *or* take risks?"

There was a faint smile playing on their lips. There was a look of expectancy in Jenny's eyes as she still held close to Harvinder who was beginning to feel a little uneasy. Sarjit managed to put his embarrassment behind him and say, "America is not for the weak-and also not for those who just think scoring high grades in exams is the answer to making millions. America is for those who are in for the long haul. America is for those of us who believe in a dream and are prepared to suffer for it."

We all seemed to have sobered up. Now there was this other dialogue starting. About America. About the great US of A. About us who were brought up on Hollywood movies. Jenny, Sarjit, Harvinder and I looked at Amarjit who had been silent.

"Alright Harvinder. I think Mah and Pah are right. You are right. America is not for me. I should return to Malaysia. The *bunga raya* still smells good. My days of whisky and rye are over. The beer here is cheap. But dreams are expensive. Let us go."

Well, what could we say or do after these odd remarks from Amarjit but slowly move away from each other after wishing 'goodnights'. Jenny held Sarjit's hand but I knew the clasp had been weakened. Harvinder put his arms around Amarjit as he slowly steered towards a taxi. And I, well, I thought about my Columbia interview and slowly trudged towards my hotel thinking, 'If Columbia offers me a job, that will be my risk.'

GLORIA
Suchen Christine Lim

She wraps her brown brawny arms around him, holding him between her knees, hugging him close against her breasts. He leans back, sinking into the fold of her arms, his eyes fixed on the tv screen in the living room. But her eyes are not on the tv. They're gazing through the black iron grille of the balcony, gazing at the distant lights of the ships anchored out at sea, gazing towards where the brightly lit buildings shine like altars to their Chinese gods, and beyond that to the dark sky, the same dark sky that arcs over Manila City, the same dark sky with the same bright moon shining on the garbage of the Pasig River. Oblivious of the glances of her ma'am, seated in the armchair in the living room, her hand is stroking the child's back. The family is watching tv after dinner, and she has slipped out of the kitchen to join them. But she does not sit with them. Although her ma'am has not said anything, she knows that it will be regarded as presumptuous if she sits with them in the living room. So she sits on the cane chair in the balcony, and the boy, Timmy, the youngest of the two boys and a girl under her charge, has come out to sit with her. She wraps her arms around his warm tubby belly, inhaling the lavender fragrance of the talcum powder she has rubbed on him after his bath. When she has saved enough, she will buy a small tin of the same Johnson & Johnson talc powder to take home to Migoy and Amy, her two youngest. She kisses the boy's head.

"Timmy! Come in here!"

With a start, her arms drop to her side. The boy runs to his mother.

"What're you doing in the balcony, darling? Full of mosquitoes out there. Sit here with Mummy. Gloria!"

"Yes, Ma'am."

"Have you finished washing the dishes?"

"Yes, Ma'am."

"What about the kitchen towels? Did you wash them and hang them up to dry?"

"Yes, Ma'am."

"Bring out the chocolate cake in the fridge. And don't forget the plates and forks this time."

"Yes, Ma'am."

She goes into the kitchen and returns with the cake, the plates and forks on a tray. She sets it on the coffee table.

"How am I going to cut the cake without a knife? And you forgot napkins."

"Yes, Ma'am."

She goes into the kitchen again, returns with the cake knife and some napkins.

"No, you don't cut it. I'll cut it. You still have laundry to do tonight, don't you?"

"Yes, Ma'am."

"Well, what're you waiting for then? I don't need you here."

She retreats into the kitchen, and sits on the floor of the narrow alcove where the laundry is hung and where she sleeps at night. She sits beside her suitcase, the green and brown canvas suitcase that Tita Flora had lent her when the village knew that she was coming to Singapore to work. She sits beside it, her brown brawny arms wrapped around her shoulders, rocking her upper body back and forth, back and forth, as though she was rocking her baby. Her little Migoy.

"Good morning, ah, Mrs Ling."

"Good morning, Alice. This is my new maid."

"Oh, your new maid, ah?" The receptionist at the clinic looks at her. "What happened to the old one?"

"I had to change her," her ma'am replies.

"To change maids, you got to pay extra or not?"

"This maid agency is very good. The employer is allowed to make two changes. No need to pay. You pay a transfer fee only at the third change."

Her ma'am hands over a sheath of official papers across the counter.

"Glori-ah An-ton-nia Bern-na-dette San-tos," the receptionist reads out her name in the singsong lilt of the Chinese in this clean and green city where even the trees look neat and tidy, very different from the unruly trees back home. But the sunlight is the same, the same. The sun that shines in this rich city is the same sun that shines on her *barangay*.

"Glor-ri-a!" the receptionist turns to her.

"Yes, ma'am." Her voice squeaks like one of those tiny white mice in the pet shop. The clinic is full of watchful eyes. The eyes of these strangers are scrutinising her, eyes that say she's the stranger, not them. She keeps her head down, suddenly ashamed of her shabby blouse and faded black pants. The receptionist continues to address her in a loud voice as if that will help her to understand better.

"You, *ah*! You take this cup and go to the toilet. You pass urine into the cup, okay? Make sure enough urine is inside the cup, not outside; otherwise cannot do the pregnancy test. You got pee or not? If cannot pee now, you drink some water."

The woman turns to her ma'am.

"Must always tell them to drink water. Some of them, no pee, also go inside the toilet and stay there a long time. And their employer is out here waiting and waiting, and the maid is still inside the toilet. Many people complain to me. Other patients also want to use the toilet. So now I tell all the maids. Go drink some water first."

Her ma'am smiles and shakes her head. "I know. You've got to spell out every single step before they do it right."

"Ya, *lor*! Glor-ri-a, you go pee now."

Head down, she walks across towards the closed door.

"*Oi*! Not that door! The other door! That other one!" the receptionist shouts across the crowded waiting room.

A young man rises from his seat and points her to another door. He gives her an embarrassed smile. She nods, goes in and locks the door. The words, 'thank you', are stuck like a fishbone in her throat. She leans over the sink, turns on the tap and cups her two hands to drink some water. It's only when she unzips her pants and squats over the plastic cup that she lets her tears fall.

A mother since age sixteen, she's thirty-six but looks fifty-six. This is the medical examination to decide her fate. Make sure that she's not pregnant before they will confirm her employment. What they don't know is that she doesn't want to get pregnant any more. She'd pushed Alex away. After the first four, she didn't want it any more. Didn't want more babies. But how could she keep saying no to her Alex? He wanted her even when they already had ten mouths to feed. And the wife should submit to the husband and not push him into sin, Father Paolo Biviendo had preached. These priests. They know only God's will. She cleans herself, zips up her pants, and washes her hands at the sink. She's through with these priests. It's up to Suzie and her now. Suzie will take care of the others. They will have to depend on their eldest sister. It'll be five long years before Alex is out of prison. In the meantime, she'll work and make money. Make lots of money. Pay back the agent; pay back the lawyer; pay back Tita Flora; pay back Ma Lulu and the others. She opens the washroom door, carefully holding with both hands the white plastic cup half filled with yellow urine.

"Speak up, Gloria. I can't hear you."

"Yes, ma'am," she repeats a little louder.

"Now the maid agency says you can cook. Is that right?"

"Yes, ma'am."

"Good. I want you to cook simple nutritious meals for the children. One meat, one vegetable, a soup and rice. I myself don't know how to cook so you take charge of the menu. If you don't know anything, ask. See this stack of cookbooks? You can look at them. I bought them for the last maid. You can read, can't you?"

GLORIA

A slight movement of her head. Neither a 'yes' nor a 'no'. She's unsure of the consequences if she should admit that she'd only been to school up to grade four.

"I'm very particular about cleanliness. When I come back from the office, I don't want to see oily stains all over the stove or walk on an oily floor. This kitchen must be clean and spotless. You understand?"

"Yes, ma'am."

"If you run out of detergents, cleansers or anything, tell me. Don't keep quiet like the other maids. Don't tell me at the last minute or when I ask or when I find out we've run out of food and things. I'm busy working every day. I go to the supermarket once a week so you must let me know in advance. Here. This notebook and pen are for you. Write down all the things I've got to buy for the week. You understand?"

"Yes ma'am."

"See this box? I've put fifty dollars inside. It's for little emergencies. You run out of condiments or the children need to buy something in school, then you take the money from this box. Always ask the shopkeepers downstairs for a receipt. Put the receipts inside. I'll check the box once a week and replenish it. You understand?"

"Yes, ma'am."

Her head is reeling. Fifty Singapore dollars. How much is that in peso? That is… that is… that is two thousand peso. She's amazed but she's careful not to smile. Two thousand peso for her to buy things each week. She has never had so much money before.

"Let me see. What else do I have to tell you? Oh yes. Do you know how to use the washing machine? I've pinned up the instructions here. Just read and follow the instructions. If you don't know how to operate it, ask John. He's the oldest. John! John!"

"What?" The boy is surly at being called into the kitchen.

"Show Gloria how to operate the washing machine, and the other electrical things if she doesn't know."

"Very simple to use, what! Just read the instructions."

"I will teach Gloria, Mummy!"

"Timmy! You teach Gloria?" Sarah runs into the kitchen, wagging her finger at the little one. "Hahaha! He'll teach her all the wrong things, Mummy!"

"But I know! I know!"

"Quiet. You children, out. Go on. Out of the kitchen. I want to talk to Gloria."

"Yes, ma'am."

"The agent has explained things to you. But I will go through it again. You get three hundred dollars a month. The agency will deduct two hundred and seventy every month for ten months until you finish paying back what you owe them. So I will give the agency two hundred and seventy dollars, and give you the remainder, thirty dollars, each month. Do you understand? You get thirty dollars every month. The rest goes to your agent. So you must spend within your means. I'm sick and tired of maids borrowing money from me. No borrowing. My last two maids always borrowed. Father ill. Brother sick in hospital. Mother dying. Sister getting married. Brother going to college. Or uncle lost his harvest in floods and typhoons. All sorts of stories I've heard. I lost six hundred dollars just listening to the stories of the last two maids. Sir said, no borrowing. No advance payment. Do you understand?"

"Yes, ma'am."

"Are you clear about the meals and kitchen? And the schedules of the children?"

"Yes, ma'am."

"Don't just say 'yes ma'am, yes ma'am' when you don't understand. Do you understand?"

"Yes, ma'am."

"Eeee! The pork tastes funny!"

The girl spits out the meat on to her plate. Timmy follows suit.

"You don't like pork, Sarah?"

"This pork tastes funny. What is it?"

"Pork adobo."

"Yuks! I don't like it. I want fish fingers."

"Me too! Me too!" Timmy claps his hands. The doorbell rings. She runs out to open the door for the eldest boy back from school.

"What's for lunch, Gloria?"

"Yukky pork!" the girl giggles. "We're having fish fingers instead."

"Yeah, I want fish fingers too, Gloria."

Without a word, she goes to the freezer. "How many you want?" she asks.

"Ten," the eldest boy says.

"Me too," the girl follows.

"Me too, me too," Timmy clamours.

But there are only fifteen fish fingers in the box. She heats some oil in the frying pan, and empties the whole box into it. When the fish fingers are a golden brown, she gives the eldest boy seven pieces, and the two younger ones four fish fingers each.

"It's not fair! You gave John more!"

"Cos I'm the eldest!"

"You're not!" the girl shouts.

"I am!"

"You're not!"

"I'm the oldest!"

"I was the oldest before you came to live with us!"

"You think I want to live here with you? You lizard face!"

"I'll tell my Mummy you called me lizard face!"

"Tell-*lah*! Tell-*lah*! Cry baby! This is my Dad's apartment!"

"It's also my Mummy's apartment!"

"Children! Children!" She tries to calm them.

"Mummy!" The girl is already calling her mother on the phone.

She is summoned to the phone.

"Yes, ma'm. No, ma'm. Yes, ma'am." The children watch as her eyes brim over. "I understand, ma'am." She puts down the phone and goes to the moneybox.

She takes out the fifty-dollar note. She likes the crisp, clean feel of the white and blue note. It's not limp, dirty and crumpled like the red *Limampung Piso*, the fifty peso note that she's used to handling. Fifty dollars. She can buy so many sacks of rice, so many kilos of fish, especially the bangus and tilapia that her children dream of eating, and so many yards of cloth to sew shirts for Bet and Vern, may be a blouse and skirt for Mol and Suzie, and buy shoes for Ninoy and Beng. Ahhh, a great many things she will buy with two thousand peso!

"Gloria! Where're you going?" the girl asks.

"The shop downstairs. Your mummy says to buy more fish fingers."

"I want to go too," Timmy insists.

With the two children leading the way, she has no trouble taking the elevator from the 21st floor to the ground floor. She doesn't tell them that the speed makes her dizzy. But she will tell her children when she sends a letter home. Timmy and Sarah lead her across the empty car park which, in the evening, will be filled with shiny clean cars parked in neat straight rows. Everything is clean, neat and orderly in her ma'am's condo. No one says sub-division here. Not like in Manila. She will write and tell her children. They walk past the rows of palm trees, the swimming pool and the tennis courts. What Sarah calls 'our neighbourhood shop' is in fact a small air-conditioned supermarket like the ones back home where the rich people in Quezon City shop, and where she has gone with Tita Flora to deliver the laundry. She's working in a rich neighbourhood for a rich family. Her ma'am scolded her just now because she didn't spend the fifty dollars.

"What's the matter with you, Gloria? You know there's only one box of fish fingers. You know it's not enough. Why didn't you go downstairs to buy another box? What's the money in the box for? I don't want the children to quarrel just because there's not enough food. For goodness sake! Use your brain. Go to the shop and buy another box of fish fingers! What's so difficult about that? I'm in the middle of a meeting. I don't want the children to call me about these little things. Do you understand?"

She walks down rows of bottled soft drinks, cans of beer, bottles of soy sauces, fish sauces, tomato ketchup, spices, condiments, and boxes of cereals she'd never seen or eaten before; and milk powder packed in tins, pasteurised milk in packets and bottles, and jars of jams, tins of meat, chicken and fish crowded the shelves. The tins of Spam, and sardines in tomato sauce make her mouth water even though she's still full from her lunch of rice and pork adobo. Ahhh, she feels blessed. She's walking through this wonderland, armed with the knowledge that she has money power. She has fifty dollars. But the shopkeeper doesn't understand her when she speaks. He behaves as though she's not speaking English.

"What, *ah*? You new, *ah*?"

"Uncle, she's our new maid. Her name is Gloria," Sarah, the little busybody, explains.

The shopkeeper looks at her. "Oh, *Glori-ah*. What you want to buy, *ha*?"

She opens one of the glass doors of the refrigerators and takes out a big box of Bird's Eye Fish Fingers. Then for good measure, to show that she's in charge, she walks over to the other side of the shop, and picks out two pink kitchen towels, a mop and a red plastic pail. When the children ask for ice cream, she lets them choose what they want. Two years, may be three years, from now if her ma'am extends her contract, she will let Migoy and Amy choose what they want in the supermarket in Fairview. One day. Some day. She hands over the fifty dollars to the Chinaman shopkeeper.

That night, her ma'am tells her not to cook pork adobo any more.

"The children don't like it. You have it for lunch tomorrow."

"Yes, ma'am."

Her brood would've rushed for the adobo. When there was enough pesos, she would buy the leftover fatty pork from Jong Boy's meat stall on the corner of the narrow lane between the tricycle and motor repair shops and Nana Ahchut's *sari-sari* store. Nana Ahchut had refused to let her buy on credit, not even the stale bread loaves and egg-sized *pan-de-sal* for the children's breakfast. *If I do that, Gloria, I will have to close down. Touch wood! I've many mouths to feed like you!* Nana Ahchut shouted through the iron grille, her fat face framed in the small window through which all the store's transactions were made. No one was allowed to enter the tiny store. *Been robbed too many times.* Nana Ahchut glared at her as if what Alex did was all her fault. The kids learnt to go without breakfast. They learnt to make a bit of rice and salted fish last until dinnertime when she returned from the laundry where she waited with other women to do the washing. If she were lucky, she had more kilos of clothes to wash, and earned more pesos. But that was not enough. Never enough to feed ten mouths. Her children were always hungry and scrawny like the chickens in Tita Flora's backyard scratching the dirt for scraps.

She scrapes into the bin the chunks of half eaten pork, rice and vegetables that the three children and their parents have left on their plates.

"We don't eat leftovers. Throw them away unless you want to eat them for lunch tomorrow," the ma'am said.

Why should she eat leftovers in this island of plenty? For once in her life, she will not eat leftovers. She'll even have an egg for breakfast.

Her new radio alarm rings. She gets out of bed and starts to dress. At six-thirty, just as the sky brightens, the ma'am comes out of her bedroom. They leave the apartment together, and take the elevator down, she carrying the basket and the ma'am carrying her purse and car keys. It's Saturday, the day when the children have tuition classes instead of school. It's also the day she goes to the fresh food market with the ma'am. She looks forward to this weekly trip although the ma'am dislikes the wet market, and would rather shop in Cold Storage, but Sir does not like the meat from the supermarket.

She sits in the front passenger seat with the basket on her lap. The ma'am starts the car; they rarely talk in the car. When they reach the market, the ma'am parks the car and strides ahead in her tee shirt, denim shorts and high-heeled slippers. She follows with her piece of paper and the blue plastic basket. Their routine has not changed this past one year. But today, she intends to vary things a little.

"Two chickens." She points to two large freshly slaughtered chickens. By now, the chicken man is used to her. Then she points to a bag of chicken bones and adds it to her usual order. "To make soup, ma'am," she says. "Timmy likes chicken soup."

"Ok. Is this enough?"

"Enough, ma'am." She keeps the pleasure out of her voice.

They move on to the Malay butcher's stall to buy beef, and then walk to the other side of the market to buy pork from the Chinese butcher. By now, she's used to this funny arrangement of selling meat in the markets in Singapore. Only the Chinese sell pork, and only the Malays sell beef. Back home at Jong Boy's stall, things are easier. No one makes a fuss if a leg of mutton or beef is hanging next to the head of a pig. When she mentioned this to the other maids at the church she goes to on Sundays, they laughed. Last year, when she was still a new arrival, they had told her that all Chinese in Singapore are Buddhist, and all Indians are Hindu, and they don't eat beef.

Of course, we eat beef, Gloria. Cook beef steak for us if you know how to do it. As long as the children eat what you cook, and Sir does not complain, that's fine with me. I just don't want to come home and hear a host of complaints from the children. You understand?

Her ma'am does not care how much food she buys and cooks these days.

"Pork one and a half kilo," she points to the rump, which has a bit more fat. "And lean pork one kilo. The bones four dollars."

At the fish stall, she adds two kilos of fish and half a kilo of shrimps, and tells herself to stop; don't over do it. The ma'am might ask questions even though the ma'am's mind is always busy at the bank, and she works late like Sir. Both earn a big fat salary. They won't mind paying extra. They won't even miss it. She knows because the ma'am and Sir talk at the dinner table. Last Christmas, the ma'am's bank gave her six extra months' salary as a bonus. The family bought a new car, and went to America for a holiday. During the two weeks they were away, she worked for the ma'am's mother, and the old lady gave her fifty dollars. When the ma'am returned, she also gave her fifty dollars on Christmas Day. It was the first time that she'd received so much money. The money is in the bank now. She can't touch it. The ma'am had made her deposit her money in the neighbourhood Post Office bank.

Don't be stupid, Gloria. You maids always sent your money home. You shouldn't. How do you know that your family is not wasting your hard earned money? You must save for yourself. Put the money in the bank here. Earn interest. I'll use my name to open a joint account with you. Don't worry. I won't run off with your money. And you keep the book. At the end of your contract, you can withdraw all the money and go home with a lump sum. Do you understand?

"Gloria! What're you thinking? Are we through?"

"Sorry, ma'am. I forgot to buy sweet *tauhu*."

"You're still saying *tauhu*. People here will think you want bean curd for frying. It's *tau-huay* for sweet bean curd."

"Sorry, ma'am. Timmy wants."

"Here's ten dollars. Go quickly. The market is getting crowded. I'm tired."

The ma'am will let her buy anything if it's for the children. Her ma'am walks ahead carrying her purse and car keys. She follows with the blue basket loaded with food and two large pink plastic bags filled with enough meat and veg to feed eight adults for a week. And the ma'am hasn't questioned her. Is this a sign? Is God being fair at last? Maybe God knows her troubles and gives her this chance. She can't be choosy. If she's given the chance, wouldn't she be a fool not to take it? Suzie is gone.

I know this will break your heart, Gloria. Suzie has left home. She didn't tell anyone. Not me. Not her brothers. Not her sisters. Not a soul. Oh, Gloria, she left them in the dark. Such a shock to me when Migoy came running to say their sister is gone. Tita Flora wrote.

She remembers holding that letter in her hand as the tears gathered and the news sank in. Bent over the kitchen sink, she had clutched her breasts. Her heart was broken again. How long could a heart remain a heart? Her heart had been hacked too many times. First, by Alex, then Ninoy and her drunken *Tatay*, the father she wished she'd never had. All day she was poorly. The ma'am, thinking she had caught the flu, had taken her to the clinic where the nurse had made her take a blood and urine test. *Just to be sure*, the ma'am said to the nurse in Chinese. *Just to be sure*, the nurse's silent nod agreed. Did they think she was stupid and diseased? That she would infect them with her broken heart? That she was too stupid to understand their *Chink-chong* code? Did the ma'am think that she'd caught something and would pass it to the children? Just to be sure. Always, it's just to be sure. The ma'am who has everything wants to be sure of everything. She who has nothing is never sure of anything. She cannot even be sure of the child who dropped out of her womb. Suzie's gone. Her flesh and blood has left her.

No letter. No phone call. Not even a note. *Did Gabriel Jose leave the village too? Did she elope with him? Did you check with Gab's family? Did you ask them?* She had cried and screamed into the public phone at the post office till her phone card ran out of money. How did this happen? Who could tell her? Would Suzie have run away if she were there? If her Papa were there? Alex. Alex. He was a fool to think he could leave the warehouse without the guards knowing. A fool to get himself arrested. A fool that no lawyer would defend because there was no money! Fool! Fool! Fool! Suzie. Her child! Her baby. The first in the family to graduate from high school. Her pride.

She had to ask herself: What do you do when your only hope runs off because she's afraid of the burden you placed on her thin shoulders? She runs away because she doesn't want to end up like you and her aunts sleeping, eating and shitting in the hovels under the bridges of Pasig and Quezon City. Cardboard palaces that the typhoons blow away and the floods wash away. Can you blame Suzie for taking off? Can you blame your daughter if she doesn't want to be like you? What do you do? Where can you find her? O God! Where can I find her? Is this why You have given me this opportunity? This skill? These men?

Carefully, she wraps the extra pieces of fried fish and pork sausages in sheets of tin foil and pushes them to the back of the freezer behind the Tupperware boxes of frozen pork, prawns and fish. No one will bother to look into the freezer. On Sunday, her day off, she will take the bus to Lucky Plaza in Orchard Road and pass the package to Ramos and Roddy, and they will pay her.

Sarah runs into the kitchen waving an envelope.

"*Glori-ah!* Letter for you! From Japan. Can I have the stamps?"

"Later, later. Go and play."

The girl runs out. Hands trembling, she tears open the envelope. She sits on the floor in the alcove of the kitchen beside Tita Flora's suitcase, and stares at the two photographs. She brings the letter to her nose and inhales its sweet fragrance. The letter is written on pink perfumed paper with a border of tiny flowers in pale blue. *Dearest Mama.* Her eyes start to brim. Nine months and eleven days after she's run away, Suzie writes, *Dearest Mama, how are you? I am well. I am working in a hotel in Tokyo... Dearest Mama. Dearest Mama.*

"Gloria! Sarah says you've a letter from Japan. Do you have anyone working there?" the ma'am asks her after dinner.

"Yes, ma'am. My eldest daughter."

"Oh. Is she working as a maid too?"

"No, ma'am. She's a secretary in a big hotel in Tokyo."

She takes out the photographs as proud proof of her daughter's new status.

"My daughter graduated from high school."

"Oh. Very pretty girl. Did you say she's a secretary in a hotel?"

"Yes, ma'am."

"And she's dressed like this?"

Something in the ma'am's question has poisoned her eyes. Her sight is maimed. She stares at the photos. She can no longer see her daughter. Instead she sees a young teenage girl in a bright red negligee reclining on the large bed. A bright red sunny smile plastered on her face. The other photo shows her in a black mini skirt and high-heeled black leather boots outside a grand-looking building with bright lights and Japanese men in the background.

"It's her bedroom, ma'am," she insists, barely able to control the tremor in her voice as she thrusts the photos back into the envelope. No. She will not tear out the stamps for Sarah.

One year, eleven months and twenty-nine days later.

"Mummy, where's Gloria?" Sarah asks licking her fingers clean.

Linda has ordered in home delivery of two large pizzas, three orders of garlic bread and salad for the children.

"Gloria has gone shopping, dumbo," John reaches for the largest slice of pizza. "She's flying home tomorrow."

"I will miss Gloria, Mummy."

"Don't be daft, Timmy. Miss her? For what? We'll get a new maid soon." Pause. Then, "Right, Mum?" John turns to her.

"Yes." Linda gives him a bright smile. It's so seldom that he calls her 'Mum' that she's willing to overlook his comment about not missing the maid. But it's not right. She'll have to correct him later.

"It's okay, Timmy. You can miss Gloria a little."

"I'll miss her a lot, Mummy."

"Then you're stupid!"

"Mummy!"

"It's okay, Timmy. *Kor-kor* John is just teasing you."

"But it's stupid to miss the maid. They always leave. I don't miss any of them!"

"John, that's enough," George says.

The boy stuffs his mouth with garlic bread and ignores his father and the rest of the family.

"It's okay, John, if you don't want to miss anyone. Here. Have another slice of pizza."

She pushes the pizza box towards him. The boy makes no move. She rises and hands him a slice of pizza on a plate.

"Thanks," a pause, then, "Mum."

Sarah giggles. George smiles. Ack! She's worrying too much as usual. John's just a bitter boy ever since his mother left him. And there are all sorts of stories about wicked stepmothers. George said that she shouldn't force the pace; let things happen naturally. But she likes to nudge things forward a little. She glances at the clock.

"Da, it's nine o'clock. Gloria's not back yet."

"Don't worry. It's her last night in Singapore. Maybe she wants to paint the town red. Didn't you go with her to close the joint account, and she withdrew all her money?"

"*Ya*. That woman has saved quite a bit. Nine hundred and ninety something. Times that by thirty pesos. How much is that?"

"Hey, you're the one who works in the bank," George laughs and turns on the TV to watch the news.

"Thirty-one thousand six hundred and forty-five peso," John announces.

"Not much for two years' work," George turns around.

"Not much here but a lot in the Philippines. Luckily I asked her to open the account. She sent quite a bit of money home. So many children. Ten. She's packed two large suitcases. She muttered something about opening a stall. What they call *sari-sari*."

"Did you check her bags?"

"What? You think she might've squirreled away some of our things to take home to sell? I gave her all the children's old clothes and some of yours and mine too. But I'll check her bags tomorrow before we leave for the airport. If I check tonight, she can still re-pack while we're asleep. If a maid wants to steal, she'll find ways to do it. What can you do? She lives with us, and we're not home all the time. Hey. You three! Go to bed! This is adult talk. Go to bed! Brush your teeth! If she's not back by eleven, I'm going to lock the door and go to bed."

"What time did she leave the house?"

"After lunch. I gave her the day off. She said she wanted to buy gifts for her family."

"If she's not back by midnight, we'll call the police and report her missing."

"You think she doesn't want to go back to the Philippines?"

"How do I know what she wants? I just don't want to lose our deposit at the Manpower Ministry if she goes missing."

"I hope she doesn't get into an accident or something. The next maid we get must be younger and unmarried."

"*Aha!* Not scared she might seduce the Sir?"

"George, be serious. You don't joke about such things, okay?"

"Hey, read the papers. The media is always biased against us. They always highlight the man doing the seducing. What about the woman, *eh*? A young maid."

"Okay, enough. You go and quarrel with the media about it. I'll get a fat and ugly one for us. But young and single. Not another mother."

"You're the one who insisted on an older woman and a mother."

"I know; I know. My mistake. Have you seen Gloria with Timmy before I put a stop to her hugging and kissing? She likes to cuddle my darling."

"Our son likes her."

"It's not healthy. All this hugging and pawing! That's why I stopped her from bathing Timmy."

"*Ahhh!* A case of maternal jealousy."

"Shut up, George. I don't like maids to hug and kiss my kids. I can do that myself. I told her before. Chinese people. We don't like strangers to kiss and hug our children. She said Filipinos do it all the time. I told her I don't care what she or other Filipinos do back home. But in my home, I set the rules. I don't want the maid to hug my kids."

"*Aye*, women and mothers!"

"Sexist!" She throws a cushion at him. George ducks. He clicks the remote and switches on the tv. She switches it off.

"I want to talk. Did you hear John call me 'Mum' just now?"

A tired "Yes, I told you he'd come round if you give him time."

"*Ya*, claim credit for it. You think it's so easy to be your son's stepmum? I noticed a change when I stopped Gloria from hugging the two younger ones. I mean just see it from John's angle. He's the oldest. Already he sees himself as the outsider. The other two are my own, and what does the maid do? She's always hugging Timmy, and Sarah when Sarah allows it. I know she misses her own kids. I've heard her telling Timmy about her ten children."

"Okay, what? What's your point?"

"The point is that John felt better after I stopped Gloria from hugging Timmy and Sarah. He's eleven. Too old for Gloria to hug him. But he's still a child and feels deprived. Seeing the maid hug the other two and not him makes him feel even worse about being my stepson. Got it? So, no hugging except by me. I'm the mum who hugs all three of them. I hug John whether he wants it or not. Just to show that I treat him as my own. And you think I'm acting like a jealous…"

"Come here."

Her husband wraps his arms around her and plants a wet kiss on her lips. The phone rings. George picks up the receiver.

"Yes. Yes. That's right. Please wait a sec. I'll check with my wife. Is her name Gloria Antonia Bernadette Santos?"

"Yes. What's wrong?"

"*Shhh!* Yes, she's our maid. Okay. Okay. We'll be there in half an hour."

It's almost two in the morning by the time they are home again. They were silent throughout the ride home from the Tanglin Police Station. Linda clasps and unclasps her hands. George had told her expressly not to say anything or ask any question until they got home. He didn't want a scene. He handled everything at the station. But the moment he shuts their front door, he sits down beside her, and they confront the bovine face of their maid.

"Sit down, Gloria. Take the chair opposite us. Now take out your handbag. Show us how much you have in there," she begins.

The woman empties the contents of her purse on to the dining table.

"Count your money."

They wait till she has finished.

"How much do you have? Come on. Tell us. How much do you have inside your purse? You've just counted the money. How much?"

The brown sullen face wears a sheen of sweat and oil; the dark eyes are averted; they would not meet her eyes.

"I'm not budging until you tell us, Gloria."

The woman looks at her, stupefied.

"I mean it, Gloria."

"Three hundred and twenty-eight dollars and seventy-five cents, ma'am."

"You have three hundred and twenty-eight dollars in your purse, Gloria. More than three hundred Singapore dollars! Why the hell did you have to steal? Why did you do such a stupid thing on the eve of your departure? Tomorrow you will be charged. Do you know that? Tomorrow, you will go to jail and miss your flight! Sir will forfeit his deposit with the Ministry of Manpower and I don't know what else will happen to you! You're a fool!"

She feels the pressure of George's restraining hand as she stared into the stupid woman's unweeping eyes till shame makes the woman look down.

"Put your money back into your purse, Gloria," George says. "Where were you when you were caught?"

A long silence. Then she says, "Scotts Shopping Centre, Sir."

"The police told us that the security guards searched your bags and person. They found two bras unpaid for, two packets of AA batteries, a transistor radio and three shirts for men. All not paid."

"I was going to pay, Sir."

"Don't lie to us, Gloria!" she yells. How good it is to yell at the cow! She's been bottling up her anger all the way from Tanglin and up the East Coast Expressway till they reached home. "The guards stopped you at the exit! If you were going to pay, you should've been at the cash counter! What were you doing at the exit with all the unpaid goods? *Ha?* Tell me!"

Again she feels the press of George's hand, restraining her.

"The police have impounded your passport. Tomorrow we have to take you to the subordinate court where you will be charged," George tells the brazen liar. "You know that in Singapore, shoplifters are jailed. Depending on how seriously the judge views your case, Gloria, you could be jailed for one or two weeks. Do you understand? We will not bail you out. You will miss your flight home tomorrow. We have already paid for this flight. If you want to go home after serving your jail sentence, you will have to pay for your own air ticket. Do you understand?"

The woman nods; her eyes are dumb as a cow's waiting for the butcher's knife.

First published in *Asiatic: IIUM Journal of English Language and Literature*, International Islamic University of Malaysia (IIUM), Dec 2007 (http://asiatic.iiu.edu.my or http://asiatic.iium.edu.my); anthologised in *SASTRA ASIA*, Universitas Pelita Harapan (UPH): Indonesia, 2011; and translated into Spanish in *Hermano Cerdo* (hermanocerdo.com), Multicultural Writers' Association: Australia, 2011 (http://hermanocerdo.com/2011/09/gloria).

BIRDS OF PARADISE
Minfong Ho

Once upon a time, there was a lovely little island in the middle of the Southern Seas. Blue skies, palm fronds, sandy beaches—it was a tropical paradise. Healthy plump chickens lived on this island, clucking quietly in contentment as they spent their days pecking at the dirt and fluffing up their feathers.

Every morning, the chickens would each lay a big brown egg, and every evening their eggs would be collected. They didn't mind this—after all, weren't they fed high-protein chicken feed and housed in rows of neat little chicken coops? As chickens go, they had a pretty good life and they felt as happy as chickens can feel.

Oh, there was the occasional tugging over a fat earthworm, of course, and sometimes two old hens might start squawking about who had laid the bigger egg—but then a stern rooster would strut on over and in very short order, sort everything out.

The years went by, and everything was fine. Brown eggs were fetching a high price in the market, the chickens were laying contentedly, the sun was always shining. The island could remain a tropical paradise forever, right?

Wrong. Nothing ever stays the same forever, not even a tropical paradise. At first the changes were so small and so quiet that nobody even noticed them.

It started one day when a shy small-boned little hen who was walking around the beach looked up at the sky and thought, *What if I could fly?*

The thought startled her so much that she just stood there, blinking rapidly in the sunlight. Then, feeling a little foolish, she lifted one wing and—slowly, slowly—flapped it. A small rush of air fanned against her. A rather pleasant sensation, she thought. She flapped her other wing. The same thing happened. Delighted, she tried flapping both wings at once, and this actually lifted her a few inches off the ground.

She was just getting a running start and flapping both wings, when she heard somebody shout behind her, "Hey! What do you think you're doing?"

Lani—for that was the little chicken's name—looked back and saw a bantam rooster sternly staring at her. With a twinge of alarm, Lani recognised him as The Chief Rooster of the whole flock. She swallowed hard.

"I'm... I'm trying to fly," said Lani, shyly.

"Fly?" the Chief Rooster said. "You can't fly. You're a chicken. Chickens lay eggs."

"I know," Lani said politely. "I've just laid my egg for today. But I want to fly too."

"Well, you can't," the rooster said, and strutted away without looking back.

Thoughtfully, Lani watched him walk away. *So I can't fly*, she thought sadly, tucking in her wings. A passing sea breeze ruffled her feathers, sending a thrill through her. *If only I could feel the rush of wind against me as I soared into the sky*, Lani thought. *And why not?* The challenge ruffled her mind as silent and suggestive as the sea breeze. Lani squared her shoulders and jutted her beak out at the sky. "Why not?" she said aloud. "Why can't I try?"

And so, in the next few days, little Lani would lay her egg in a cubicle just like all the other hens and then go off to a quiet corner of the beach, and practised flying.

She flapped her wings, she ran around in circles, she jumped off rocks. At first she never got more than a few inches off the ground, but as her wings got stronger and her movements more coordinated, she managed to half-glide, half-fly off the larger rocks onto the sand a few feet away.

Lani liked the feel of the wind against her feathers and the sheer sense of space around her, and she especially liked exercising her wing muscles. *So wings aren't just for warming a nest of eggs or sheltering scared chicks,* she thought. *They can be used for flying too.* And the thought thrilled her.

Even engrossed as she was in trying to fly, Lani couldn't help but notice that other chickens were also coming out to spend their afternoons on this quiet stretch of beach.

Curious, she would watch them between her practice runs. Those other chickens weren't trying to fly, but they were doing some rather strange things.

One chicken would crane her neck up, point her beak at the sky, and cackle loudly. It wasn't a melodious sound, in fact it sounded as if an earthworm had gotten stuck in her throat, but at least it was more interesting than clucking.

"What're you trying to do?" Lani asked politely.

"Sing," said the other chicken.

Lani was intrigued. "Why?" she asked.

The other hen shrugged. "I'm tired of just clucking all the time and my throat itches so much I need to make other sounds." She looked at Lani curiously. "What about you?" she asked. "Why are you trying to fly?"

Lani stretched her wings and laughed. "Because I feel like it," she answered.

"Well there you are," the other hen said. "I sing because I feel like it, too."

Her answer satisfied Lani and with a polite bow, they parted ways.

On another day, Lani saw a young cockerel gather bits of seaweed and ferns washed up on the sand and stick them in his tail, before swaying down the beach in his new plumage.

"What're you trying to do?" Lani asked, flapping alongside of him.

"Dance," the little cock said. "I have some gorgeous new feathers growing by my tail," he turned around to show her the delicate plumes sprouting there, "but they aren't big and gaudy enough, so I'm adding some leaves and stuff back there. Don't you think I'm beautiful?"

Lani thought he looked rather ridiculous, but she didn't want to hurt his feelings. "You look… er, interesting," she said diplomatically, before going off to practise her flying.

The more Lani practised, the better she got at it, and the more she enjoyed it. She shed some of her fat, and big new feathers grew in at her wings, making them even stronger. She found that if she made a running start off a small slope, she could flap her way up quite high before gliding—more or less gracefully—back to the beach.

One afternoon, borne on a particularly good wind, she saw the Chief Rooster below her and, exhilarated by her flight, called down to him. "Look!" she cried gaily, "I can fly! I can fly!"

He looked up at her in amazement. "But chickens can't fly!" he shouted up at her. As Lani winged past, she saw the expression on his face change from amazement to anger, and then to fear.

Why should he be afraid of me? Lani wondered. Puzzled, she tried to land next to him, but just then the wind changed and she was swept to the other end of the beach. By the time she had flapped —rather awkwardly—to a stop to look for him, the Chief Rooster had disappeared.

Uneasy, Lani made her way back to her chicken coop, where, tired out from her long flight, she soon fell into a deep sleep.

That night, she was rudely awakened by the sound of knocks.

Drowsily, she glanced outside. Between the wire mesh of the coop, it was still pitch dark. "Who is it?" she asked softly, not wanting to wake up the hens roosting next to her.

"Nest builders," came the reply. "We want to see if you need new straw."

It seemed to be a strange time to be changing the straw, Lani thought, but she got up, flexed her wings because her muscles were rather stiff, and opened the door a crack.

Immediately a troop of fowl barged their way in. Quietly and methodically, they started to examine her nest, straw by straw.

"Careful," Lani said. You're messing up my nest." But they continued to rip at it. "Stop it, or I'll call the police."

"We are the police," one of them said. "We are officers from the Island Submarine Division. And you're under arrest."

Lani was stunned. "What for?" she gasped.

"For being a hawk," said the bantam cock.

Before Lani had a chance to protest, she felt something being tied tightly around her eyes. She realised that she was blindfolded.

Suddenly Lani was gripped by a cold fear. "Where're you taking me?" she asked.

"Where we take all hawks and other subversives," the bantam's voice answered. "To the Submarine."

It was very cold inside the submarine. Lani had lost all sense of time—even though the submarine was deep under the sea. Overhead spotlights beamed down on her from all sides, so brightly that she could barely make out the familiar face of the Chief Rooster staring at her behind the glare.

She was rather cold and tired. For a long time now, she had been standing there, her wings wrapped tightly around herself for comfort as much as for warmth, as the Chief Rooster bombarded her with questions.

"So you do admit you were flying?" the Chief Rooster asked her, for what seemed the hundredth time.

Lani nodded wearily.

"Then you're a hawk," he declared.

Lani shook her head.

"But you just admitted that you flew. Chickens don't fly. If you fly, you must be a hawk."

Confused and bewildered, Lani remained silent. The Chief Rooster sounded so logical that Lani did not dare to question his reasoning. Yet, deep down, she knew there was something wrong somewhere.

"And if you're a hawk," the Bantam persisted, "you must hate chickens. All hawks hate chickens."

"No," Lani protested weakly.

"No, what?"

"No, I am not a hawk. And I don't hate chickens," Lani told him.

"But you were flying. That means you're a hawk. And that means you hate chickens!"

And so the whole cycle of questioning would begin again. Sometimes the Chief Rooster would be severe, at other times quiet, almost gentle. But always he insisted that there were only two kinds of birds in the world: hawks and chickens.

And since Lani was not a chicken, she must be a hawk. Hawks were dangerous creatures, he told her, hawks were the sworn enemies of the chickens. In fact, hawks almost took over the island once, long ago, before Lani was even hatched. Since then, hawks had established themselves in a large colony up north, too far to be seen of course, but always there—perhaps circling overhead right now, ready to attack, ready to kill the chickens, and ready to take over the island.

"Perhaps you were flying up to meet your fellow hawks," the Chief Rooster suggested.

"No," Lani would answer, her eyes so heavy with fatigue she could barely keep them open.

"Then you were flying down to spy on us chickens," he would insist.

Lani shook her head miserably.

"Is it possible that the hawks were using you in their conspiracy?" the rooster suggested.

"I don't even know of any conspiracy," Lani said.

"Is it possible that the hawks were using you in their plot," the Chief Rooster said cajolingly, "without your realising it?"

Lani sighed. "Anything is possible," she said.

Anything but the simple truth, she thought. She realised that no answer she could give would satisfy him. In fact, the more truthful the answer, the more dissatisfied he was. Dispirited and exhausted, she closed her eyes and fell asleep.

From somewhere in the shadows, a bantam cock splashed a bucketful of ice-cold water on her as another cock reached out and yanked out a few of her feathers. Lani jerked awake, squinting at the bright lights in bewilderment.

"Look, we're getting tired of this too," the Chief Rooster said impatiently. "We'll leave you alone to sleep—just as soon as you promise me you won't ever fly anymore."

Lani sighed. Her head throbbed, and her thoughts whirled round and round in crazy spirals. She wanted to sleep, but she wanted to fly too. Could she fly in her sleep? Could she sleep while she flew? Would she turn into a hawk in mid-flight? Or into a chicken in her sleep?

"Go on, just promise," the Chief Rooster said. "Promise you won't fly again. And I'll let you sleep."

Lani opened her beak. "I promise," she murmured thickly, closing her eyes, "to try…" But so quickly did she fall asleep that she wasn't sure if she had spoken aloud the last two words, or merely thought them.

Left alone in a little bare cell, Lani slept for a long time. It might even have been days, but that was only a guess because all the lights were left on, so that she had no sense of time other than the intervals set by her own sleep patterns.

To keep up her spirits, she would flap her wings for exercise and talk to the little crabs and fish that would swim by outside the tiny porthole of her room.

Then one day, the door of her cell was unlocked and a bantam officer beckoned her to follow him.

He led her down a long corridor and into a large dark room. At first Lani thought that she was the only chicken in it, but when her eyes got accustomed to the darkness, she realised that there in a line-up were two other chickens. With a start, she recognised them. There was the chicken who had started making those strange throaty noises, and beside her was the pretty cockerel who liked to dance and show off his blue-green tail feathers. They both looked dazed and there was a tired, dull look in their eyes. She realised that they recognised her too, but no one dared to acknowledge the other.

The silence in the room was broken by a familiar voice. It was the Chief Rooster. "As social deviants, you are all a threat to our island," he said sternly. "However, since you show signs of repentance, and since I am after all a forgiving chief, I have decided to give you a second chance."

He paused dramatically and looked from one to the other. Lani held her breath. "That's right, you will all be freed."

Freed! Lani thought. *Free to feel the sun on her wings and hear the ocean waves lapping at the sand again—how wonderful!*

"Of course, there is one small condition for your release," the Chief Rooster continued smoothly. He lifted his wing, and in his claws was a sharp, gleaming knife.

The sun had risen high above the ocean by the time the submarine rose above the waves, depositing the three chickens onto the beach. A crowd of hens had gathered around to watch curiously as the three scampered onto shore, but nobody looked at them, much less welcomed them back. Head bent, Lani walked down the beach alone back to her coop, avoiding the eyes of the other hens as they clucked quietly among themselves.

For such a long time now, Lani had looked forward so much to the open sky and the sea breeze, but now that she was actually free, she felt strangely dispirited. As the other two made their way back to the coops, Lani stood on the shoreline alone and thought back to what had happened in the submarine just before they had surfaced.

The Chief Rooster had smiled at the three of them so genially that Lani had been caught off-guard for the steel blade which he suddenly held up in front of him.

With the knife glinting in his hand, he had stepped up to the little chicken who liked to sing. She had whimpered, trying to tuck her head under her wing. But with a quick move, the Chief Rooster had reached into her open beak and deftly sliced off her tongue. "No more singing, understand?" he had said pleasantly.

Then he had stepped up to the chicken whose tail feathers had started to grow blue-green plumes and slashed them all off. "No more preening and dancing, you hear?" he had said.

And finally he had walked up to Lani. She had clamped her wings tight behind her, but even so, he had pried them and drastically clipped back the feathers of her left wing. "And you, no more flying. Agreed?"

The three mutilated chickens had looked at him wordlessly.

"If any of you show the least sign of any deviant behaviour again, you know what will happen, don't you?"

Like a patient schoolteacher, he had smiled kindly at them. "You'll all turn into hawks, every one of you. And then..." he had shaken his head sadly, "I'll be forced to stop you, once and for all." He had held his knife up in front of their faces, briefly, before walking away, his bright red comb bobbing on his head.

Thinking of this now, Lani shivered, even though the sun was shining high overhead in a cloudless blue sky. Beneath her claws, the sand was warm and gritty, and a fat worm wriggled nearby, but Lani's heart remained heavy.

Out of the corner of her eye, she saw the submarine retreat into the distance and sink beneath the sea. Even after it had disappeared however, Lani noticed the glint of a glass lens poking above the waves, like a glass eye on a metallic stalk. And it was this distant periscope which gave Lani the unsettling feeling that though she was free now, she was still being watched.

The next day, Lani felt better. Waking up nestled inside the warm straw of her cubicle, Lani listened to the morning clucking sounds of the other hens around her, and breathed in the smell of the fresh straw lining their nests.

She wandered outside the chicken coop and looked around. The sun was shining, a light breeze rustled the leaves and all around her stretched rows of clean, neat chicken coops. *What a quiet, well-ordered, happy little place this island is*, Lani thought, as if she was seeing it for the first time. With a flash of recognition of love, she realised that this was her home and that she loved it with all her heart.

She stretched and flexed her wings. There was a twinge of pain where her feathers had been clipped. And suddenly the yearning surged through her again, stronger than ever.

She wanted to fly.

No, she told herself. *No, no, no, no.*

A wave of panic seized her. *I don't want to turn into a hawk*, she thought. *I just want to be a good chicken, laying my one egg a day and clucking in my coop. Please, don't let me turn into a hawk.*

Confused and scared, Lani kept these thoughts to herself. For the next few weeks, she did exactly what the other chickens did—cluck, lay eggs, peck at the dirt. But with each day her wing feathers grew back a little more, and her desire to stretch and flex her wings grew stronger, until she felt an overwhelming desire to fly again.

One evening, when she couldn't stand being cooped up anymore, she slipped down to the beach where she had once practised flying.

It was deserted there and Lani walked on the sand half-heartedly. If only she dared to stretch out her wings and fly again! But that would make her different from the other chickens and that would be wrong. Soon she saw another chicken in the distance and recognised her as the chicken who liked to sing.

"How have you been?" she called over to Lani.

Lani could hardly believe her ears. Was this clear sweet voice really the chicken who'd had her tongue sliced off?

"I'm lucky. My tongue grew back," she said, as if reading Lani's thoughts.

"But... your voice," Lani whispered, awestruck. "It's... it's so different."

The other chicken laughed and the sound was pure music. It's nice, isn't it?" she trilled. "I've always hoped it would turn out this way." She looked at her curiously. "And what about you?" she asked.

Lani hesitated. "I'm... I think I'm different too," she said miserably. "I know it's wrong, but I still want to fly."

"Why would it be wrong?"

"Because it would make me different from the other chickens," Lani said. "It would make me a hawk."

"But can't we be different without being hawks?" she asked gently.

Lani stared at her. "What do you mean?" she asked.

"Well, chickens don't sing, but as far as I know hawks don't sing either. So if I sing, I can't be a chicken or a hawk. Maybe..." she looked around her to make sure no one was listening, "maybe there are more than two kinds of birds in the world. Maybe there are three, or even four or five. What do you think?"

Lani drew back, startled. All her life, she had been told what to think. Nobody had ever asked her what she thought before. She hesitated.

What if this was a trick, she thought? *What if the other chicken was really a hawk and was drawing her into some conspiracy?* "I... I don't know," Lani said cautiously. "I... I don't know what to think." *Or how to think*, she admitted silently.

The other chicken smiled. "Never mind, I have something to show you. Come with me," she said.

It did not take long to find him. Even though he was partially hidden behind some big rocks, they could easily see his wild plumage from a distance.

How daring, he's stuck ferns and flowers in his tail again, Lani thought as they approached. *And they're even bushier and gaudier than the ones he chose before.*

But when they approached him, Lani was amazed to see that it wasn't ferns but real feathers fanning behind him, green and gold and glistening magnificently in the afternoon sunlight.

"You look so... so different!" she exclaimed.

Startled, he looked up and abruptly lowered his plumage, as if he was suddenly ashamed of them.

"Please, I didn't mean 'different' in a bad way," Lani said softly.

He smiled then and fanned out his tail feathers again, a shimmering rainbow against the blue of the ocean. Swaying majestically, he approached her. "It's good to see you again," he said. "How do I look?"

"You look beautiful," Lani assured him, with total honesty.

"And you, have you started flying again?"

She looked up at the vast blue sky above her, and slowly stretched her wings. The feathers which had been clipped off, had gradually grown back in, and her wings felt stronger than ever now. Lani burst out into a joyous laugh. "Fly again? Why not?" she said.

She lifted her outspread wings and drew them down. Another stretch and flap, and she was aloft.

Oh—the sheer ease with which she surged upwards with just a smooth sweep of the wing! She was soaring higher and further than she ever had before! The wave sparkled under her, a rippling reflection of the starlight sky. Far away were the neat rows of chicken coops, like tiny matchboxes.

I don't belong in those chicken coops, Lani thought. *I'm not a chicken, I'm a skylark! I'm a skylark.*

Like a flash of lightning, the knowledge came from deep within her. How could the Chief Rooster or anybody else tell me what I was, or what I would become, when I didn't know myself? *And now I know*, she thought, *I'm a skylark, I'm a skylark!* And in sheer relief she soared higher and higher into the sky.

She did not know how long she stayed aloft, but finally even her strong wings began to tire and she honed in to the beach. As she glided lower, she saw the two other birds below.

One was singing to the rising moon, while the other was dancing and swaying with his rainbow feathers.

Lani the skylark swooped over them.

"I'm a skylark," she called down to them.

They understood.

"I'm an oriole," the songbird called out, her voice clear and sweet.

"I'm a peacock," the one with the beautiful plumage shouted, displaying his gold-green feathers.

It was a magic moment.

Together, in perfect and effortless harmony, the skylark and the oriole and the peacock performed for each other and for themselves, secure in the knowledge that they were who they were, and that nobody could ever again have the power to tell them what they were supposed to be.

Nothing could stop Lani and the other two birds from spending their free afternoons down by the beach after that. As Lani practised her swooping and gliding, the oriole would burst exuberantly into song and the peacock would gracefully fan out his tale.

With each day that the three birds were there, more young chicks strayed out to join them. They would wander out of their chicken coops to the beach, watch the other three for awhile and then start doing their own odd little rituals on the beach.

A few of them seemed interested in singing and would crane their necks up so that strange throaty noises would well out of their beaks. These soon gathered around the oriole, so that together they became a ragtag choir of sorts. The jumble of noise they made was harsh and discordant at first, but as they practised more, their songs actually began to sound sweet and harmonious.

A few of the young cocks wanted only to preen and parade around. They too stuck leaves and flowers into their tail, as they gazed at the peacock and his fantastic plumage. If a few of them got discouraged with the bits of soggy seaweed that kept falling off their tails, the peacock would come over and help put frangipanis and ferns in their feathers until they all looked quite striking as they paraded about in their finery.

As for herself, Lani couldn't help but notice that there were more and more small-boned chickens who were flapping their wings about, trying to fly. Some of them managed to learn on their own, running off the gentle sand dunes for a flying start. Others would crash land time after time, then with wistful envy watch as Lani glided by high overhead. Soon Lani was showing a few of the clumsier ones how to tip their wings for a steadier turn, or how to tuck their feet tight under them as they took off. They listened to her with interest, but for the most part they were off practising on their own—which was fine with Lani.

And so that stretch of beach bustled with activity, with little chickens trying to sing or dance or fly, sometimes in large groups, sometimes in small groups but most often alone.

Even the placid plump hens would collect on the beach after laying their daily egg, clucking appreciatively as they watched all the activity about them. Once in a while they would even call out, "Well done!" or break into spontaneous applause, but for the most part they seemed content watching and pecking at the occasional worm.

As Lani glided above them all one glorious afternoon, she had a sudden vision of the island—her island, their island—teeming not just with plump egg-laying chickens but with soaring skylarks and gorgeous peacocks and warbling orioles as well. The island was really becoming a paradise, she thought, and they were all living out full, happy lives as birds of paradise.

So enchanted was she with this thought, that for a long time she did not notice the submarine breaking the surface of the sea.

It was only when she was about to glide back down to the beach that she became aware of the sudden stillness below her. Broods of chickens had gathered in a large semi-circle on the beach, surrounding a big rooster who was angrily gesturing up at her.

Oh no, it's the Chief Rooster, Lani thought with a stab of dread. Reluctantly she swooped down and alighted at the edge of the circle. She saw then that the oriole and the peacock had all been assembled around the rooster too.

The rooster looked at them sternly. "What's going on here?" he demanded.

Only then did Lani realise that it wasn't the Chief Rooster after all—or at least, not the one she had known before. This rooster was leggier, younger—milder-looking. Surprised, Lani blurted out, "Who are you?"

"The Chief Rooster," he replied with dignity. "The new one."

"Where... where is the old one?" Lani asked.

"Where all good old Chief Roosters are, of course," he said. "Roosting."

Lani wasn't sure what 'roosting' consisted of, but before she had a chance to ask, this new Chief Rooster had flicked out a knife and was advancing toward her. "Enough questions," he said impatiently. The blade glinted in the twilight.

Lani gasped and stepped back. No one else moved.

"We warned you," the new Chief Rooster said quietly, almost apologetically. "We told you not to fly anymore and yet you persist in this dangerous, deviant behaviour. Why? Aren't you satisfied with being a chicken?" He sounded almost hurt. "We worked hard, especially my predecessor, to provide you with everything a chicken could want. You were eating good feed, living in clean coops, laying big brown eggs. Why do you still want to become a hawk?"

Lani tried not to look at the gleaming knife in his hand. "I know you worked hard for us, sir," Lani said earnestly. "And I'm grateful for everything you've done. It's not that I want to be a hawk, but..." she paused, and took a deep breath. "But I don't want to be a chicken either."

His response was as immediate as it was predictable. "If you're not a chicken, you're a hawk," he said.

"I'm not a hawk, or a chicken," Lani said in a loud, clear voice. "I'm a skylark."

"But there are only two kinds of birds: chickens and…"

"You're wrong, sir," Lani burst out. "There are more than two kinds."

The new Chief Rooster looked stunned. "Wrong?" he echoed. "But we are never wrong. Either you are a chicken or a hawk. Either you are for us, or you are against us."

"Times have changed, sir," Lani said quietly. "Things aren't so clear-cut anymore. I'm not a chicken, but I'm not a hawk either."

"I have heard recently," the new chief conceded, "that the hawks up north are really harmless little sparrows," he said. "So maybe we have nothing to be afraid of after all. Not of the 'hawks', and not of you." For the first time, he looked uncertain and his wings drooped a little. "Maybe," he said so softly that no one but Lani could hear him, "maybe times have changed after all."

"Yes sir," Lani said. "So please, can't I fly? I won't hurt anybody with my flying. The chickens all know that. They're not afraid of me."

The plump brown hens nodded their heads jerkily and made reassuring clucking noises. "Lani flies," they murmured. "She flies up high. We like her, we like watching her." They shuffled up to her and nuzzled her gently with their warm feathers. "Fly, Lani," they clucked. "Fly for us."

The new Chief Rooster looked at the hens around him anxiously. "But you don't know what's good for you," he said. "You're just trusting young fools."

"No they're not. They know what they want," Lani insisted. "And they want me to fly." Impulsively, she spread out her wings and was on the verge of taking off in flight when he stopped her.

With a quick decisive move, the new Chief Rooster had reached out and pinned Lani's wings behind her.

"I'm sorry, but I can't let you fly off. It's safer for everyone of us to make sure that you will never, never be able to fly again."

He raised his knife.

"No, wait!"

The murmur of protest arose from the edges of the semi-circle, soft and gentle, but like a tidal wave rushing onshore, it gathered force until it crested into a loud roar as it reached Lani and the Chief Rooster. "Wait... wait... stop... no!"

As if with one voice, the plump brown hens who had been watching from the side protested with such force that the Chief Rooster staggered back in amazement.

"Fools!" he said to the hens. "Don't you realise she may actually be a hawk? Don't you know better than to trust her?"

"We know better..."

"We trust her..."

"Let her go..."

"Let her fly..."

Gently, Lani extricated her wings from his grasp. "Please listen to them," she said. They're right, you know."

For a long moment the new Chief Rooster did not say anything. Then he shrugged, stepped back and dropped the knife onto the sand. A small, slow smile touched his face. "All right," he said finally, "I'll listen to them. Go ahead, then. Fly!"

Lani felt a surge of relief so strong that it was as if her heart had suddenly sprouted wings and was soaring out of her throat. "Thank you, sir," she said.

Without a backward glance, she stretched her wings and took off.

Higher and higher, over the waves and into the sky, she flew, winging towards the horizon. It was dawn and the first pale tint of morning light filtered through the clouds. And as she flew, she noticed down below her, the peacock was starting to fan out his shimmering tail feathers, and perched on a tall branch, the oriole was bursting into song.

Far beyond the shores and high above the waves she flew. And it was only as she started her descent, that she caught a glimpse of a single periscope rising, absolutely motionless, above the waves. Suddenly, she knew with a calm certainty that beneath it, roosting in the submarine, was the old Chief Rooster, keeping a vigilant eye on her.

Gracefully, she flew toward the periscope and dipped her wing at it in salute, before soaring aloft once more.

EVERY DAY WILL BE LIKE SUNDAY
Don Bosco

Tai Thong was Chew Tai Thong for six days a week. Monday, Tuesday, Wednesday, Thursday, Friday, and Saturday. Mondays through Fridays he attended classes as a Business Administration undergraduate at the local university. He was already in his third year and doing quite well. No girlfriend yet, though he did get involved for a while with a petite freshette named Nicole. But Nicole was also a part-time model, and after she did that credit card advertisement she had stopped hanging out with him. She had become too hot too handle. As a macho shit idiot, Tai Thong did not like to deal with the situation. It made him feel insecure. And so, like a big fat truck reversing out of a Loading/Unloading bay, he backed off.

On Saturdays, Tai Thong was also Chew Tai Thong. Saturday mornings he spent on campus with the faculty club, organising student activities and fulfilling his share of the Computer Room duties. As a member of the faculty club's executive committee, he felt rather important. For years some evil students around would get sarcastic and say that such activities were only for losers who needed to get a life. What the heck, Tai Thong felt, it had its own prestige, and gave him an opportunity to work closely with a bunch of girls. Tai Thong is so solid one, computer hang he also can repair, they all said in front of him. On Saturdays, being Tai Thong gave him satisfaction.

However, on Sundays Tai Thong was Michael Chew. He had been Michael on Sundays for almost eleven years already, since he started attending church services in primary school, with his second auntie, who was staying with them at that time. She had since married an insurance agent, and moved off to a three-room apartment at Marine Parade. But with or without her, every Sunday without fail Tai Thong was Michael, and he still went to church.

Tai Thong was Chew Tai Thong six days of the week, except on Sundays, when he was Michael Chew.

Since Tai Thong was so very enthusiastic about music, Second Aunt had brought him along for church services on Sunday mornings because she thought he would enjoy the songs they sang during worship. The place was only a short bus ride away, and it would give his parents some quiet time at home on Sunday morning. Tai Thong ended up really liking it. When it was time to sing, he clapped his hands with a commendable sense of rhythm, and soon memorised all the words, singing along happily in all his pre-teen innocence. When he got comfortable enough, he joined the classes they had for kids his age, and besides listening to bible stories and learning new songs, he and his church friends would spend some time after service colouring posters and making various props for Easter or Christmas productions. One year there was a Christmas play, and Tai Thong got a role in it, playing one of the three wise men. It made the kid very happy.

Along the way it was felt that he needed a Christian name to reflect this new church-oriented lifestyle of his, his religious rebirth. Second Aunt decided that Michael would suit him pretty well. She was a fan of Michael Douglas, and she was also dating an ex-classmate at that time, who was now an insurance agent, and his name was also Michael. All this led Second Aunt to think that Michael was a damn cool name. And so Tai Thong became Michael.

Two years after that, Second Aunt married Michael the insurance agent, and the couple moved off to their own apartment in Marine Parade. Tai Thong continued to attend the same church, though Second Aunt was no longer available to keep him company. Still, he had made a lot of friends, and had comfortably settled into the community. In church on Sundays, he had come to introduce himself as Michael. Hi, my name is Michael, he would say. Call me Michael. I'm Michael. Eventually it sounded so natural to him. When church friends called his home, they would ask for Michael. At first his parents were confused. "Ah boy ah, why your name become Michael, ah?" they asked him. But they soon learnt to deal with it. His younger sister teased him for a while. Michael Jackson, got phone call. Michael Jackson, do moonwalk show me. Cannot do moonwalk where got Michael Jackson one. But soon she too began calling him Michael. That was probably around the same time she started calling herself Janet.

Halfway through Secondary Three, Tai Thong had a bright idea. In March that year, he suddenly started writing his name as Michael Chew on all his school work. His Maths exercise books, his biology lab workbooks, his test papers, everything, everywhere. At first there was major confusion. After one test, Mr Tay the form teacher could not find Michael Chew in the class register, and caused some inconvenience as he tried to sort out the matter. Who in this class is called Michael Chew? Got new boy, is it? How come I *dunno*?

The kids all laughed at Mr Tay's wit. Ha ha ha, Tai Thong! Tai Thong, they roared. Tai Thong raised his hand, stood up timidly, and said, Teacher, I am Michael. What you Michael? Since when? How come I dunno one? Eh boy, you trying to be funny or what? My Tay was clearly enjoying himself. Who give you that name one? Cannot anyhow give yourself you know, otherwise I also tomorrow call myself Elvis Presley. Tell me quick, who give you that name one?

Ha ha ha ha ha, the entire class roared, bursting into inspired hysterics.

Teacher, 'Michael' is my Christian name. My auntie give me one, Tai Thong said hesitatingly. Suddenly calling himself Michael did not seem like such a good idea after all.

Okay, you say is your Christian name, got proof or not? My Tay was serious now. He would not stand any nonsense from this little bugger. Your birth certificate, your IC, got 'Michael' or not?

Don' have, Tai Thong admitted.

Then you don' anyhow give yourself names, okay, boy? My Tay told him.

And so that was that. Tai Thong could not call himself Michael in school because his birth certificate and his IC never write that name.

His grades were always pretty good, and before long Tai Thong found himself in junior college. He had heard a lot about the orientation activities, which were supposed to be a whole lot of fun, and Tai Thong was looking forward to getting blind-folded and made to do the Lambada with a convent girl.

His neighbour Gurmit was older by a year, and had been in a college for the first three months, until his 'O' level results came out and he didn't qualify. But during the first three months he had a wild time, especially during orientation. They called this the 'honeymoon period'. Tai Thong like the sound of that. Honeymoon indeed. So romantic one. Gurmit told him that during his first three months junior college orientation he had to do a forfeit, and they blindfolded him and another girl, who was still wearing her old convent pinafore, and made the two do the Lambada vigorously, while the kids from the other orientation groups cheered them on. Damn *shiok* one man, Gurmit reported. Can feel her whole body, wah, horny like shit, man. After hearing his story, every time Tai Thong came across a convent girl in a pinafore, whether in the bus, on the MRT, or at the shopping center, he would study her very carefully. After all, who knows, he might have to do the Lambada with her one day.

And so Tai Thong went to junior college for the first three months. When his orientation group councilor gave him a blank name tag for him to write his name and his orientation group, Tai Thong had deliberately written Michael Chew, Eagle Group. This was a fine time to let people get used to this Michael thing. Yes, it was a good idea.

Unfortunately, his orientation group councilor was an old neighbour of his, used to stay two floors above him, and they had played football together on the void deck for a couple of years. They were very pleased to see each other. Tai Thong was glad this guy was his councilor, then he could take cover whenever he didn't like the orientation activities.

Alas, this old neighbour had always known him as Ah Thong. He immediately introduced Tai Thong to the other new students, who were already gathered and sitting on the floor in a semi-circle. Okay, everybody, this is my old friend, we used to play soccer together last time. The girls better be careful, he quite *buaya* one, ha ha ha. Please welcome another member of our group, Ah Thong.

Damn shit, Tai Thong muttered in resignation. He had spent so much effort writing his name as Michael, and now this *goondu* went to spoil it all. Ah Thong, for goodness sake. This kind of name where got romantic? Where can do the Lambada and get horny? Tai Thong sat down gloomily.

Hello, Ah Thong, welcome to our Eagles Group, the girl next to him offered. He glanced at her name tag. It said Susan Chan. She, on the other hand, did not bother to check out his name tag. After all, she had heard the councilor announce his name, and since they had been bosom childhood buddies, how could he get the name wrong? Ah Thong, what school you last time from, ah?

But Tai Thong did not hear her. He felt numb. He decided that he would kill himself if the kids around him called him Ah Thong for the rest of his junior college days. He wished he had never played football at the void deck with this idiotic old neighbour of his who used to live two floors above him.

And so Tai Thong was still Tai Thong six days a week, and on some bad days he was Ah Thong. Sheesh.

During his national service days, Tai Thong was neither Tai Thong nor Michael. For a while he was T. T. Chew. Hey Recruit Chew, come here, the Corporal would yell. Chew, why so blur one? Never wake up yet is it? his platoon commander would shout. Chew this, Chew that, Chew everything. Later he got sent to Officer Cadet School, and when he passed out his non-officer peers had to call him 'Sir'. At last, this was something he could get used to. But he was aware that it could not last forever.

And so for two and a half years Tai Thong did not have to worry about being Tai Thong or Ah Thong or Michael. It was either Chew, or Sir.

On Sundays, however, he still went to church, and people there called him Michael, except for old friends, who had begun calling him Mike.

The feeder bus was rather empty this Sunday morning, and Tai Thong sat next to the window just after the exit door. He stared out of the window, and contemplated the fierce sunshine outside. It was a bright and sunny day, very, very hot. That previous week had been particularly satisfying, and Tai Thong was happy. He had done rather well for his second year Human Resource Management test, and the Biz Ad club had nominated him as 'Mr Personality' at the coming Dinner and Dance. Really, this was more flattery than he expected, or was used to.

He was now on his way to church to praise and worship, and give thanks to God. Every Sunday for the past eleven years he had been making this trip to church without fail. Every Sunday he would make his way down the aisle and ease himself into the same seat, week after week, and sing and pray and worship his heart out. It never failed to make him feel so spiritually recharged. Life was confusing, so full of disappointments, but Sundays were always so reassuring.

As Tai Thong pressed the buzzer for the driver to stop after the next junction, he wished to himself that every day could be like this Sunday. So fulfilling, so bright and sunny. Tai Thong was grateful that despite everything else, his Sundays had remained constant for the past eleven years. Second Auntie was now living her own life on the other end of the island, his childhood football *kaki* had all moved out of the block, all his school friends were far away living their own lives. People and places had come and gone and passed on. But Sundays had always been the same. Never mind Tai Thong, Ah Thong, Chew, Sir, or whatever.

As he collected the week's song sheets and made his way through the aisle, Tai Thong mentally made the switch. Ah, he was Michael now, and it felt good. Tai Thong wished he could be Michael more often. And then every day will be like Sunday.

THE PHENWICK PHENOMENA
Simon Tay

"Hullo, is the head in?"

"He's outstation. Who's calling?"

"Outstation?"

"Ya, conference in Hawaii. Who's calling?"

"He won't be back today by any chance, will he?"

"Ya."

"What time?"

"What time? He's coming back next Thursday."

"I thought you said today."

"No, You asked if he won't be back and I said, 'Yes, he won't be back'. Who's calling?"

"Professor Phenwick."

"Oh, Prof Penwick of the English Dept."

"Yes, but it's Phenwick with an F, like 'Philosophy'".

"Philosophy Dept?"

"No, English Department, but with an F."

"English Dept with an 'F'?"

"Oh, just tell the Head, Phenwick. He'll know."

"Okay, I tell him you called."

John Phenwick put the phone down heavily. He should he used to it all: the Head being abroad, the habit of answering yes to a negative question, words like 'outstation' and most of all, the inability of almost anyone to pronounce his surname correctly. He had known the Head for twelve years, before he had been appointed Head, and even then he had always been away at some meeting or conference; as for everything else, Phenwick was a Professor in English and had even published a paper on words, usages and omissions which were peculiar to Singaporeans; a philology. He knew these things. But they were facts held in the deliberate, conscious part of his mind that organised his days and fell away whenever he was preoccupied or in a hurry or upset, as he was that afternoon. In such moods, John Phenwick might wake up and dress as he would for a bright spring day and wonder why he was sweating even before he left the house. He might walk straight in, with his shoes on, before Su Lin would point them out. Or bite into a *sambal* sandwich at tea time and wonder why the watercress stank his mouth.

The computer hummed beneath the hiss of the air-conditioning that, through shiny metal sheet tubes, poured out cold air all over the university. He settled himself at the keyboard, picking up the only thing on his otherwise clear desk, the play script he was analysing. By the side of his desk was a shelf and on that shelf were other scripts, students' essays, a club membership form, the draft hand-out for his next class, the minutes of the Department committee he was chairing, and the car advertisement he'd drafted. So many things to do today, he thought, and tomorrow, more.

He approached them methodically, systematically, as only a person who is not by nature methodical or systematic, could: everything on the shelf had been carefully organised in the sequence he would need them—even the play scripts were in the order they would be analysed in his paper. He would, he determined, be ready by tomorrow or, at worst, the day after. But that afternoon, through the studied veil of concentration, he felt the pinpricks of small irritations. He should never have let the other John make him promise to write the paper for the annual publication or, together with the Head, put him up for membership in that club. And why did he have to draft the advert on the mere hope that Su Lin would, this time, agree to sell the car? And why did these have to compete with the full plate of things he had accepted as given—term papers, the notes he churned out for class after class after class?

He put on his spectacles. They were silver wire, half-framed reading glasses be had affected from the day he had started teaching, so he could peer down his nose at his students. Now he really needed them. He peered down, not at the scripts, but at the single white type-written sheet which had upset him and re-opened that long closed door to the irritation at things he should—he knew, he knew—be used to. He re-read the poem. It was the one he had just been discussing with the Head.

> Haze upon water,
> how long we have travelled
> how hard the way, to this place
> where trees are a barrier
> and the river, a glade.
> We can rest here.
> No one will find us,
> mistaking the shadows we huddle,
> the reflection we cast,
> for the flesh we used to burden.
> Listen,
>   The wind upon water,
> the slow lifting dazzle of the haze:
> water on water,
> Until we are as still as the water.
> Come I will form this reflection,
> ripple in the pool of you.

Other than that there was typed only, at the top of the sheet, 'For John Phenwick', and at the bottom, 'Love'. No name and no handwriting. He looked at the sheet more closely. If only it had a defective 'F' or something, lifted half way off the line. That could indicate a manual typewriter with a bad key had been used and be the invaluable clue which would solve the mystery. Since there was not, he did not know where to begin.

So he had jumped to any possibility and called the Head to ask if, for some reason or other, it was he who sent the poem, leaving it on his desk, rolled and tied with a pink ribbon, and marked 'Love'. Luckily, the Head had been abroad, He sighed, opened the drawer of his desk and put the poem away with the other one. He didn't want to think about them, because he had work to do, and because it was some silly, unimportant prank. He was phlegmatic.

He reached across for another script he suddenly thought was needed and rummaged clumsily through, disarranging everything until he found it. The shelf and table were now a mess, as if a fresh, strong wind had come in, under the door or through some gap. On the computer screen he saw that, under the paragraph of his paper arguing that the use of English in Singapore Drama had matured, the title of each poem, the name of the poets and the place where the sheets had been found, were typed in. He deleted them from the screen. He sighed and began to tidy his desk.

He opened a drawer to put away something but the poems came out instead. Each had appeared mysteriously. On a bright, windy afternoon the first had been stuck to the windshield of his grey Honda. A damn parking ticket, he'd thought, did I forget to put my stupid 'Lecturer' sticker on again? It was a poem from the book *Against the Next Wave* by another lecturer. Why had the poems been sent? Who could have sent them?

His mind turned to the faces in the classes he took. The sixty plus students who sat quietly in the large new lecture halls, each having taken a copy of Phenwick's computer generated notes, passively chewing gum or sweets as they listened to him and jotted down more notes: No, not one of them. The smaller tutorials when eight to ten of them would troop into his office, now large and clean enough to accommodate them. That would be more likely. One of them. A girl. A girl who had a crush on him. A secret love. This fed his vanity. His mind started to sort out the names and faces of his students, replaying their actions, their expressions when he spoke to them or they spoke to him. It has to be quite a nice, sweet girl he thought. Slightly foolish perhaps, hut not without good taste. Susie, the fair girl with slightly brown hair who always sat right in the front. Or

Carla of the short skirts, sneakers and dark sunglasses. Or Mimi, with the long black hair and dreamy look.

John Phenwick sat there, at his desk with these thoughts, amidst the growing mess, with the poem in front of him, trying to peer through the shroud of the mystery and knowing, even as he did, he had insufficient clues. In front of him, the smoked-glass window which looked out into the afternoon threw back his partial reflection. But he did not see it.

Su Lin stopped typing only when she heard his car pulling up their driveway and, although she rushed, she was still between setting out the things for tea on the bougainvillea-covered patio and boiling the water in the kitchen when she heard his key rattle in the lock and the door open. His footsteps echoed in the cool stone corridor as they did every morning when he left and each evening when he returned, although this afternoon, more loudly. He knocked ceremoniously on the open kitchen door and smiled.

"Hullo."

"Oh, hi. It's not 4:30 yet. You're early, John."

"Sorry. I wasn't getting anywhere with that paper so I thought I'd come hack. There's no need to hurry with tea."

"Thanks a lot, I didn't intend to. How was your day, John? Anything interesting?"

"Just one class and that was a ruddy pain."

"Ya? What happened?"

"You know the student, Samuel, the one I told you about?"

"The one you said was quite bright?"

"As bright as a bite on my bum. He spent the whole time distracting the class about *The Tempest*; how it's Third World drama in which Ariel is left in charge of the island when Prospero left and that we arc all Calibans and must re-take the island once we recapture our mother spirit from the tree. Prospero being the colonialists, Ariel being the elite locals who can speak English and rule and Calibans being, I suppose, The People. A real philippic. He went on about cultural colonialism, Literatures in English rather than English literature, as if I didn't know all that."

"Well, he must have thought he was being bold. I mean, the class was about Shakespeare and an *angmoh* was teaching—even if you have been here twelve years, you're still an *angmoh* you know, John. At least, you look like one. Must be some strong stuff John Lim's been teaching in that Singapore Lit class to have that kind of impact on him."

"My fist would like to make an impact on that boy. But yes, I see it. John Lim—your old classmate, my former student, now Associate Prof—preaching cultural colonialism and revolution in his Oxford accent. How does your mother put it... makes me want to vomit blood."

"Anything else happen?"

"Oh, Ah Lee called. The car is finally ready."

"Can you pick it up tomorrow before class?"

"Su, I was thinking we should sell it. '32 year-old car, same owner for 12 years, new brakes, cassette player.' Sounds like a good ad."

"Don't you dare think of it. Ah Lee always say something needs to be done—that's how he stays in business, You talk to that man as much as you want, John, just don't listen to him. We're keeping the car."

"It's just that it keeps breaking down."

"Well, that's why we bought the Honda."

"But you know I got the car only because it was the only thing I could afford when I came..."

"No, John."

"... I didn't really want to get caught in the rain..."

"No."

"OK. I'll pick it up tomorrow."

"Well, except for that, nothing else happened?"

Stoically, she waited for him to regale her, as he always did, with a blow-by-blow account of the latest meeting of the committee he chaired.

"No, it was quiet," he said instead. "Well then, off for a quick shower."

She hid her surprise. He turned to go.

"And dear..."

"Yes, Su?"

"Take off your shoes."

He looked down at his thick-soled, brown Church shoes sheepishly, bent over like some wading bird (or one of the phalarope), unlaced them and half threw both socks and shoes into a corner. Mr Organised was still so forgetful sometimes. As he walked away, his now naked feet padding lightly in the corridor, Su Lin turned from the stove to watch him through the open kitchen door. But she did not see Professor John Phenwick, the department committee head and note-giving lecturer; she saw him as he had been. A Phantom in a Phantasmagoria.

Twelve years ago, a tall, lanky *angmoh* with a strong hooked nose, curly brown hair and a pale skin which was slightly red patched from the sun, stood in front of his first class where Su Lin sat in the front row on the extreme right, his large slim hands resting on the back of file chair he leaned on, their stillness belying what happened after perhaps a minute of silence, when he'd cleared his throat and those same hands quickly became semaphores, gesturing, signaling wildly, his voice taking on a higher, more excited tenor as he first read poetry and then barked out: questions about what he'd just read, the questions on questions escalating the pace of the lesson, involving everyone in the quest for the answer, getting the students to find their own, rather than having the teacher give it to them.

"I've forgotten," he then said, back to the lower, calm Englishman's voice with which he had starred, "I've not introduced myself. John Phenwick—'*Ph*' giving an *F* sound, like 'Philharmonic'." And so, in no time, he had a secret name, 'Phil'.

Su Lin and the girls would have tea at the Union House and talk about him, their voices like a gossiping wind, listened to in the sleepiness of the campus, in the overhanging trees, in the hot half-cylindrical metal sheds where tutorials were held, in the narrow, warped stairs which lead up to the English Department and cramped offices of each lecturer, and in the large, now silent, courtyards where Student Union leaders once held rallies.

"Phil had an open top sports car. Li Huan saw him coming to Uni in it one bright morning, his longish hair wind swept; Gina Rodriguez passed him parked under a flyover, drenched and trying to get the top up in the midst of a thunderstorm. 'Phil' wore either the Oxford Cotton shirts and light wool trousers he had come in on that first day or outlandishly colourful batik shirts. 'Phil' had had his own book of poems published in England some years ago and was rumoured to have hopes of finding inspiration in the tropical heat like other expat writers had before him. He read his poems at a small event to mark Arts Day that year and Su Lin and the girls had gone along to hear him (few others went—the philistines). Finally, he taught like no other lecturer at that time did, and with that Socratic style, his class was always buzzing, noisy. They could not help but be intrigued by him, a splash of *angmoh* pink in their grey days.

Other students were not as enchanted. Quite a few muttered complaints—what a mess their notes were, full of questions, jumping from one subject to another, and how were questions supposed to help them to answer exams? The boys were it little jealous of the attention he received from the girls. Some even started referring to him as, Phenwick—Ph as in 'phallus'.

It was unjustified. John Phenwick didn't encourage the girls in anything other than their work. In this he was as much assisted by his professionalism as by the fact that: he was blind to any effect he had on the girls and could get lost within 100 metres of his office. Su Lin and the girls appreciated this and didn't bat eyelashes at him. When that flirt Sandra Cheong did, corralling him in the narrow corridors and obstructing his passage with her considerable chest box, they cut her with *jeleng* looks and plotted ways of putting her in her place. But then—on her own accord, for want of progress—she put an end to it. On their part, the most they would do was to connive ways of visiting him in his office. They would work out: questions with some help from the star pupil of their class, John Lim, intricate and intelligent questions to better veil the fact that their curiosity was more with the lecturer, than what he lectured.

John Phenwick received the four of them kindly, moving the piles of books and crates around to clear a spot for each of them to sit in the tiny, book-shelved room. He'd make them mugs of tea. Answering their questions, he'd often quote this or that book and then rummage through the piles and shelves again until he found it, holding it up like a newly excavated treasure, his hands dusty from the search, his hair in a tangle with a long lock falling over his blazing eyes. He would always mutter apologies about the mess but the books—strewn across the desk, in piles on the chairs, occasionally tumbling to the floor, stuffed on the sagging shelves—were always there, and the crates which Su Lin at first excused as having just arrived from England, were still unpacked by the end of the year when they had graduated and come to say goodbye.

John started dating Su Lin two years later. They met at a huge house-warming party given by a lecturer both hardly knew. It was the first time they'd met since she had graduated and all they did was sit and talk in the kitchen, chomping on cashew nuts and sipping white wine. Still, John had sought out advice on the ethics of this, the teacher-student relationship, from the Head. The Head laughed, slapped him on the back and poured two glasses of sherry. It was perfectly all right he said and the drink was to celebrate him asking; she was no longer his student after all. Court the girl, marry her—the Head enthused—become a Singaporean.

With this blessing, John and Su Lin proceeded.

He bought her a scarf to tie up her hair so it wouldn't be mussed by the wind when they went out in his car. She spent weekends trying to organise his office, tidying and shelving the books before giving up when she realised that just when she had organised one section, a new mess was being created in another. They went to French movies every Tuesday until they discovered neither of them understood or appreciated them as each thought the other did. She bought him copies of books by Singaporean poets and he would sometimes read some to her, the ones he'd liked, over coffee at Moonlighter's, a small cafe-restaurant on the riverside which had become a regular haunt.

It was a quiet, short courtship and their intention to marry surprised everyone. Gina and Li Huan gasped and agreed to be her bridesmaids so long as they could wear fierce green eye shadow as a sign of their jealousy. John's widower father said he was happy and would fly out once his travel agent knew in which part of China Singapore was. As for her family, Su Lin had expected resistance: John was white and more than ten years older, he wasn't a Singaporean citizen and might go back, taking her with him. Her parents were apprehensive at the start for these very reasons but, to their credit, knew their lively but serious daughter well and counting on all the times she had never caused them the problems with boys and love, they agreed.

They even grew to like John once they got used to his accent and he began to tryout his Hokkien and Malay with them. The only thing Su Lin's parents insisted upon was that: the children be given Chinese names and learn to speak Hokkien. "*Suka-lu*", John acceded, more Singaporean—albeit in an odd sort of way than most Singaporeans. As for Su Lin herself, she had no doubts about the marriage except what she might be called: Mrs Phenwick-Cheong Su Lin? Cheong-Phenwick Su Lin? Cheong Su Lin Phenwick? Phenwick Su Lin? Phenwick Lin? Su Phenwick? Lin Phenwick?

She surprised herself by being so certain about him, He was different from the 'Phil' she had gossiped about. In spite of the cheeky sports car and lively style of teaching, he was quiet, almost demure. Not uninteresting and certainly capable of talking lip a storm when a favourite subject—usually poetry—was broached, but otherwise a man who would contentedly listen to her over a cup of coffee, asking questions, comparing his experiences to those she mentioned, embroidering the conversation with comments, but not taking over and controlling things as a lot of men did.

From the first date silences were not awkward and therefore conversations were not confined to the stultifying choice of either being fuelled with lots of energy or flagging; they could lapse or meander, rush on or be deflected, as if both knew they would have lots of time to resume, redirect and come to those points again in the future. They enjoyed an immediate intimacy from the start.

In other forms of intimacy, they progressed much more slowly; again surprising, given the image of that sports car and what people expect of *angmohs* in general and *angmohs* 'lecherers' in particular. Their honeymoon was their first time. Not because John's appetite for her was wanting—as he laughed with a roar on that first night, "Phenwick, as in 'Phoenix', I will rise again"—but because, us he later told her, he wanted to show in the most old-fashioned way, how much he respected her and to belie all those prejudices of which he was aware. Not a big talker or a playboy, not wanting to play *tuan* to a colonial, or teacher to a student. And also not all job and car like too many of the Singaporean men she knew. Kindness and care, intelligence, wit and honesty was how Su was won over. And poetry.

> I would come to you out of the north
> if a promise would purse your lips
> and not feel the sun for your warmth:
> at this equator the world has woman's hips.
> My old world face, my master's tastes
> and learnings would melt away,
> I will wake surprised in the moist dawn
> that water winter hands once called warm
> chills me, as a baby just born. Re-born.

Published two weeks before their wedding. The last poem he had ever written. She shook her head at the memory and corrected herself with a decade old optimism: the latest poem he had written to date.

"The pot's boiling over, Su."

She looked up at him, out of the pool of her memories, through the cloud of steam. Just out of the bath, his hair wet and neatly combed, its receding pattern starting to make itself clear, his eyes still that bright blue hut focusing on something else, not her, not this room, their attention missing in spite of having seen the jet of steam her memories had obscured, her husband, John Phenwick, as he was.

She turned off the fire, brought things out, and called the children to come for tea. They sat down. The two boys—Chester Kar Gee Phenwick and Charlie Kar Gay Phenwick—ran in from the garden, chasing each other around, going faster and faster, nearer and nearer the glass and wrought-iron table where the tea things were. At other times, either John or Su Lin would have stopped them, reminding them the tea set: was a delicate and expensive wedding gift from John's Aunt Helen of Exeter. But that evening as the darkness grew out of the trees and shrubs around their house, set behind the campus where they had met (now given over to another institution), and the mosquitoes started to come out of the small pools of water even the most vigilant inspectors had missed, they did not. Su Lin was wrapped in more of the past. John was thinking of the poems.

"Moonlighter's Cafe and Restaurant."
 "Yes, Moonlighter's. Can I book a table please?"
 "For tonight?"
 "Yes. 8:15 for two. Phenwick."
 "That's F… E…"
 "No, PH. P… H…"
 "Oh, I know, like 'pheasant under glass'. Is that Mrs Phenwick? Hello, it's Henry the captain here. Long time no see."
 "Henry, hello, Nice of you to remember us,"
 "Nice to have you visit us again."
 "Not at all. It's our tenth anniversary and I immediately thought of the café."
 "Ten years already? Congrats. Would you like a cake for your anniversary—on the house, of course?"
 Su Lin saw the Bomb Alaska Henry had brought out of the kitchen last year. Blazing with brandy flames, it was a beautiful sight or would have been if it had not shown off John's reddening been when he finally realised what the dinner and the cake were for.
 She remembered the hot mixture of anger, humiliation and sadness she had felt as John tried blowing out the flames and singing 'Happy Birthday'. That was why they had not returned to the cafe since.
 Before, they had gone as often as twice a week to sit at their usual table by the window with the mismatched chairs, the paintings and bookshelves on either side, knowing that they had gone there from their first days of courtship, knowing that they could count on bumping into someone they knew, to chat with and catch up, or else that they could read or talk between themselves over good coffee and some new dish on the ever

changing menu. She remembered the Marquez book she'd bought there—her first-and how John would buy *Singa* quite regularly when he had still been writing. The cafe and its incorporated bookstore had been the scene of many good memories and she suddenly felt ashamed for abandoning it just because of one had one.

The shame provoked her.

"Would you like a cake, Mrs Phenwick?" Henry repeated.

"Yes, a cake Henry. That'd be wonderful, thank you."

She said it and put down the phone before she realised she'd bet on John again, doubling the emotional stakes in a replay of last year's fiasco. Would he remember?

Committee meetings and an urgent report had been his excuses last year, as she railed that he'd forgotten in spite or all his computer-generated schedules and lists when, ironically, no matter how disorganised and absent minded he had been previously, their anniversary was at least one thing he'd never forgotten. And this time? He'd said nothing about either the dinner or his work. Perhaps he was pretending so he could surprise her. He had played tricks before, she reminded herself, and hopefully he was still capable of such things. When she'd scrawled a large note about the dinner in the kitchen diary, her pencil had poised in the air. She thought of putting in the reason for the dinner. Then she'd shaken her head, thought, "Let's see if Mr Organised remembers," and closed the book. She looked at the photograph of John on the telephone table (Ph as in Photograph), wondering if that had been the right thing, if she was not just setting herself up again for disappointment, to be crowned with the bitterest Bomb Alaska.

She gazed at his captured smile, so far away in time, and wanted to believe he would remember. She remembered another day John had surprised her.

He must have heard her key in the lock, then her footsteps in the corridor but remained where he was continuing with what he was doing, instead of going to greet her. She stood in the doorway of the study for a few minutes without saying a word as he went on rearranging the books and papers which had become more or less a fixture of the room, piled on the floor. He dusted the shelves and books, picked out books in separate piles to throw or relegate to boxes to be sealed and placed in the storeroom under the stairs, or return to friends and libraries. "What are you doing, John?" That was all she could find to say.

And she had no retort when he replied, "Oh, just cleaning," as if it was something he did habitually. When her parents next visited, her mother trooped upstairs almost immediately she was in the door. "This I must see for myself she said loudly and Su Lin could see John trying not to smile in triumph. When they next came over for tea, Su Lin's friends, Gina and Li Huan, asked to drop in on the library too, ostensibly wanting to borrow some books. It was the miracle of their house—John cleared his things and, lo and behold, there was a floor underneath after all.

She waited for John to falter: for the study at home and his office to slowly sink back into the swamp of books and papers they'd been for so long, for him again to give firm instructions that the maid was just to dust around the hooks and not, never, to touch anything because there was a fragile order to what seemed like mess. He seemed to know that and delighted in disappointing her. Nor only did he keep it up but he started ordering where his slippers and shoes were kept, where the car keys were placed on the mantle, the cutlery and crockery. A computer was bought and installed on John Lim's recommendation, and it kept lists of everything and churned out the tidy committee minutes and lecture notes John began producing. He was not the same absent-minded, carelessly human professor she had married.

She sighed, went to the study and restarted typing as if each word, each letter that the old typewriter struck onto the white page, was part of an incantation that would bring hack that past.

John Phenwick lingered too long at Ah Lee's garage that morning. Despite Ah Lee first calling him 'Fenwich' like 'sandwich' and then, 'Pros' rather than 'Prof', they had got on from their first meeting and John could spend entire Saturday afternoons there, jabbering away in an unholy mix of English, Malay and Hokkien about the cost of living, the rising cost of cars and Ah Lee's son who wanted to work in some boutique.

That morning, John tried to keep the conversation short but Ah Lee was telling him about some part he had had the good fortune to find which would help make the car more original. And then there was no time for John to go home first, drop off the car, change to the Honda and still make his class. He could take a taxi—as he had getting to the workshop—but he hated even the thought of it.

Twelve years and taxi drivers were still offering him nice, clean women and copy watches. He'd give them directions in the Hokkien he'd learnt from Su Lin's father or in Malay but they would always assume he was a tourist out for a good time. It didn't help that his name was John. "Hey, John", they would start, using the common name for want of knowing what his name actually was—like how *Roti John* was named—and he would automatically lean forward and listen. Then he'd have to decline their offers for the rest of the trip.

Most friends refused to believe these stories, preferring to think vice was available only to those who went out of their way to knock on certain Geylang doors and that being white meant only easier admission to certain private clubs and better service in restaurants. Ah Lee knew better—he was an ex-taxi driver himself—and this was one of the reasons John liked the bulky, sun burnt man.

Would the old car make it to University without overheating, he asked, and would it rain? It was in good condition, came the cautious non-answer, and as for the weather, Ah Lee laughed gruffly, that was as predictable as the next government ruling. He laughed, said the ISD was going to get Ah Lee for the joke, started the engine and gunned away.

He was late for the Shakespeare class despite running down the corridor. It hadn't rained once in the last week, and he hadn't driven the car to university in over six months, but since he did, it rained. By the time he pulled under some trees to get the top up, his shirt was soaked. By the time he got the top up, he was sweating. Wet with rain and perspiration, John did his best to ignore the students' stares. He began the class.

But as he did, he found, edging itself to the front of his mind, the sweet mystery of the poems and their sender. He couldn't help himself: his three prime suspects were in this class. He spoke about Singaporean poetry, hoping to draw out clues to the identity of the mysterious sender. The students were a little mystified at his departure from Shakespeare, turning the two-page hand outs he'd given them over and over to see how this or that Singaporean poem might fit in with *The Tempest*.

Then they responded. Samuel the champion of Third World culture, led, quoting John Lim on this and that and the other. Of the prime suspects, Mimi and Carla followed the discussion quite quickly, cutting in with some points and even some quotations. Susie was quiet: was it because she didn't know much Singaporean poetry or because she was frightened of giving herself away? He asked questions to provoke their thinking and the unexpected forum spiraled, like his classes of old. And just like the classes of old, John could see some students, the ones in the corner, fall away, their pens lapsing on their notepads since there was nothing to copy. These were the same breed of students who had filled in their assessment forms with such negative remarks those many years ago that he had abandoned his original style of teaching. He looked at their lost eyes and reined in the discussion. Turn to page two of the handout, he said. As they did, he had looked his prime candidates over again: which was the mysterious sender?

He left the class angry with himself for pursuing the mystery at the expense of the proper lesson, excited and curious about the effect his questions and general behaviour might have on the mysterious sender and somewhat bitter about how some students could never appreciate his Socratic style and, instead, had a vivid respect for John Lim. It was not a pleasant or orderly mix of emotions. He was also at once quite cold from being wet in the air-conditioned room and still hot and clammy from running to the class. His room reflected those states of mind and body.

One pile of poetry books was by his chair. Others were strewn across the shelves and his signed copy of *Down the Line*, poems by another lecturer, lay on the desk, its pages stuck with yellow flags and paperclips to mark poems he thought the mysterious sender might send. A stack of mid-term papers by unmarked under a half-finished cup of coffee. The books he was using to prepare the handout for the next class and the scripts he was writing the paper about were mixed in a fan of disarray, not leaving a single clear space on the desk. The computer printer was ON, his window left half open. John was struck by the mess he had left the previous day.

He tried to rearrange the Singaporean poetry books in alphabetical order on the shelf next to the last, sun-faded copies of his own book but, as he diet he started flipping the pages of the boob he had meant to reshelf and reading the poems again, sitting down on another pile of books as if un a low stool. Which would be the next poem, he wondered, where would it be and would it provide him more clues? Who was the mysterious sender? He brought more books down, leaving them in another pile next to him. His mind turned to this question again, not in the least bored by the same speculations which had no answer and he sat there, leafing through the pages of the strewn books, taking down more books from the shelf, reading some poems aloud, imagining the face behind the typewriter.

It was then that the slip of paper scraped against the bottom edge of the door as it was pushed in. He would not have heard it normally, he was facing the other way and the cold air whirred ceaselessly out of the vents, but—because he was reading the poetry aloud—his senses were keener. It was a squashed plastic wrapper in a silent theatre, the digital watch alarm during a concert and the whispered "excuse me-s" of latecomers getting through to their scats. The paper passed over the threshold of both his room and his imagination and at first he was irritated. Then he jolted on his precarious seat of piled hooks.

It was the solution to his vexed question. Another poem. The mysterious sender had been right at his door.

The pile of books collapsed under his agitation and he fell. He jumped back to his feet and leapt over them to the door, grabbing the piece of paper on the uprise, the door handle at the apex of his leap and crashing into the door as he pulled it open and tried to go through in mixed order. The bump on his forehead quickly reddened but was barely felt. Out in the corridor, he heard the click clack of high-heels moving away. He paused for a second, gathering dignity to him as two students went by, nodding their greetings. He mumbled a reply and played with his spectacles so his raised hand hid the red hump. When they passed, he ran headlong in the other direction, following the sound of the high heels, holding the slip of paper in his right hand and swinging it like a baton, taking the stairs two at a time.

There was no one at the top of the stairs but like a blood hound, John felt instinct lead him up the short cut to the canteen. There they were: Carla, Mimi and Susie together at a table near the juice stall—all the suspects in one place.

Mimi was sipping watermelon juice while Susie talked, ignoring the glass of pineapple in front of her. Was Susie confessing to it all to her friend? Was Mimi taking Susie's advice on the mad and secret love? Were the drinks both Philters? He walked nearer and when they noticed him, stopped. He cleared his throat coolly, nodded and looked them over for more clues.

It was Carla, he realised—she had no drink at all and from this it was obvious she had just arrived, hurrying back from his room. He looked down at her legs and found, as expected, the high heels he'd heard. "Dropped something, Prof Phenwick?" He ignored the question and looked at her, smiling. The sly minx licked her lips; an obvious provocation. Carla of the short skirt, a pretty thing, drawn inexorably to him. He was flattered and embarrassed but even in the seconds he took to move towards their table, rehearsing the words with which he would gently break her hopes, he realised his main emotion was disappointment that the secret love had come to an end—no matter how satisfactory the answer.

"You got my note, Prof Phenwick?"

"Yes I did, Carla."

"I hope it's okay,"

"Well, it's very nice,"

"The least I could do. Couldn't help it. Sorry, Prof."

"There's no need to be sorry. It happens, especially to you young people. And I understand. But this can't go on."

He said it as gently as possible—but firmly—and looked at her face, imagining it stripped of the stylish make-up and sunglasses, looking child-like again with pain and embarrassment.

"Well, Prof, would it be all right if I gave it to you in about two weeks?"

"What?"

"How about ten days?"

"Ten days?"

"Well, like I said in my note, there are two other essays and I hope you won't mind giving me an extension on the term paper you asked for. I know everyone else has sent in theirs already, so if I could just have a few days more..."

John looked down at the three bright young faces, Carla's note crumpled as his fist tightened around it.

"That is what you wanted to see me about, right, Prof? I looked for you in your office to explain but I heard you talking so I thought I wouldn't disturb you."

"I was reading poetry."

"Aloud? Oh, I thought..."

"Two weeks is fine Carla,"

"Phew, thanks so much."

"Don't mention it."

"Join us for a juice? You look hot."

"I've been running."

"But I thought you were reading poetry?"

"I'll take you up on that offer of a drink another day, thanks."

"Thanks for the extension."

"Don't mention it. I remember what it's like to be young."

John's embarrassment didn't last the 150 steps back to his office. Along the path, he read Carla's note and all he saw written was the word 'essay', almost highlighted in his eyes. Essays handed in by all his students were sitting on his desk. Typed essays. Some on computers, others on electronic typewriters but a few still on manual ones. Maybe one might match the poems. He started running. His heart pumped freely.

After his search, the essays lay in disarray over his desk, chair and sidetable. None of them matched. And he was in no mood to mark them or to try to get things organised so he could begin his other work. John Lim called. He asked about the progress on the paper and about the application form. John made vague promises and, straight after, went back to reading poems. After a while, he picked lip the old, battered copy of his own book, the special copy he set aside for doing all his readings, and read to himself—as if he was hearing everything new again. And then he was ready to leave.

The next poem was tied to the short gearstick of the car. He sat ill there, feeling conspicuous as students walked past and looked at the odd, old, red open-top car. Or perhaps the odd, old, red-faced, slightly-balding lecturer sitting and reading in it. He read the poem again, with a heady mixture of nervousness and pleasure.

> Come red with identity out the night,
> Headlights staring into the blind corner,
> We arc focused instantly,
> polaroid, two in a two-seater
> Knowledgeable with speed:
> No one need tell us who we are.
> My car will hold in any bend,
> On a pin, a thought, is
> Existential.
> Hold on tight and let the wind
> Blow out consciousness
> Like a candle, that's what
> Open tops are for.
> We go
> go go

The upsetting things of the day faded away as he looked at the poem again, smiling. In this careless, happy mood he hastily over-pumped the accelerator and the flooded engine turned without sparking, condemning him to wait for it to clear. He smacked himself on the forehead for stupidity and then laughed, not minding what more students, passing the parked and stalled car, might think.

John was late coming home (and early the day before), when usually, these last few years at least, she could set her watch by his return. He hurried through and was ready while she was still at her dressing table, and then he went to the study—she watched him in the mirror through the open door between the study and their bedroom. He rummaged through looking for this book and that. He asked her for the typewriter and said nothing when she told him it was on her desk. She told him John Lim called to remind him about the application form for club membership and, raising her voice above the typewriter's click-clack, asked if he was doing it then. He said, No, and continued to type and when he was finished and she was ready and they left in the car, with the top down and with her wearing one of the old scarves he had given her.

In the few seconds when the fine, familiar dinner was over and only coffee and the cake were to come, Su Lin reviewed everything that had happened that night. And then she waited. There was a mirror in the wall to her left and she could see them both there, as others saw them, and she looked, as trying to memorise how they were that evening, at that moment:.

John wasn't thinking about the membership form, his paper, the students' essays or even the dinner they had finished. Neither was he thinking about the mysterious poems, Carla, Susie or Mimi. Outside, beyond the riverside window, the tall buildings faced him, Parliament House was lit-up, white through the darkness, and the river flowed, When he first came, there had still been bumboats and half-dressed, sun-wrinkled men waiting outside the go-downs, chatting in dialect; now that was the nostalgia of water-colour paintings. Except for UOB, those tall buildings hadn't been there; soon, that Bank would finish off another skyscraper to match its rivals'.

He knew that beyond this immediate scene there were planned towns sitting on whole coastlines which had been sea at the time of his arrival. The pace of change here surprised him, as it did every time he paused to consider it. And then his focus shifted nearer, to the half reflection in the window: the restaurant, the table, Su Lin and himself. It was something he now knew had been following him, floating like a phantom at the edge of his vision.

Just as Su Lin finished her review of the immediate past and John smiled at what he recognised in the window: Henry came out of the kitchen with the flaming cake. But the poor man was last year's ghost to Su Lin and she could not bring herself to look either at him or across the table at John, to see if he had remembered. She looked only into the brandy flames. She heard John singing, "Happy Birthday" and turned to him sharply. He stopped when she did and was smiling, with a white envelope and a small, brightly-wrapped present on the table in front of him.

"Happy Anniversary."

Su Lin wasn't sure whether she actually heard the words or just thought she had, and said nothing until he repeated himself and, leaning across, kissed her.

She was not sure when he had remembered and did not: know what the present was. When they went out to the car, it might: be full to the brim with flowers (phalaenopsis?). They would get in and drive to the beach, where the sea was working its slow changes, or straight home to watch their sons sleeping or make love or go straight to sleep, holding each other. And tomorrow, they could decide to keep the car for another twelve years or sell it, and John might either join the club or not bother, and she might tidy his study or leave it, or he might tidy it or might try and fail or just not bother anymore, ever again. He might know who had been sending him the poems, he might know and tell her he knew, he might not know and keep trying to figure it out, he might know but never tell her he knew. None of this mattered to her for now, John had pushed the present and the envelope across the table.

She looked down at down. Like everything else, she did not care exactly what the present was—just that it was given. But, the envelope...

Despite and because of its plainness, Su Lin had only to touch it: to know, surely, confidently, like the best of optimisms confirmed, that it was a poem, and that John Phenwick, Professor Phenwick, 'Phil', the lecturer, the poet, and her husband, had written it.

PAINTING THE TIGER
Philip Jeyaretnam

Ah Leong had taken his son to the zoo. The boy had devoured an orange Frutti ice cream, a grubby handful of chocolates and a packet of biscuits. He munched while the macaques chattered, swallowed as the sun bears yawned and dragged his feet as the orangutans slumbered. He was no more interested in his surroundings than when one or other of his grandmothers placed him in front of the television with a packet of cream crackers. Power Rangers, Pokemon, Digimon, Sakura—marathon sessions of animated combat that left him in a belly-up, eyes-glazed stupor by the time Ah Leong got home from his insurance calls. Ah Leong was beginning to wonder if he shouldn't just have stayed home and flipped channels after all.

Then they met the polar bear. No snow. No ice. But still, a real polar bear. It caught a fish. It swam on its back. It ambled across the rocks and dived into the blue water. In front of the glass panel, the boy's eyes widened. He pressed his nose against the pane. The bear swam up, and almost vertical, belly to the boy, touched his own nose to the glass. David (for that was the little boy's name, chosen by mother and father after watching a very informative programme about Michelangelo on Arts Central) squealed, alarm turning quickly to delight.

Now the boy was hooked. He ran ahead of Ah Leong from one exhibit to the next. At last they reached Ah Leong's favourite animal, the creature he admired more than any other, and ran into the viewing gallery that is built out over the mock river at the front of their enclosure.

The biggest of the three tigers stretched and yawned, and meandered down to the water's edge. He tested the water with each of his front paws and then slid in. Ah Leong whispered in his son's ear. "That's the King of the Jungle. Look at his muscles rippling beneath his stripes." The boy repeated his father's catchphrase, shorn of genitive and article: "King Jungle, King Jungle." From behind them shrill voices intruded: "See how he checked temperature first." "*Aiyo*. Missed it. This one can send to America's Funniest Videos." For a moment Ah Leong tried to block his son's ears, to save him from this urban mockery of the magnificent beast, a mere fifteen metres away, whose race, the Sumatran, is doomed to extinction in the wild within thirty years. Then he realised that to his son's two-and-a-half-year-old eyes, the tiger's majesty is irrefutable, and no intervention was necessary.

Ah Leong's own fascination with tigers had begun as an eight-year-old. At first it was just the impression of power and freedom that he got from its size, its arrogant gait and muscled torso. Then as he learned more about the animal, its habits and character, it was in the end the tiger's patience in the hunt, its slow stalk and final pounce, that he most admired.

He hoped that David too would learn something from tigers. And when the boy was older he planned to take him to the spot in Choa Chu Kang, where the last wild tiger in Singapore was shot in the 1920s. Do they know what they're doing, he suddenly thought, those Indonesians and Malaysians, happily following our lead in the taming of swamp and jungle, eliminating untidiness in the name of progress? Do they understand the loss of spirit that follows the destruction of wildness? Once there is no big predator out there, we puff up with pride, believing ourselves invulnerable. But worse than that, our minds narrow. A country with neither wolf nor lion nor tiger is a country that will always think tame thoughts, that sinks softly into comfy sofas at the end of the day, hooked on soaps from Hong Kong or action from Hollywood. The nearest it comes to the wild is through nature documentaries of another time and place, safely boxed off by the television's confines.

In the middle of this reverie, a couple of *kretek*-smoking gentlemen thrust their way to the barrier. "No more trees," said one, and Ah Leong half-turned to him, wanting to make contact with this kindred soul, this rough-looking Indonesian lamenting the loss within a single generation of almost the entirety of his country's heritage. Then the other one laughed, "I'm told Liberia's the place to make money these days. Plenty of forest for the next ten years, and no one to complain about how you cut it down." "No one to make noise about the smoke, eh?"

That night, sleeping next to his wife, Ah Leong dreamed that the tiger had escaped, that it had swum across the reservoir and made its way to the landscaped grounds of his executive condominium, that even now it was prowling among the rectangular planter boxes in the lift lobby, padding across the polished granite tiles. He dreamed that zoo keepers and policemen and military were swarming the area and had the tiger in their sights. But he, Ah Leong, convinced them not to shoot, to let the tiger go free. "There must be a tiger in our darkness," he argued. "Let's not just bring discos to the zoo. We must bring tigers to our discos. Let that tiger go."

In the morning, he opened *The Straits Times* expectantly. Had a tiger escaped? And if it had escaped, did it make it to the cover of Mandai jungle or had it been shot before it reached the protection of the trees? And if it had made the jungle, how would it survive? Each tiger needs a range at least half the size of Singapore, and Mandai jungle was tiny, with hardly anything to stalk. A few macaques perhaps, if they could be surprised digging for seeds on the forest floor. Or wild boar? Perhaps the tiger would have to swim to Ubin or Tekong to catch anything worth eating. And if it got that far it might as well just keep going, onward to Johore and the fragments of jungle that form the vertebrae of Malaysia's highland spine.

But there was nothing in the newspaper about an escaped tiger. Just the usual stories celebrating top scorers in examinations, tut-tutting over new liaisons between celebrities or lauding upgrading projects in heartlander districts. Ah Leong drained his coffee and turned to his file of insurance prospects. Make the calls. Do the rounds. A medical check late morning for a proposer who signed up last week. A free afternoon. He could take his paints and easel to Mandai Park. He had an idea for a big canvas, but needed to do some sketches first. A sharp-edged diamond, the hardest and most durable of all things, spiraling from its core into a green vortex, the shape of a tiger just discernible, rising from the swirling lines.

Later that day, as he sat in the shade, looking out across the water, he traced the outline of the tiger in his mind, first imagining the sweep of his hand in one fluid motion from tail to nose, and then contrasting that emergence with a single stroke from head to haunches, so that the tiger changed direction, disappearing into the depths instead. And the tiger itself? One of those he had seen in the zoo, and if so which one? Or else that tiger on the dirt track in Choa Chu Kang, the hunter's boot pressed against its bullet-riddled neck? Or an ideal tiger, the archetype of all tigers that have ever lived, just as its creator pictured it, unchanging and eternal, the ideal that even extinction will not erase. But what would that ideal tiger look like? As big as a Siberian tiger, but with the close stripes of the Sumatran? Or exactly the other way around?

Where did his pictures come from? From what part of his body did the impulse speed to his hand? From the eye, presenting what he could see? From his mind, some construct of reason and memory? Or from his heart, the bloodlines of feeling? He was convinced that only when it came from his heart was his painting any good, worth the high sticker prices the galleries placed on his work, and which on occasion it transacted at. But how could someone born and bred in this city paint a tiger from his heart? Six hundred years ago the lion had been chosen for us, even though no lion had ever walked our land, as if our destiny as an imperial outpost had already been determined. When a few hundred years later the British came prowling, sniffing round the islands of the Riau, the lion was a perfect fit for the projection of the British crown's power. The contrast between the lion (who dominates his pride by force of will, hunts in the day and overwhelms prey with the strength of an entire pride) and the tiger (who hunts at night, alone, relying on cunning as much as strength) illustrated the difference between Singapore's orderly streets, with the first street lighting and sanitation in Southeast Asia, and the dark jungles all around. Not surprising then that tigers were ruthlessly exterminated.

Naturally enough, as we passed from imperial outpost to modern nation, the lion matched our own image of ourselves: one people gaining strength through working together, bright reason our constant guide. The lion has even survived being fitted out with a peculiar tail: by rendering the mouth bigger and teeth sharper (so that the on-looker is at once struck by fear) the absurdity of that scaly torso, flicking up from frothy waves, is hidden from sight. Triple its size, give it flashing green eyes, and any kid will be terrified (David, not yet a slayer of giants, certainly was). One has not time to grasp the simple silliness of it all, the impossibility of such a beast ever being able to pounce, to catch anything, on land or water. But after all, neither lion nor Merlion is of this land, this water. And without a real beast, the image is only an idea, something for the mind and not the heart or soul.

So could his drawing of the tiger bring it back to life on our soil? Could its rebirth on his canvas stir the souls of Singaporeans too?

That night the tiger's spirit seized him. He dreamed he was a tiger, prowling in the forest. The thrill of the hunt coursed through him, and when he awoke, in mid-pounce, he went immediately to work. "As I paint the tiger, I am the tiger," he whispered to himself. By morning it was finished and drying.

The next night he did not dream that he was a tiger. Instead, sleep took him to a fallen tree. He sat astride it. Melancholy descended upon him. It was dusk, and the trees cast long shadows. A tiger came to him, and placed a paw on the trunk beside him. Ah Leong observed the perfection of its unsheathed claws, and then gazed into its majestic face. Unafraid, he saw how this feline's colours were a brighter gold, a deeper black, than those of any mortal tiger.

"We leave you behind, but we will never really be gone. Our spirit will linger, in the wild places of this world, as emissaries from the next."

"Even when I go blind from all my painting, I will not forget you."

When Ah Leong awoke, the dream fell away like a cape untied after a long journey, leaving the weight of his years heavy upon him. Half his life was gone, and all that he'd done was secure insurance cover for clients, paint pictures, marry a kind woman and produce a son, a son who would never see a tiger in the wild because by the time he was a man there would be none left outside zoos or safari parks. Sitting on the edge of his bed, he felt it beyond him to rise to his feet, stagger through the door and begin another day. Every day is greyer than the last, he thought, picturing the smoke swirling from Indonesia's forests.

Then his son appeared. In that soft gentle state of the just awakened, he pattered across the parquet floor. He looked at his father's new painting, stretched across the frame of the easel. His eyes lit up. A smile, like a falling tree, cracked his face. "Tiger," he said, "King Jungle."

CROSSING DISTANCE
Tan Mei Ching

I wanted to see what Gran's China was like. After all, I came from China, in sorts, via my grandmother. And it was now or never—Gran said this was probably the last time she would come here. She would be 'too weak' to do it again another year ("no, *lah*, Ah Ma, don't say that"). Then our connection to China would be lost. I didn't want to see China on a tour bus; I wanted to see China with Gran, I wanted her to show me her village, her world, I wanted to see it through her eyes.

I met my distant cousin, Ah Hia (the son of the daughter of Gran's father's sworn brother), who had got out to push the tricycle uphill. The boy whose tricycle it was, stood up on the pedals and ground them down. When we came to a part of the road which had sunk in and become a mud bank, the mud sucked in one of Ah Hia's slippers. Gran said we could walk the rest of the way. The boy agreed. He was soaked with sweat. Gran gave him ten yuan, two more than he asked for. "Poor thing," she said, "small boy working so hard. Next time," she told Ah Hia who found his slipper, "get someone bigger." I told Gran that if everyone didn't want to take the boy's tricycle because they felt sorry that he had to work so hard, he wouldn't earn any money. Gran considered and said, "See how lucky you are?"

When we got to the village, I met another distant cousin, Ah Hee (the son of the son of the daughter of Gran's grandmother), and both Ah Hee's and Ah Hia's families—mothers, grandmothers, wives, children, nieces and nephews, all crowded into Ah Hia's stone house and spilled out onto the courtyard.

They were all happy to see Gran. Everyone in the village, related or not, was happy to see Gran.

They grinned at me with bad teeth and the men broke out cigarette packs and passed cigarettes around generously among themselves. I made a mental note of this discrimination to tell my friends in Singapore, then was surprised when someone offered me a cigarette. I declined. I think it was because I was a 'foreign guest'. Either that or I looked like a man.

With my autoflash, autofocus, automatic "idiot" camera, I took pictures of Gran seated in the hall of Ah Hia's stone house, surrounded by the villagers as she sorted out into separate piles the clothing we had brought from Singapore.

"In Singapore, people have so many clothes and they don't want to wear them all. See, how nice these are?" Gran held up a white shirt, long outdated in fashion. The villagers murmured assent. "Nobody wants to wear them," Gran said, folding the shirt and putting it on one pile. "In Singapore, there are so many vlothes, if I were to bring them all, it would take a big ship. I'm not bluffing. Two ships even."

I took pictures of children carrying other children piggy-back, the younger children bare- and black- bottomed, most shoeless like the adults. No one in the village had a camera, so they were all interested in this little black box that flashed and captured time. Everyone wanted me to take pictures of their family. When I pressed the button on the camera and said, "Okay," people kept still and always asked, 'is it okay?' meaning they wanted me to take the exact same picture of the exact same pose two or three times before they were sure that the picture was absorbed by the idiot-camera.

"Yes, yes," I always said professionally, and quickly had other families pose. I also took pictures of old men and women who wanted pictures to put on their coffins when they died. It was after I had taken their pictures that someone told me that these pictures could not be taken with the altar of gods in the background (because gods could not be placed on coffins with the picture of the deceased and prayed to that way), and I had to retake the pictures again, this time making sure the people were surrounded by nothing but wall and furniture. By the thirty-ninth shot, I fiddled with my camera and tried to tell them that I couldn't take any more because I needed to save film to take pictures of what China looked like and bring them home to my family.

I opened my mouth and got stuck. My Hokkien was the pits. It was what Gran originally spoke, but some of it had been lost in the ocean between China and Singapore, and a lot more between what Gran gave to my mother and what my mother gave to me. I didn't know how to say film, or pictures, or save, so I just said, "Cannot use. Don't have enough."

I wandered about the house, taking snapshots of whatever looked interesting, like a professional photographer working for *National Geographic*. I took a picture of the grass shack—a squarish room with grey walls and a little window with wooden bars. Dried grass piled up almost to the ceiling. Leaning against the wall by the window was a smooth wooden ladder. Gran had told me about this room. Curious. I couldn't figure out what I had imagined the room to be before I came, as if seeing it now had merged its image with my mind's picture so that they were inseparable. I wanted to climb up the ladder to the top of the grass stack and lie there, but then I saw myself falling off the stack, followed by an avalanche of grass. I wandered into the courtyard. The villagers had put a main door here, wide, leading into the courtyard, and from the courtyard, the house started, with another door. The doors were thick slabs of wood and on all the doors in the house, plastered near the top, were red papers with fortuitous sayings like 'Enter and exit with safety', 'Spring', and 'Long Life'.

In a corner of the courtyard near the main door was the toilet which didn't have a roof. I could probably look into it if I stood on the balcony upstairs. I asked if I could go upstairs and take a picture (I couldn't see much of the inside of the toilet after all), took another of the bedroom— it had a dresser and a bed made of planks—and went back down to the courtyard. It was quite ingenious how they had improvised a toilet door, using oneside of the main door that swung open to partially block the entrance to the toilet. I guess if you didn't have enough, you just used what was there. I had to stand on guard outside the toilet when Gran had to go.

She had asked Ah Hia's mother where the *jamban* was. Ah Hia's mother looked puzzled.

"Gran," I said, pulling her elbow, "that's Malay."

That was the third time she had used a Chinesised Malay word from Singapore.

When Gran was done, she showed me where the urine went. It flowed in a little drain in the toilet right out to an open hole beside the front door. I contemplated taking a picture of the cesspool, but it didn't look particularly enlightening. It would not be something I would forget telling my family about.

"Won't people fall into it?" I asked Ah Hia, whom I was to call 'older brother'.

He gave me a strange look. "No," he said.

"Did anyone ever step into it accidentally?" I asked.

"No," he said.

"Children?" I asked.

"No," he said.

What a wonder, I told Gran, who said I was silly to think anyone would step into it. "It's used for fertilizer," Gran told me. "See how lucky you are? When I was a child, I had to carry this to the fields and fertilize the plants. They still do it now." Ah Hia's wife gave me a shy smile as she manoeuvred past us with a yoke and two buckets of steamy, murky looking liquid. "Is that... is that..." I said. What Hokkien word did Gran use for 'fertilizer'? Gran said, "Water from washing hot pans out after cooking and rotten vegetables. For the pigs."

I wanted to wander around the compound but Gran was certain I would get lost, be killed or kidnapped, so she insisted on going along. I wanted to see the site of the old houses, where Gran used to live, and also the sea she had talked about so many times. Although it had been raining recently and the ground was wet and in many places flooded, some villagers and Ah Hia decided that there was a route dry enough to be taken. While negotiating some flooded areas, something caught Gran's attention.

"What's that?" She pointed uphill.

"That's the old temple," Ah Hia said.

"That's near where the old houses are, right?" Gran asked, and was about to go on when I reminded her I wanted to see the old houses. "I want to see where you used to live, Gran," I said. "I want to see where you lived for the first sixteen years of your life."

"Okay." She started up the sloping ground and I followed, giving her my arm which she leaned on more heavily as we went on.

"There, there," she said at the sight of a brown roof peeking out from behind the foliage of a crooked tree. When we stepped onto the old village ground, my eyes seemed to refocus—the air quavered, the ground shifted—as if time was bending and the future was touching the past as I crossed the same boundaries that my gran had some fifty years ago. I was almost surprised that I did not metamorphose into the girl who had been living the stories my gran told me. I looked at my gran and tried to imagine her here, living in the stone house by the yew tree, "With the cow" she said, the house which had now fallen in and creepers had taken over. I searched her face for emotion, but all I saw was mild interest.

"Are you okay, Gran?" I asked, digging out the camera from my bag. She seemed a little breathless. She nodded and waved her hand around. "Look, look."

There was a little temple right ahead. Unlike the sprawling temples near the marketplace, it was just one room and had one figure of a god, the Earth God, on a small table. The villagers waited outside while Gran and I stepped in to look. In front of the god was a small urn filled with used joss-sticks. Ash had overflowed around it. The walls were grey and dark in the corners. It felt like no one had been here for a long time, as if people had forgotten about the little temple in their village and instead went miles to the big temples which were always crowded, filled with warm bodies and incense from joss-sticks and burning paper offerings. My eyes always watered as soon as I stepped inside those places. In this blurred state, I would try to avoid getting holes in my side from smouldering joss-sticks sticking out from people's hands. At every big temple there would be people kneeling in front of some gods or goddesses, shaking a bamboo container filled with flat sticks—they made a chi-chi sound—until a flat stick stuck its head out of the pile and dropped onto the ground. Then thanks were said and the stick was brought to one of the few fortune-tellers for deciphering. But here, there were no joss-sticks or chi-chi sticks, and all we did was put our hands together and bowed our heads.

We had to jump over several pools en route to the sea; Gran waded through them as she had rubber slippers on and water wouldn't hurt them. I had leather shoes. I kept asking Gran if she was feeling all right. Maybe we shouldn't have walked so much, just because I wanted to look around. But she said she was fine.

Gran asked Ah Hia if the houses where fishermen from other villagers stayed during the fishing season were still around. Ah Hia nodded. "But more run down now than a few years ago," he said. "People nowadays prefer to spend time on more crops, or a side business, like selling cigarettes. Fishing is not very reliable, not much money in it."

"Didn't you go to the sea two years ago when you last came?" I asked Gran.

"No," she said.

"When did you last see the sea?"

"Oh…" She thought for a minute as we manoeuvred around a ditch. "Since I left here."

I was aghast. "Since you went to Singapore?"

"Yah."

"Fifty-six years ago!"

"Yah."

"Why?" I asked, helping her across some muddy ground. She, in turn, stopped midway and tried to help me across. "Gran, you go first," I told her, giving her a nudge. She thinks I'm ten years old.

"Why?" I asked when she seemed to have forgotten.

"Oh, just never had the chance to go to the sea."

Ah Hia said, "Your grandmother was busy when she visited us. She was visiting everybody."

"You didn't have time?" I said when what I meant was, "You didn't make time?"

She said, slightly rebuking, "I've only been back here twice, and only stayed in this area for two or three days each time, too many things to do."

I could smell salt in the air. It smelled like the sea. This salt was a heavier, grainier salt—the real thing—I could tell. Somehow the salt from Singapore's sea was softened, diluted by the perfumes of modern society. We approached squat buildings which Ah Hia said were houses for fishermen.

"Too bad we don't have fishing now, or you can watch them at work, pulling nets. Very nice to see," he said.

The sea was a light shade of turquoise, dotted with fishing boats crescent-like and motionless. The sky was blue, the mountains in the far distance dusky, indistinct but ever present. I turned my head to the side, and saw, near the shore, a several-storeyed rectangular, pale grey, ugly building. "What is that?" I asked, frowning.

"Probably an administrative building," Gran said.

I took a few pictures of the sea, which looked very much like the sea I saw once in Australia, and some of the fishermen's houses and a few of the villagers who came with us. They stood several feet apart from each other, posing as naturally as they could. They looked like some incongruous pop group. One had on black rubber boots and had rolled up his T-shirt exposing his stomach, another had a black umbrella and blue rubber slippers. Ah Hia himself wore a T-shirt with the face of Michael Jackson on it, which nobody would wear at home in Singapore.

"*Mya Jahsen,*" Gran told Ah Hia, who gathered him to be an important person in Singapore. I picked up a few seashells for mementoes. They were pale peach, spiral in a flatish way, with dark lines following the shell round and round, ending in a dark spot. I wondered how Gran was feeling, being at the sea again, the sea of her childhood, of her stories, her memories. How many times had she, as a young child, stood on these shores and wondered what lay beyond this sea? How many nights had she lain awake and heard the sea's whispers? How many times had she marvelled at its magnificent storms, awed by its power? How many times soothed by its tranquillity? How many times did she see it in her dreams of fifty-six years?

"Gran, do you miss the sea?" I asked.

"What's there to miss? A sea is a sea. Singapore has a sea."

"Well, yeah... but it's different, you know..."

She turned to look at me, smiling. "Silly child. Have you seen enough?"

When we got back to the village, dishes were set on a square, foldable table. Around it, chairs and stools, wooden, plastic, bent, limpy. A gourd of some species, cut up and fried, had begun to exude its water content and spill over the plate. The table slanted to one side. Gran scouted the ground outside and found a flat piece of stone and stuck it under one table leg. The gourd plate stopped dripping. Two plastic containers with fish soup were set on the table.

"This is a feast for them, too. You think they would eat like this if we weren't here?" Gran told me in a whisper. I wiped the bowls, spoons and chopsticks with tissue from my bag, and sat down, fanning around the dishes to prevent flies from landing on the food. Once we started eating, the flies came back I was careful not to touch anything the flies landed on.

After dinner, Gran asked Ah Hia where we could take the bus back to the hotel.

"Huh?" he said.

Gran repeated herself, louder this time. I rolled my eyes. She was doing it again. I reminded Gran that they didn't understand the English word 'bus'. She used the dialect word.

"Come again! Come again!" all the villagers said when we were leaving. Ah Hia was escorting us back to the hotel. The villagers held our hands, patted them, and touched our arms. Gran had two people on each arm as we walked out the village, and the whole village walked behind us. I looked at Gran, dressed in a pants suit of green and blue, a watch on her left wrist, a gold chain with a jade piece (which she hid from view inside her blouse) round her neck, and I looked at the villagers. There were actually two foreign guests here, I realised, not just me. For some reason I felt sad.

On the bus, which was a van with very worn down seats and a plank for a bench in the front, we met our neighbours from the hotel. They were also Singaporeans. One of them was Mrs Wu who was the mother of my neighbour back home, the others were Mrs Wu's sworn sister, Ah Mui, and Ah Mui's brother. Three of their relatives from a nearby village were with them.

"Singapore's roads are never so bumpy," Mrs Wu was telling her relatives. "Here, before they complete one part they start another. Everything is all over the place, so ugly and dusty. In Singapore, they never start another part till they've finished one part, then, you see, you can transport the materials to the next part more easily. What do they do here? How do they get materials over this bumpy road? Really, no sense." The relatives nodded acquiescence. "And people in Singapore," Mrs Wu continued, "don't spit all over the place. Really this place is quite dirty." She made a face at me. The relatives nodded again.

"*Aiyah*," Ah Mui said to my gran, "you don't know. This afternoon, the tricycle I was in fell into a hole and toppled over. I was thinking, *aiyah*, lucky it's me and not you, you with your high-blood. Almost scared me to death. My heart is still jumping. *Aiyoh*, I told the woman who was handling the tricycle, a woman shouldn't be doing this, you have not enough strength to handle this. Men are stronger."

The bus stopped and picked up two women with straw hats and a basket of vegetables. Mrs Wu waited for them to move to the back before getting up and tapping the driver on the shoulder. "Don't take the passengers with fertilizer," she instructed.

Mrs Wu's relatives were recommending another way of transport to Ah Mui—motorcycles. The bigger ones could seat two people and the driver. Mrs Wu said she didn't dare ride on those.

"Where do the drivers get their..."—how do you say licenses in Hokkien?—"papers for driving here?" I asked Ah Hia.

"What is that?" he asked.

"You know, papers that say you can drive. Where people learn to drive and get a paper that says they can drive? Don't you have places where people learn to drive?"

"They just learn to drive. From someone who drives. Then they drive," Ah Hia said.

"Huh? You mean no driving schools?" I exclaimed.

"*Aiyah*," Mrs Wu told me, "they don't have that here. You think like Singapore?"

During the next few days, Gran kept worrying about whether I was enjoying myself.

"Don't worry, Gran," I told her. "All I really want to see on this trip is your village. Did you take your pills?"

I asked her this about four times a day, afraid I'd forget again. When both she and I forgot about taking the morning dose of medicine two days ago, I almost panicked—it was afternoon when I thought to ask her—but she wasn't worried and just took half a tablet then. I watched her anxiously. In my mind several accusing voices floated around—ask you to do such a little thing, making sure your gran takes her medicine, and you forget, just once in the morning and once at night, so simple, how can you forget…

Mrs Wu came in that afternoon and introduced us to her relative who professed to be a bit of a home doctor. He produced a dog-eared book and went on to talk to my grandmother about her illnesses and symptoms. I was introduced to this man's granddaughter, Ah Zhen, a slim woman with a ponytail and red ribbons. She was a few years older than I and we struck up an immediate liking for each other, bonded by the common decade we were born in, and by our gender. She was an elementary school teacher in her village and she earned the Singapore equivalent of fifteen dollars a month , with a bonus though, she said when I expressed shock, of three dollars.

"Three dollars per month?" I asked, sitting by her on the hotel bed.

"Not per semester."

"How long is a semester?"

"Twenty-weeks," she said.

"Oh." *My god.*

She smiled at me, and for lack of anything cheerful to say, I asked,

"Does every woman in the village have to marry?" I looked at her to see if she took any offence at my question. That wasn't very cheerful either.

"Eventually." She nodded.

"Could you not marry?" She didn't seem to mind this topic.

She shook her head and said, "No, not in this society. I live in this society, so I have to follow its customs."

"In Singapore... " I started, then hesitated. I sounded like Mrs Wu and Gran. But I needed to convey to her the choice women could and should have. "Back home," I said, "we could choose." She nodded.

"What if you don't find anybody you like?" I asked.

"You keep meeting people, your parents and relatives would keep a lookout for you, until you meet someone and had some time to get to know him and if you think you could live with this person and you like him, then you set a date for the marriage." She leaned towards me. "Women who don't get married by a certain age are looked upon as strange. It would affect the whole family. But this was not as bad as ten years ago. Back then, when you received news of a possible match, you arranged to meet the person at a public place. Your relative or some guardian would go with you and the woman would stand on one side of the street and the man on the other and if they liked the look of each other, it was done."

"Just like that?" I said. "It is better now."

She smiled again. I ran my finger down the dark blanket between us and looked at the imprint I made. A great divide, I thought, separating different worlds.

That night, when the lights were dimmed and I was copying down the prescriptions in the 'medical handbook', I reminded gran that she had to check these with my auntie, the nurse. Gran said she wouldn't take Chinese medicine with Western medicine. That was a load off my mind. I didn't want any accidents. Then I worried that she'd stop taking the Western medicine altogether. I made a note to contact my aunt when we got home.

"Gran," I said when I was almost done. She was lying on her side in her bed, facing me, her eyes closed.

She opened them.

"Ah Zhen, that man's granddaughter, told me that about ten years ago, people still married people they didn't know. Isn't that terrible? She said they can choose now, but they must still marry, whether they want to or not."

"China is like that," Gran said.

"When did you marry Grandpa?"

"Two years after I went to Singapore."

"Did you really know him, I mean, did you get to know him a little?"

"What's there to know? I was brought into their family as a baby to be his bride when I grew up, so I saw him every day."

"But did you talk to him?"

"Of course."

"About what?"

"About the crops, the fields, work." She smiled.

"You think what? In those days we didn't do anything but work. No time and no mind for anything else."

"Ah Zhen said she'll bring me some shells from the seashore near her house."

"Don't you have enough shells? Haven't you collected enough? When we go somewhere else, there might be other things to buy."

"Gran," I said, "don't worry about going to other places. I told you all I want to do here is see your village."

"Well, see more then. You will have many opportunities to see other things later. Me, I cannot already. But I am satisfied. I have seen the whole world, so can stay home now. That's why before I stop travelling, I come here one last time, to give them all the clothes and to give them some money when we leave and then all matters will be taken care of." She swept her hands outwards as if sweeping everything away.

"Won't you come back any more?" I didn't know why I asked since she had made it clear.

"What for? Clothes give already, everything taken care of, nothing more."

Nothing more? Here was her childhood country, the place where she first set roots, and there's nothing more?

"Won't you miss this place?" I asked, wanting her to say yes, of course, this was where she buried her father and mother, where she had her first friends, where she grew up, but she said, "Miss what? All matters are settled." And I couldn't figure it out. I felt as if I had been digging for something and when I found it, it wasn't what I had in mind.

She had closed her eyes once more and had turned over to the other side, her back towards me. I turned off the lights and got under the blankets.

In the middle of the night, she woke me up and asked me why the air-con was so cold. In my fuzzy state of mind, I was slightly irritated. Could they turn it down, she asked. I muttered that it was the middle of the night and I doubted if they would come to the room with the remote control to turn it down, the service personnel in China being generally moody. I didn't want to call hotel personnel in the middle of the night. I dreaded their response time and having to wait up for them. We could wait until daybreak. Why not sleep until daybreak then? I told Gran to put on a cardigan and pull up the blankets. She didn't argue.

I looked over to her after a short while. She had a pillow on her head. She seemed very still. I couldn't see her face at all. My heart went a funny thump. I sat up, leaned across to her bed and put my face close to the pillow. Was there breathing? I thought I saw a rise and fall under the blankets. Still too sleepy to worry much, I lay back on my bed and closed my eyes. I wasn't awake, but I didn't sleep.

In the early morning, I heard a voice saying, why was the air-con so cold, why couldn't she sleep more, this sickening habit of hers, why did she have so much phlegm and why couldn't she seem to cough it all out, why was the air-con so cold, why was it so cold...

I opened one eye and saw Gran making a drink with something draped about her, her blanket probably. She looked like she was playing dress-up. Why was the air-con so cold, she went on talking to herself, or indirectly talking to me, making me feel more guilty. I tried to ignore it, but soon I got up and called service personnel.

Her talking every morning started to pervade my sleep like a hypnotist. I saw her shadowy figure many times through my hazy eyes and in those early hours I thought how unlike Gran this figure was, so restless and unsure, so... vulnerable. During the day, when she held my hand as we walked in her China, I found myself holding her tighter.

On our last day in China, Gran wanted to visit another relative of hers. She said that this woman, my great-grandaunt, ninety-seven years old, was the one who had taken her to the dock when she was leaving for Singapore.

"We go back a long way," she said. Ah Hia was around, as usual, and we took the bus heading towards Gran's village and it dropped us off at the village before Gran's. It was a larger village, the houses were bigger and there were more lanes. Ah Hia took us to a three-storeyed house with opened doors. Two women came hurrying up when they saw Gran and expressed how happy they were to see her and her granddaughter; then one of them, Ah Hua, left to get great-grandaunt. The other woman led us into the house and offered us wicker chairs. Gran admired the red-tiled floor and told Ah Hia that when he was able, he was to have his floor made too, instead of leaving it the rough cement it was.

A wizened, bent woman in dark blue, with scant grey, fizzy hair, came into the hall on the arm of Ah Hua. Great-grandaunt looked up slowly and her eyes widened, and her veined hand reached shakily for Gran. When Gran went to her, she almost fell on Gran, hugging her and stroking her arms and back, mumbling Gran's name like Gran was a little girl. Gran led her to the wicker chairs where I was standing by stupidly and sat her down. When I was introduced to great-grandaunt, she pulled me down by her with a surprisingly strong grip, and mumbled blessings. Gran told her she had clothes for the family and some gifts from friends in Singapore. Great-grandaunt kept nodding her head, saying good, good, and stroking my hand. Gran said to me, "She is the one who brought me to the dock when I left for Singapore all those years ago."

Great-grandaunt spoke tremulously, "Yes, yes, I couldn't let her go alone, so that night we left for the dock. We travelled a day and a night by bus, then I left her at the dock. That was very long ago, ah, but I remember it very well, one woman and a child. She was so young, fifteen or sixteen, with a timid face."

"That was very long ago. I'm not so young now," Gran smiled. "This granddaughter here wanted to see Grand's China. Mountain-tortoise-child, never seen a place like this. Very interested, always asking me about what China was like, what did you plant, how were you picked up from the roadside when you were a baby... "

Great-grandaunt smiled toothlessly, "Yes, yes, I remember that. Ah, your gran," she stroked my hand, "when we found her by the village roadside, she was surrounded by big, wild dogs ready to eat her. It was all very scary, but your gran here, she cried and cried..."

"I've told her that story," Gran said.

Great-grandaunt made an 'O' with her mouth and went on, "And when she was growing up, she was treated so badly by that female relative after her parents died. *Ai*, I always felt bad for her, so when she was leaving, I brought her to the dock. *Aiyah*, your gran had a very hard life, very hard. You must treat her well now, you know."

I nodded yes, I know. Then she turned to talk to Gran, holding one of Gran's hands and one of mine. I sat there and listened, watching Gran and the woman who gave her passage across the distance of time.

When we were leaving, great-grandaunt's eyes brimmed with tears as she held onto both of us and muttered blessings—safe passage home, everything goes smoothly, good health—and Gran took her hand in both of hers and told her to take care. I thought I saw Gran's eyes glisten. Great-grandaunt stood at the door until Gran, Ah Hia and I were out of sight.

We were waiting by the roadside for a while when two motorcycles drove up.

"Need a ride?" the man asked. "I can take one and the other motorcycle can take two."

I thought Gran would refuse, but to my surprise, she pointed to the bigger motorcycle and said, "This?" which was an acceptance. "For both of us?" She indicated me and her. The man on the bigger motorcycle said, "Sure." Ah Hia got onto the first motorcycle.

I watched with open mouth as Gran climbed in behind the man. He told her to put her feet on the little stands by the side. I sat behind Gran and had to share one metal stand on the left side with Gran's foot and my right foot I had to put on the tailpipe.

"Will it get very hot?" I asked the man about the tailpipe.

"No," he said.

I hoped he knew what he was talking about. Gran clutched her handbag close and I gripped my own bag, leaving one hand on Gran's shoulder. The man told Gran to hold onto his shoulders and we were off. I realised we had no helmets, but then most people on motorbikes here didn't have helmets.

"How old are you?" Gran asked the man.

"Seventeen," he answered.

"*Wah*, see," Gran told me, "seventeen and out to work." Then she addressed the boy (that's what he was!), "How long have you been driving this thing?"

"Don't worry, nothing will happen, you'll be safe, this is very safe."

"Don't go too fast, boy, you have an old person on board."

"I won't," he promised.

The motorcycle was very steady. Maybe because it was going slowly, and the boy (the term seemed inappropriate) was negotiating the bumps along the muddy road. When we came to the long road towards town, he told Gran to hold him at the waist. "You'll be more secure that way," he said.

"You don't mind, do you?" Gran said. "You won't be embarrassed?"

"No," he said.

"After all, I'm old enough to be your grandmother," Gran chuckled.

"Yes," he said. I saw him smiling as he turned his head to answer Gran. Gran told me to hold tight. I put my hand on her waist.

We gathered speed, riding down the centre of the road, no line dividers telling us we were breaking rules. The wind whipped through my hair, but the boy-man didn't go so fast that I had to strain my neck to keep my head upright or that I couldn't have a good look at the fields and trees around us. *We wouldn't be able to do this in Singapore,* I thought. My parents would disapprove—ride on a motorbike? With a seventeen-year-old?! No licence?!—and we would not be able to ride without helmets in Singapore—what a laugh, the police would be down on us in a minute.

I felt the graininess of the road under us, the heat of the tailpipe. I felt the wind on my face, in my hair, around my arms and legs, on my back, the glorious air about us, uninhibited, full of the smells of salt and crops and earth. How things have changed, for the child-grandma and the woman-grandma. What I picked from the seashore, they could not be mine. But this was mine, this ride I was in motion with, so smoothly, Gran between me and China.

HELL HATH NO FURY
Claire Tham

The road to Damascus for Grandma occurred on a hot Sunday morning in the church of St. Aloysius, Roman Catholic, 10:30 A.M. Father Le Mesurier, the old French priest who normally conducted Mass in a thickly incomprehensible French accent, was away on holiday. In his place was Father James Hsien, newly graduated from a Taiwanese seminary.

Father Hsien was so short that nobody in the congregation realised he had streamed in until an admonitory reedy voice piped over the sound system, "Brothers and sisters in Christ, PLEASE STAND!" Startled, the congregation leapt to its feet. Over the top of the lectern, the beginnings of a crew cut and thick tortoiseshell glasses of a type not seen since the 1950s could be glimpsed. From what they could see of him, he appeared to be all of twenty-one years old. (He was, in fact, ten years older). He looked like an infant swaddled in sacerdotal robes for a joke.

In his opening remarks, he told the assembled throng there was much sin about and little grace and redemption. With this unpromising start, he steamed into a sermon that managed to antagonise everybody from the large expatriate American community ("America is a land of sin and fornication, plagued by crime, drugs and AIDs"), to the society ladies who organised charity lunches and thought themselves remarkably benevolent ("And I say to you, think of how you treat your maids. For the gospel says that the meek shall inherit the earth, so how will your diamonds, your cars and your travels avail you?"), to Grandma ("And I know of old ladies who waste their last years playing mahjong and living from one meal to the next, instead of reflecting on their sins and the life that is to come..."). With that last salvo, Grandma came awake with a look of murder on her face. It was all the Tan family could do to prevent her from marching up the aisle and clouting Father Hsien around the head with her handbag. Quivering with indignation, she refused to go for communion; she wanted nothing to do with 'that man'.

On the ride home, she fulminated against the Catholic Church, its bossy patriarchy and above all Father Hsien. "I should never have sent you to the convent," she told her daughter, Mrs Tan. "I should have known that colonial institution would have you rushing into the church. What does that man know about anything? He's still wet behind the ears. I've given birth to six children—"

"Mother," said Mrs Tan, patiently, "I don't think he was referring to you personally."

"He was looking," said Grandma, "right at me."

Her grandchildren, Peter and Jonathan (good Biblical names) groaned. Mr Tan drove on with a long-suffering look on his face. He was thinking that if Father Hsien managed to wean his mother-in-law off her marathon nocturnal mahjong sessions, he would, like a good disciple, drop all and follow him. Not exactly drop *all*, of course, but he would certainly be a lifelong devotee. Mr Tan was an engineering lecturer with a propensity towards migraines who craved above all peace, quiet and tranquillity. There was very little of any with his mother-in-law around.

The next Sunday Grandma announced that she was a fully paid up member of the Renewal Charismatic Free Church for All Brethren. She had washed her hands of the Catholic Church.

"She's joined *what*?" said Mr Tan.

Mrs Tan, close to hysterics and convinced her mother was doomed to hellfire, repeated the name of the church. Again, Mr Tan, good at engineering terms and bad at civilian discourse, missed it by a mile.

"Oh," he said.

"It's one of those fundamentalist Protestant groupings where they speak in tongues and insist that everyone pays ten per cent of their income."

"She hasn't got an income."

"That's not the point. The point is, she's been led astray."

"Oh, now really," said Mr Tan. "We all believe in the same things in the end."

"No, they don't. They don't believe in the Virgin Mary or acknowledge the Pope or—this is *horrible*."

As it turned out, Grandma had very little idea what her new brethren *did* believe in. She had joined the renegades because her friend Mrs Sinnathuray was a member and because the pastor, the Reverend Michaels from Peoria, Illinois, was so handsome and so kind. Not at all like the vituperative dwarf at St. Aloysius. And she liked the rousing services, where there was a good deal of arm-waving, breast-beating and being born again. ("Everything short of Mardi Gras," said a distraught Mrs Tan.) So very different from the Catholic Church, where people slumbered through Mass in an agreeable stupor and had only the foggiest notion of the Bible's contents. Grandma, in a most moving personal testimony to a packed assembly, laid the blame for her years of waste and error squarely at the door of the Pope.

But Grandma was nothing if not broadminded. She went right on reciting her rosaries and praying to the Virgin Mary. And her mahjong parties increased in bonhomie and amplitude, as her new church members took to her like ducks to water, in spite of her theological shakiness.

"So delightful!" they said to Mr Tan. "At her age, with her energy, her mind, remarkable!"

Mrs Tan resolutely stayed in her room during these proceedings. When she did appear, she drifted through, wraith-like, hollow-eyed. The Brethren left her alone, recognising that here was a woman who had closed her mind to the Message. Mr Tan's chief emotion at these times was a wishful desire that his wife would stand up to her mother, but that, he knew, was beyond her. It was beyond him, for that matter. Grandma was an Act of God.

However, no matter how much the Brethren smiled, chirped and wolfed down the food in the refrigerator, they never shook off the air they carried with them of venturing into the home of infidels and pagans. Mr Tan recognised the familiar battle-light gleaming in the eye of the keen proselytiser as, one by one, they bore down on him.

"Don't you want," they invariably began, "to join a church where you feel you belong, where you know you're at home?"

Mr Tan, a man of limited spiritual needs, felt his head beginning to throb. They wouldn't leave him alone in the office and now they were invading his home as well. "I do go to church," he pointed out.

They smiled disbelievingly. They never stopped smiling, but there was a range of meanings compressed into those smiles. This was the gently humoring smile. Did the secret of their success lie in those never-ending, fixed smiles? Come to think of it, Catholics generally went around dour and indifferent, hardly beacons of light for their faith.

"We believe," they said, "in a participatory church. Where you take part in a service that glorifies God. We don't believe in passively following ritual."

Mr Tan waved a feeble hand at his sons, returning noisily after football practice. It was a signal for help but they ignored him. "Gosh, hi, Dad, bye, Dad," they said. "Got to rush, Dad." They bolted themselves in their room.

Mr Tan was not a particularly religious man. It had to do with the fact, he sometimes thought, that he was a man of little imagination; the thought of death, the afterlife, the sense of a higher, divine being, seldom disturbed him. He wasn't given to asking why. He was a Catholic by marriage and that, it seemed to him, was as good a reason as any. The histrionics, the sheer *energy* involved in becoming a born-again Christian, appalled him. And there were times when he told himself that if the Europeans hadn't flooded Asia with their missionaries and their schools, he would still be a Buddhist, comfortably subsisting in the darkness where there was supposed to be weeping and gnashing of teeth. What if the so called act of faith was nothing but a historical accident?—He realised, with relief, that it was time to go to bed.

Grandma's rebirth was akin to lobbing a stone into a still pond: it created ever-widening ripples. One of its immediate effects was that Grandma became tremendously interested in the Apocalypse and the Antichrist.

"You will know the end of the world is nigh," she reported, "when there are earthquakes, famines and volcanic eruptions."

"They've always been around," Mr Tan said dampeningly.

Grandma gave him a shirty look. "The point is," she said, "that we always have to be ready, no matter where we are or what we're doing. Imagine! If the Lord came to earth while I was in the bathroom, what would I do?" (Nobody could find a ready answer to this either.)

Then she discovered that the Proctor & Gamble trademark was thought by some to be depicting the Antichrist. She hot-footed it home, determined to eradicate all use of their products, but *everything* in the nature of a cleansing agent was apparently manufactured by P & G or a subsidiary. This struck Grandma as even more sinister. How could a single multinational have a monopoly on all the soap circulating in the world?

"I guess it's a case of being clean or being pure,' Jonathan said. The whole family soaped away, P & G-style, doing its best to boost capitalist exploitation and ignoring Grandma's warnings.

Next, Grandma took it into her head that Ronald Reagan was the beast himself; 666 was the number of the beast, was it not, and there were six letters in each of his names. 'That only makes 66," Mr Tan pointed out; in spite of himself, he was becoming quite interested in all this.

"This is totally infantile," Mrs Tan declared. "Numerology under the guise of Christianity—honestly!"

There was nothing she could do, however, to stop Grandma from giving a delicious shudder every time the avuncular features of Mr Reagan appeared on the screen, or to prevent the boys from yapping and howling in dire imitation of a werewolf whenever his name was mentioned. Mrs Tan, who was supremely rational in every area outside Catholicism, told anyone who would listen that it was simply mind boggling that the man who had acted with Bonzo the Chimp could in any way be associated with the forces of evil. She was discovering the labyrinthine and peculiar byways of Christianity and they appalled her.

The next Sunday, Peter Tan, fifteen, electrified his family by announcing that he had became a Buddhist and wouldn't be attending Mass any longer. After a heated argument about transport convenience (the family usually went for lunch after Sunday Mass) he sulkily accompanied the rest to church.

Later, in his room, they discovered a book called *Zen and the Art of Motorcycle Maintenance*. "Have you been corrupted by this book?" Mrs Tan demanded.

Peter shrugged sleepily. He was tall for his age, slender, and surreptitiously growing his hair whenever his parents didn't notice. Dreamy and dissociated, his parents feared he might never become the lawyer/doctor/ accountant/banker they wanted him to be. Jonathan, sixteen and aloof, said, distantly, "Don't ask *me*," when cornered. He was going through a family-phobic phase and his whole manner implied he was not his brother's keeper.

"*Why* are you doing this?" Mrs Tan asked her son, with a sort of petrified tranquility.

"I just happen to find Buddhism a lot more compatible, Mum."

"Compatible!"

"Catholicism is a patriarchal and bureaucratic religion, Mum. It's drifted away from its roots. Sure, maybe it was a good idea in its time but Jesus would be horrified if he came down now and saw what his followers had done."

Mrs Tan made a gurgling, semi-strangled noise.

"Buddhism doesn't require any structures. That's the beauty of it. It's inner-directed. It's not egocentric. You can be a force for good wherever you are—"

"*Wah*, his language improve so very much, one, *hor*, when he become Buddhist, so funny, what, what," said Jonathan. His father told him not to be sarcastic. Ostentatiously, he joined the choir at St. Aloysius as head choirboy.

Meanwhile, Peter said that animals were as worthy, if not more worthy, of respect than old Homo sapiens and he was becoming a vegetarian.

He prowled the neighbourhood collecting stray cats and dogs; he even launched a 'Stop Killing Flies' campaign. At mealtimes, he lectured his family on the unsavoury practices of the meat industry, and one choice anecdote about veal in particular had Jonathan rushing to the bathroom. The odour of sanctity carried about him, the family felt, was positively sickening. "I hope you're reincarnated as a cockroach, so I can step on you," Jonathan told his brother; Peter flew across the room and landed on him—it took both their parents to tear them apart. The situation, it seemed, was rapidly approaching West Bank flashpoint level.

"This is all your fault," Mrs Tan said, between gritted teeth, to her mother. These days she went around in a frozen calm, a self-willed deep freeze which was rather alarming.

Grandma had the grace to look a trifle disconcerted. "I don't know what you mean."

"Yes, you do, Mother! You started a revolution! You're breaking up my home!"

"Such melodrama," said Grandma, briskly. She skipped out, nimbly, with a little stack of pamphlets titled, 'Get On The Nearest Hotline To God!' (blue covers for non-Christians, red covers for Catholics). She was going to the City Hall MRT station to distribute them to the uninitiated.

"If she gets picked up by the police and spread all over the front pages, I'm renouncing her as my mother-in-law," Mr Tan said.

"This is *not* funny," said his wife.

Just then, the Reverend Michaels arrived.

It was with some difficulty that Mrs Tan could be dissuaded from slamming the door in his face. She considered him the author of, the perpetrator behind, her mother's behaviour. This large, corn-fed American with the very blue, porcelain eyes and the very white teeth, who did he think he was, leaving America to spread mayhem and dissension in once united families? She looked at him with the sort of defiance that the Catholic Mary Queen of Scots must have brought with her to the gallows, or was it the executioner's chopping block? She couldn't remember.

"Ah, Mrs Tan," said the Reverend Michaels. He took both her hands in his. It was the first time she had met him face to face since she had hitherto assiduously avoided him. He had a long, slow drawl, and a brilliant smile. He wore a short-sleeved, open-necked shirt, undone to the second button, above which tufts of luxuriant chest hair could be seen, and a pair of Levi's 501 chinos. He was very good-looking—this knowledge slowly filtered through the haze of indignation with which she regarded him. (Also the fact that his size twelve feet draped all over the front doorstep made it impossible to dislodge him.)

"It's so *varry*, *varry* nice to meet you, Mrs Tan," said the Reverend Michaels.

"Your mother has told me *so* much about what a wonderful daughter you are, Mrs Tan," the Reverend Michaels added.

By this time, he had somehow insinuated himself into the front hall and seated himself in an armchair in their living room, legs crossed, beaming in response to a somewhat dazed offer of a drink from Mrs Tan.

"Just water, if you please, ma'am. The religious life is such thirsty work."

Left alone, the Reverend Michaels and Mr Tan contemplated each other's knees. Mr Tan had met him before and had found the charisma somewhat overpowering, like musk. "Do you—er—often wear jeans?" he asked feebly.

The Reverend Michaels laughed genially. "They're my disguise," he confided, "for slipping in behind enemy lines, you know. Folks see a guy in jeans, they figure he can't be a minister and that lowers their guard. The only problem," he said thoughtfully, "are the girls. Young girls, especially."

"Have to beat them off with a stick, eh?"

The Reverend Michaels dug him in the ribs and grinned. "*Exactly*."

Mrs Tan returned with a glass. "What can we do for you?" she asked, somewhat abruptly; in the kitchen she'd had time to recover from the impact of the gaze from those eyes. "I'm afraid my mother's not in."

"*Wa-al*, actually, I was rather hoping she wouldn't be. You see, it's like this." He leaned forward, clasping his hands earnestly. "Your mother wants to donate a large, antique lacquered table to our church, to function as an altar. Now, under normal circumstances, I'd be more than happy to accept it—more than happy. As you know, we're desperately in need of what businessmen call startup capital." Flash of teeth. "We're a fledgling church and we welcome all the donations we can get—"

"Wait a minute," said Mr Tan. He turned to his wife. "Isn't that the antique table she promised to leave us in her will?" (They'd had it valued some years ago: the expert had put it at a conservative estimate of ten thousand dollars.)

Mrs Tan nodded, distracted by the slender golden hairs, glistening in the sunlight from the window, on the Reverend Michaels' wrists.

"Are you aware," demanded the Reverend Michaels solemnly, "that it has an emblem of a Chinese dragon on the surface? In gold leaf?"

"Yes, of course. It's a very good example of the art flourishing in that period..." To think of the legacy, which they had always taken for granted, going to this man made Mr Tan feel faint. Not for the first time, he thought his mother-in-law ought to be certified.

"But we can't accept it," said the Reverend Michaels sorrowfully.

"Oh," said Mr Tan, taken aback.

From the depths of his armchair, the Reverend Michaels rose to a rhetorical splendour. "How can we start a church, sir, tainted with symbols of a pagan culture? Of a pagan civilisation? Our mission is to rid the world of superstition and fear and let the light flood in. To accept such an object would be the sheerest of bad luck." He realised what he had just said and laughed, uproariously. "Oh my, I've cooked my own goose, haven't I? *Wa-al*, you know what I mean."

"My mother will be disappointed," said Mrs Tan. Her husband looked at her, wondering; she was speaking in a peculiar, constricted tone of voice.

"We aim," said the Reverend Michaels, "not to please, but to do the right thing." He spread his hands, disarmingly. "We need an altar table, ma'am. Just not one with a dragon. You *will* let her know? Thank you— And have you thought of joining your mother, and coming down to one of our gatherings?"

"Not exactly." Desperately, she focused her eyes on a point beyond him; she had the sensation of drowning.

"I understand you're a Catholic, but, please, don't be put off, we welcome everybody. As I said, we're a new church, but we're dedicated. Dedication is the word. We demand a huge commitment but we also give a lot back..."

When he was gone, an hour later, Mrs Tan rushed to her bedroom and sank to her knees. For once, praying had little effect, however; instead she splashed water on her temples and paced about angrily, telling herself to calm down and not to behave like an infatuated schoolgirl. For she had a weakness for terribly good-looking men in the old fashioned mould, which forty-odd years of living had failed to dampen. One would have thought that at her age, with two teenage sons, she would get over these attacks, which left her suffused with confusion and a burning sense of embarrassment, but no, here she was flushing again. She tried to invoke the image of her husband, placidly going through the Sunday papers in the next room, but she could only dredge up a blank. He was the ideal husband: he was safe, steady, constant and never caused her the slightest anguish. Truth to tell, he was rather dull. She smacked her forehead in despair. "Jesus, Mary, Joseph," she said aloud.

"Where are you off to?" queried her husband, as she tore through the sitting room, jangling the car-keys.

"I'm going to Mass."

He grunted. He was used to his wife's piety. As far as he was concerned, all that mattered was that the legacy was safe.

Grandma returned with Mrs Sinnathuray at ten P.M., victorious. They had pinned various quivering youths to the wall of the station and had refused to let them go until they promised to attend the next service at the Free Church. "I tell you, I'm having more fun every day since my husband died," Mrs Sinnathuray declared.

"Oh, the Reverend Michaels was here today," said Mr Tan.

Grandma sat up straighter. "Really? What for?"

He told her.

Grandma's eyes snapped. "We'll see about that," she said. She strode to the telephone and called the church; it was true. Grimly, she replaced the receiver. "Oh, darling," said Mrs Sinnathuray despondently. She recognised all the familiar warrior symptoms in her old friend.

"Mother, you promised that table to us," Mrs Tan protested.

"Yes, I know, but it's a question of who has the greater need. You and the children are comfortably off. The church is just starting. I can't tell you how *exciting* it all is."

"Mother, the Reverend Michaels has said he doesn't want it."

"That's what he thinks."

"Mother, why are you *doing* this?"

"The Greeks called it hubris," Jonathan informed everyone. "We did it in literature."

Grandma launched herself into a flurry of activity. She decided that the thing to do was to get signatures for a petition urging the inclusion of the table, but she ran into some unexpected opposition. A few people— unbelievably—shared the Reverend Michaels' reactionary views on Chinese dragons. "Philistines," fumed Grandma. "What about St. George and the Dragon? I've never heard anyone objecting to that."

That, it transpired, was because St. George's Dragon was impeccably English, a well-established part of myth and folklore and the traditions of the early church. But, in any case, the Free Church frowned upon St. George and his unfortunate Dragon, seeing that the pair of them were so bound up with the fossilised structures and rigidity of High Church Anglicanism, which, after Catholicism, was Public Enemy Number Two in the Free Church's impressive canon of objects of vilification.

"It's just a dragon," insisted Grandma. The table, after all, would be covered with a clean white cloth during the service and nobody would have to view the offending beast. In Grandma's opinion, this refusal to accept her table was nothing less than a personal insult. Her weekly mahjong parties for the faithful lost some of their sparkle, as members took sides for and against the issue; there was a positively un-Christian tinge of rancor in the atmosphere.

"Hell hath no fury like that of one Christian loathing another," Jonathan said sagely.

The Reverend Michaels tried to reason with Grandma. He sat her down in his office, fed her biscuits and turned on her the full blast of his charm. He showed her pictures of himself as an angelic little boy in Peoria, Illinois, and of his favourite spaniel, Pooch. He told her she was invaluable, *invaluable*, in the church.

"But do you remember, ma'am," he said, earnestly, "the day you testified that you had become a new person? When you promised to sublimate your will to that of the Holy Spirit?" He was walking back and forth across the carpet, fists clenched to emphasise his point. Grandma nodded, mesmerised.

"Far be it that I should try to tell you what to do. *I* can't do it; only *you* can decide for yourself what action to take. The Good Lord gave us free wills to distinguish us from the animals so that we might exercise them. But there are ways and there are ways of using our talents." He perched on the arm of her chair, smiling beatifically down at her.

At this point, Grandma's resolution wavered a little. But then she caught sight of the good-humored look in those cornflower-blue eyes, the serene conviction that *he*, Edward Danforth Michaels (a man to whom no one, and certainly no woman, had ever said no), would prevail. And the contrariness that coursed through her veins as surely as blood ever did led her to whip out the petition once again, and draw his attention to the two hundred and fifty signatures. The Reverend Michaels, his smile fading, stood, and pressed the tips of his fingers together, unavailingly. He pursed his lips; he was vexed, most vexed, and he made the mistake of saying so. They parted burgeoning enemies.

Finally, Grandma hit on a brainwave. She would hire a furniture removal company to transport the table to the church and install it while the Reverend Michaels was out fulfilling his pastoral duties. Presented with a fait accompli, he could hardly object, could he? She confided her plan to her supporters, a militant group who wanted the Reverend to take a more aggressive approach towards proselytising, and were exasperated by his high-charm, low-ferocity tactics. They saw this as a good way of registering disapproval.

So it happened that on a cloudy Friday afternoon, while the Reverend Michaels was conducting an infants' class at the home of a member, a large furniture truck rolled up to the front entrance of the church, Grandma ensconced in the front seat beside the driver, to whom she recounted the whole affair in high-velocity Hokkien. She felt like a military leader commanding a convoy. A dozen or so of her supporters milled around, hindering rather than helping in the unloading of the table. Grandma's mood was triumphal, imperial—first the table, then... the possibilities were endless.

"*What* is the meaning of this?"

The drawl, the lilting cadence, was the same, but the geniality was gone. The Reverend Michaels hove into view, blond, Nordic, towering. There was a stunned silence. A frisson ran through the assembled rebels; what was he doing here? (They discovered later that he had dismissed the infants' class early.) As he came towards them in a furious rush, the thought that was uppermost in their minds was that he looked as if he were the wrath of God personified. They fell back on either side to let him through— someone remarked later that it was eerily reminiscent of the parting of the Red Sea. He stood before the table, heaving; out of nowhere, it seemed, he produced a stick and—everyone gasped—thrashed the delicate curved legs of the table. With an almighty, ominous CRACK, it settled down with a thump, a good five inches shorter. Then the Reverend Michaels, without so much as a backward glance, vanished, leaving a distinctly post-apocalyptic flavour in the air.

Grandma took to her bed for a week. (The table, sent to the workshop, cost several thousand dollars to repair; the bill was duly despatched to the Renewal Charismatic Free Church for All Brethren.) The Tans, victorious but feeling it unseemly to crow, wore the mantle of quiet dignity as they tiptoed through the house. The mahjong parties ceased; the Brethren scattered their spiritual largesse elsewhere. Peter met a Catholic girl from the convent school down the road, and thought, perhaps, that Buddhism, well, wasn't exactly meant for him. The next Sunday, the whole family was back at St. Aloysius, Grandma barely blinking an eyelid while Father Hsien expatiated on the theme of spiritual pride. Her spirit was broken, her flesh subdued.

"I *told* you there was no need to panic," Mr Tan said to his wife.

That's what *you* think, she thought privately, though she did not answer. Absently, she fingered the crucifix around her neck. One needed a very strong faith to get through life.

POISSON IVY
Colin Cheong

It was still half an hour to lunch, but the Lieutenant noticed her three clerks putting away the confidential files and locking the steel cabinets. She was watching them through a small communication hole in the wall and she now stuck her face in the concrete square to talk to her boys.

"A bit early, isn't it?" she grumbled.

"Isn't she pretty?" the Corporal sighed to the other two clerks. "Ma'am, if only you weren't married."

"Shut up, Chin. Why are you all packing up so soon? Still quite long to lunch."

"We going to get our fish, ma'am," the Private said honestly.

"What fish?"

"Our fighting fish, ma'am," the bespectacled Lance Corporal said.

"I don't think we have space for a tank, Chong, it's already very cramped around here," she scowled as she looked around her tiny office. Fish would be nice, she thought, but she could not imagine a tank in her room or the other two officers'.

"Er ma'am, this type of fish no need tank. They'll kill each other if they were in the same tank. We will each have a fish in a jar on our desks," the Corporal said.

"What does your Sergeant say, Wee?" she asked.

"*Dunno*, we haven't told her," replied the Private as he took out his car keys.

"You boys are horrible. Better make sure the fish give no problems or else I'll flush them all down the toilet bowl."

The Lieutenant was wakened by the sound of the Alfa's engine. Oh no, the horrors are back, and what will they have with them, she thought as she straightened her uniform. The Sergeant had also heard the car and she looked up with a frown at the door. The three clerks burst into the darkened office, each swinging a little plastic bag of water with a fl ash of vibrant colour within.

"Our fish are here!" the Lance Corporal announced. They laid the packs on the Sergeant's desk.

"Oh, fighting fish. I bought one for my son once. He squeezed it until it died."

"You not going to do the same, right?" the Private asked in horror.

"See how, *lor*."

The Lieutenant walked over from her office and looked disapprovingly down at the packs on the desk, and then she suddenly smiled.

"Oh look, they're actually quite pretty."

"Like you ma'am."

"Shut up, Chin." She did not mind a compliment, but she wished they came more from her singularly unromantic husband and not this brute of a clerk.

"Eh ma'am, see," the Lance Corporal said as he held up two packs together. The fish within each pack, swimming idly around, came face to face with the other and went berserk. Their gills and fins suddenly flared with brilliant hues and shiny silver patches, and they slammed against the plastic bags, trying to get at each other.

"Stop that, you wicked boy," the Lieutenant said, "they'll hurt themselves."

"You should see what they can do when they're in the same jar," the Private said.

"You all going to make them fight, is it? So cruel," the Sergeant said.

"No *lah*. We just going to keep them on the desks. Once in a while, we'll make them have a staring incident to keep the fin muscles in shape," the Lance Corporal said. The Private came up with three ex-Nescafe jars, soon to be fish-tanks.

"Eh, stupid, can go and put in water first or not?" the Corporal asked.

"Hoi, will you all stop playing with your fishes and get the filing done?" the Sergeant asked in a loud voice. The Lieutenant popped her head through the hole and said, "Get to work or the fishes get the Royal Flush."

"Ah, ma'am we were only discussing what names to give them. Would you like my fish to be named after you, Rachel?" the Corporal asked politely.

"You dare, and you see what happens to your precious fish."

"Maybe we should name the fish after the girls in the bungalow. They same rank as us, cannot do anything to us," the Private suggested.

"Same rank as *us*, you mean. Everyone outranks you," the Lance Corporal laughed. The chubby Private threw himself against the Lance Corporal and flattened him against a wall.

"Tomorrow lunch you no need to sit in my car!"

"What is going on here?" her voice cut like a cold Taiwanese mountain wind. The Captain stood at the doorway, her trim figure cutting an aggressive silhouette. "The men were misbehaving. I will take care of them," the Corporal said quickly. She looked around the office without a word. Then she saw the jars.

"I hope your bad discipline is temporary. Or I will make them very temporary."

"Oh, the witch," the Corporal cursed as she stalked away.

"Hey, this is no fun. Everyone is using our fish as hostages," the Private said.

"I'm glad you realised that. Now will you all please show some respect for me?" the Lieutenant laughed as she withdrew her face from the window.

"I know, I know," the Corporal said. "We'll have to get things back to normal and still keep the fish somehow. In the meantime, we still have to name the fish. I like the corporal with the big tits, so my fish is Jenny. Lance Corporal gets second choice."

"I like Ivy. Got cute backside. Saw her bend over the computer last week."

"I got no choice! There's only Lilly left."

"Of course, you're only a private. And as Rachel likes to say, 'rank hath ith privilegeth', right ma'am?"

"Shut up or your fish dies," came a voice from the other side.

The next day, the clerks came in a little earlier than usual. They had actually looked forward to coming to work. It was a nice place, a colonial bungalow on a tree-canopied lane with lush foliage, steep wooden staircases and high ceilings, weeds growing through the cracks in the concrete pavement and the occasional rat, which meant great excitement because the unit was made up of mostly women.

"Feeding time," the Corporal said as he unscrewed the cap of the fish food bottle. "I wonder if any of these come with steroids. I would like my fish to get really huge, like me. Come here, Jenny babe."

The Lance Corporal watched his red fish suspended in the jar, looking at him through clear eyes, mouth ajar, the lower jaw jutting slightly. Ivy was more streamlined than Jenny, who had a biggish black head with brutal looking jaws. Ivy was a pretty scarlet thing, fairly red all over, while the other two fishes had the usual black, blue, green and silver fishes.

"You look a bit too wimpy to be a fighting fish," he told the *Betta splendens*. "I guess it's just as well you have a girl's name." Female fighting fish were very dull and hardly anything to look at compared to the males with their extravagant plumes of fins, trailing in the water like the gossamer gowns of Chinese fairies. Ivy was no exception, and he was far better looking than the other two.

"My fish could make mincemeat out of yours," the Corporal said to the Private as he shoved him out of his seat. "Come on, you wanna try?"

"No. I'm going to get mine fighting fit first, maybe even soak a bit in brandy to toughen up the scales. Then she'll kill your Jenny like nobody's business."

But it was not to be. Throughout the day, for some reason, Lilly grew more and more listless. The Private was disturbed.

"What's wrong with my fish?" he wanted to know.

"It's like you, flaccid. Don't you know? A fighting fish reflects the characteristics of its human owner. It is like a phallic symbol. Look at mine. What a stud," the Corporal said as he replaced a file in the cabinet.

"Will you all stop playing with your fishes?" the Sergeant scolded. "One of these days I'm going to squeeze them all to death."

Lilly and the Private grew more listless as the day wore on.

"I've cleaned the jar, changed the water, even put in live worms, but she's not coming round."

"Maybe she's just playing hard to get," the Lance Corporal suggested. "Girls always like that one." They had already forgotten that their fishes were male.

"Well, if that's the case, then I wish she'd just die so I can get a new, better fish."

"Now we know how you will treat your girlfriends next time," the Sergeant laughed.

When they booked out that evening, Lilly was still skulking around at the bottom of his jar while the other fishes were swimming up and down happily.

"I want a new fish," the Private whined.

"Having a fish is like having a wife, only until death do you part," the Corporal declared solemnly. "You're stuck with her."

The Lance Corporal came in the next day to find that the Private had already got to the office first. He was sitting at the Sergeant's desk, looking like someone whose rich uncle had died and left him some money, a mixture of pretended mournfulness and barely concealed joy.

The Lance Corporal went to look at Ivy. He was up and about, probably waiting for breakfast. You are so beautiful in the morning, he thought as he tapped on the glass jar and Ivy spun around to face him.

"So how's your Lilly?" the Lance Corporal asked the Private.

"She's dead."

"Huh? What do you mean?"

"She's dead. She must have committed suicide last night."

"Where is she now?"

"When I got in this morning, she wasn't in her tank. And when I looked around, I found her body in a corner of the cupboard where I put the tank. She was all desiccated."

"So what did you do with her?"

"I flushed her body down the toilet bowl."

"That's too bad."

"Yeah. I guess we'll have to go downtown again today."

When the Corporal got in, the Lance Corporal told him the news.

"Bullshit! He probably killed her himself!" the Corporal laughed.

"Waddaya mean?" the Private said defensively, getting up from his seat in a trice.

"You killed your own fish because she was sick and you couldn't be bothered to look after her. You wanted her dead and out of the way so you could get yourself a new fish, right? Even flushed away the evidence."

"No!"

"Murderer," said the Corporal.

"Murderer," said the Lance Corporal.

"Kwek, be careful of him, he's a wife-killer," they told the Sergeant when she came in. Be careful of this man, Rachel, the Lieutenant was warned.

"NOOOOOOOO! I must be going mad!"

"Murderer," came the chorus.

"Maybe it was because you behaved badly yesterday," the Sergeant said darkly. The clerks stared at her as she chuckled and walked away.

"Do you think she could have?"

"Nah, she would have killed ours. We behave worse than Wee."

"I'll never have another fish."

"A suitable period of mourning is always in order," the Lance Corporal advised. "Even if you didn't kill her yourself, maybe she heard what you said about her last night, wished she were dead and killed herself. You'd still be responsible for her death. Murderer."

The final result was that the Private never bought another fish. But the Corporal still made him drive them out on another fishing trip.

"Remember how they always threatening to do our fish in if we didn't behave right? I had this great idea on the bus this morning."

"It's no longer my problem," the Private grumbled.

"Shut up and drive," the Corporal said. "The reason why they can even think of threatening our fish is because our fish are male."

"Huh?" the Lance Corporal was puzzled.

"Think about it. They always threaten us. And I bet the Captain, the Lieutenant and the Sergeant all bully their husbands at home. Therefore, threatening us is second nature to them. Now, if we got a female fish, we would have a hostage because I think they would try to protect her."

"I don't get it," the Lance Corporal said.

"Look, our Jenny and Ivy are important to us. Now, suppose we get a fish that's important to them, we would have a bargaining tool in our tanks."

"That's cruel. Poor female fish."

"Exactly. They'll take her side, and we can go back to our usual behaviour."

They found a female fish which looked fairly healthy and robust and paid fifty cents for her, less than half the price of a good male.

"Guess what we got?" the Corporal asked the Lieutenant.

"Another fish for Wee?" she asked wearily.

"No, no, we got a playmate for our boys!"

The Lieutenant was a very devout Christian woman and she did not understand.

"You know, men need to get it off sometimes with a woman, so we got our boys a girl to play with," the Corporal said evilly, making eyes at the Lieutenant.

"That's gross!" she said when she finally saw the light.

The Corporal had bought a bowl too and he got the Private to fill it up.

"Ladies and gentlemen, welcome to the Pleasure Bowl!"

"Chin!" the officer was very annoyed.

"You have to let the female in first to let her establish it as her territory," said the Private, who had read a lot about *Betta splendens*.

She swam alone in the bowl for the rest of the afternoon, circling around a lone column of water plant, with probably no idea of what was in store for her.

"First client tomorrow, babe," the Corporal smirked as they closed the office for the night.

The next day, all three clerks got in early.

"Today's the day we get even," the Corporal laughed as the trio strolled down Sherwood Road.

"I never thought sex could be used as a weapon," the Lance Corporal said. "At least not by men!"

"You have a lot to learn, boy," the Corporal sniggered.

"What shall we call the female fish?" the Private asked.

"Well, to be as callous as possible, we should not even give her a name. But if we do, it will make it more personal for the women in our office."

"How about Lucrece? Then today's activities could be called the Rape of Lucrece," the Lance Corporal suggested.

"Not everyone has read Shakespeare, *kutu*. *Aiyah*, we'll just call her Honey."

They waited till the office had started the day's work. Then the Corporal went to ask the Lieutenant if she wanted to watch something exciting. She came over and saw the clerks and the Sergeant huddled over the bowl. The Sergeant was saying, you all very bad and the Lance Corporal was saying it's OK, fish don't have to be married.

"We're letting the stud have his way with her first," the Corporal told the officer. She was very peeved.

"Why can't you just say mate?"

"You haven't seen fighting fish mate, have you? For them, love is a combat zone. This is the arena for the battle of the sexes. You very lucky, last time even worse. They threw Christians into arenas."

"Yes, but that was to the lions."

"You're weird, ma'am. You mean you'd rather be killed than made love to?"

"Between someone like you or a lion, I'd take the lion." She thought of her own husband. Huh, I wish he was a bit more of an animal, though.

The Corporal's fish was dropped into the bowl. Disoriented, it swam about trying to regain its bearings.

"Come on, now, boy, do your owner justice. Show them what we are capable of," the Corporal egged his fish on. But it kept swimming around aimlessly, not even showing interest in the female who was swimming warily at a safe distance.

"Oh yes, what a stud," the other clerks were laughing.

"Your fish might be gay," the Private chuckled and was shoved across the room.

"Come on boy, give it to her, look she's over there, just asking for it."

"Chin!" the Lieutenant slapped his brawny forearm hard.

"Oooh, ma'am, do that to me one more time."

Then the fish went for it. A flash of black, he streaked across the bowl and hit the female hard. She twisted round and ran for it, the stud in pursuit. Round the bowl, up and down, she ran and he chased, occasionally managing to get his jaws on her fins, and she began to look tattered and torn.

"Go stud go!" the boys chanted and the Lieutenant was scolding them.

"Stop it now!" she pleaded but to no avail.

But even though she was tired, the female never submitted, running every time the male tried to curl up in a slippery embrace with her.

"Eh, your fish got no skill *leh*," the Lance Corporal said after a while. The stud was dropping back now, probably tired from the chase. It floated around, looking unfulfilled.

"You've had your turn. Now it's mine," the Lance Corporal said.

"*Aiyah*, you all so bad. Let the poor thing rest *lah*," the Sergeant pleaded. The Corporal reluctantly fished his stud out of the Pleasure Bowl and plopped him back into the jar.

"You made us look bad today," he told the fish as the Lance Corporal moved the Pleasure Bowl to a cool shady place for the female to rest.

"Once her fins get back into shape, we can try again," the Private said as he peered into the bowl.

"Look, ma'am, aren't we considerate? We even got Honey a gynaecologist," the Corporal said to the Lieutenant.

"Shuddup, you disgusting jerks. Rapists! All men are brutes!"

It was a week before her fins healed. During that time, the Lance Corporal had tried a few 'getting to know you' sessions for his fish, Poisson

Ivy, and his potential mate, Honey. He would take Ivy's jar and put it next to the bowl and Ivy would get all excited, flaring at the sight of the nubile young thing next door. Honey, on her part, acted indifferent most of the time, only going up to the glass where Ivy was magnified to take a better look at him, or maybe just to tease him a little.

"It's time," the Private finally announced. Honey was ripe, he said, look at her belly. And it was indeed swollen with eggs. She'll probably be more willing this time, the Corporal noted. Not fair. Last week played so hard to get.

The Lance Corporal transferred Poisson Ivy gingerly from his jar to the Pleasure Bowl as the clerks, the Sergeant and the Lieutenant watched.

"Go get her, boy."

"Stop making provocative remarks like that," the Lieutenant warned. She was standing with the Sergeant and the two looked on apprehensively as Poisson Ivy slipped into the water of the bowl.

"Go, Ivy go!" the clerks chanted, and the Lieutenant's pretty face was all screwed up in disgust and sympathy and she was going very red. The Corporal was about to ask if she had also looked that way on her wedding night, but thought better of it.

Poisson Ivy hung suspended in the clear water for a few moments, trying to acclimatise himself to his new surroundings. His jar had been dark and cosy, with the algae on the sides blocking out the harsh light. Here, the light was only blocked by the faces that had gathered round the bowl. Slowly, he moved his tail fin and he glided through the water easily, gracefully, his scarlet fins trailing fluidly in the water. Then out of the corner of his large eyes, he saw her and finned slowly and tentatively towards her. She was at the bottom of the bowl, just sitting there, as if she was waiting for him. The moment he was close enough to touch, she became a burst of energy and flashed away quickly. Ivy was startled and twisted around in the opposite direction.

"Real beginner. Hasn't learnt to take rejection yet," the Corporal smirked.

"It's still early. It was only the first real encounter," the Lance Corporal defended Ivy.

Ivy made another lap of the bowl, swimming near the surface while Honey hugged the bottom. Then he suddenly dropped from above as she passed below him. She sensed the sudden movement and made another spurt, Ivy in pursuit, finning furiously to catch her. He was almost upon her when she changed direction again, eluding him.

"*Tarek harga*," the Private laughed.

"Good for you, girl, don't let this stupid fish think you're cheap and easy," the Lieutenant muttered to the fish. No, men had to learn to wait till you were ready.

"*Wah*, ma'am, don't you want to see this fish have babies? We will make you and Sergeant godmothers," the Lance Corporal suggested.

"I'm not against marriage and parenthood, but I do not like this gang rape of a poor helpless little fish."

"Eh, so how come you no kids, ma'am?" the Corporal asked innocently.

"Shuddup. You're just a bunch of brutes. Look, he's still chasing her and she's getting tired. Stop this at once, I order you."

"Ma'am, that would be coitus interruptus," the Private said. "Very annoying for both parties, I can assure you as an expert on *Betta splendens* mating habits."

"But ma'am, Ivy isn't biting her, unlike Jenny the other day. Ivy's a gentleman," the Lance Corporal said, never taking his eyes from the tank. Come on fish, just a little bit more. She's getting tired with all those eggs in her belly. And she must be feeling horny too. Just stick with it, fella, you'll have her.

But nothing happened. The two finally slowed down and swam round the tank idly, Honey still in front and Ivy still chasing. But even that stopped after a while. Ivy went back to the surface and began blowing bubbles.

"He's making a nest," the Private explained to the rest.

"A bit early, right? Hasn't even got the girl yet," the Corporal said.

"Maybe this is to show the girl that he has serious intentions, not like your fish, only know how to chase, chase, chase," the Sergeant said.

Then the Lieutenant was called for and she told the rest to get back to work. The Lance Corporal sat beside the bowl as they settled down to the day's filing. Then about a couple of hours later, he turned his head towards the bowl to check on Ivy's amorous progress. His eyes widened in amazement.

"They're doing it! They're doing it!" he called in excitement. The fish were curled around each other, Ivy's long, slender, crimson body twisted into a letter 'S', around the dull silver cigar-shaped Honey. Suspended in mid-water, the couple floated in their embrace, then the eggs began to appear, tiny white ovals emerging from Honey's belly, slipping down Ivy's long anal fin, like tiny ping-pong balls rolling down a cascade of scarlet velvet, as Ivy's milt, invisible to the human beings watching, fertilised them as they passed.

"Shit, his fish actually managed it," the Corporal said. "What does that mean I am?"

On the surface of the water, Ivy had blown a nest of bubbles. And Honey had obviously approved of his efforts. Then, the flow of eggs stopped and the couple unlocked from their cold, wet embrace. Honey went for the bottom and lay there motionless, while Ivy was still curled up in an S. Slowly, he straightened himself out and began swimming around. But not for long. Even as Honey rested at the bottom, Ivy went to work. He began picking up the eggs, which had sunk to the bottom of the bowl, and putting them in the bubble nest where they would be supported near the surface. One by one he picked the eggs, going all the way down, then all the way up to the nest. And there must have been hundreds of eggs.

"See? That's a real man, not like you all," the Lieutenant scolded her clerks. "See, Ivy pursues Honey gently, but persistently. Then to prove his intentions and commitment, he builds her a nest. Then after she gives birth, he takes care of everything, including the babies. See? And you all wonder why you have no girlfriends!"

"That's below the belt, ma'am," the Corporal grunted. He looked across the room at the other two clerks and shook his head. Things were not going according to plan.

"Hey, we'll have to take Honey out of the bowl. She may start eating her own eggs," the Private said.

"But if we try to catch her now, we might break up the nest," the Lance Corporal pointed out. "And Ivy will have to start all over again!"

"Either that, or the eggs get eaten."

"*Aiyah*, what do we want with the eggs anyway? We only wanted our boys to have a good time, what," the Corporal said. "Put Ivy back into his jar *lah*, and let the woman look after the kids. That's what they're for anyway."

"Er, not in the world of the *Betta splendens*. Here, it is the male that takes care of everything," the Private said.

"Unlike some useless fellas," the Lieutenant added.

"Who asked you, ma'am?"

"Don't be rude, Chin, or I'll put you on charge."

"Huh? I thought you always threatened to kill our fish if we were bad. Kill *lah*."

"No. I will protect the baby fish from now on. You misbehave, you get charged."

The next morning, the three clerks arrived at work to find that the Sergeant had got there first. She was at her desk, the bowl in front of her with a much smaller tank. She had taken Honey out and put her in another jar and was transferring the tiny eggs from the bowl to the little tank with a teaspoon.

"Sarge! Don't tell me you're eating our fry for breakfast!" the Private shouted.

"Idiot. No *lah*. Just moving house for them. The bowl is so difficult for Ivy to move around in to keep picking up eggs. This was my son's old tank."

"Something's not quite right here," the Corporal whispered to the Lance Corporal.

The days wore on and the Lieutenant sent her boys out at lunch to get the appropriate size of fry food. Ivy worked very hard at keeping his family afloat. The clerks from the other departments began to visit their office to look at the baby fish, and all of them giggling and going, so cute, so cute, till the three boys got royally sick of them all. The girls were also very impressed with the way Ivy looked after everything.

"Where got man like this today?" was an often-made remark.

"If you want Ivy, you can take him home with you, please," the Corporal offered to every woman who compared Ivy with real men. But the Lance Corporal, of course, would hear nothing of it. He had, after all, become the godfather of all the fry and was the proud owner of Ivy, sharing in his pet's glory.

"Eh, ma'am, why don't I just flush all of them down the toilet? Save us all this hassle. I don't mind just having one fish, but this is too much, *lah*," the Corporal said after a fortnight of fry fever.

"Hallo, this is your responsibility now. You were the ones who went out to get Honey and it was your fault that she got pregnant. Now the kids are your responsibility and you'd better look after them properly," said the Lieutenant in a huff.

"And," she added darkly, "if anything happens to the baby fish, I will hold you chiefly responsible."

"It's all your fault," the Corporal glared at the Lance Corporal.

"But why?" the other asked.

"Your fish, what. Your fish got her pregnant. Dunno how to do it without getting into trouble, what. Not like my fish, the stud."

"Oh yeah, that's really prime, whose idea was it anyway?"

The Lieutenant did not stay to hear the rest of the quarrel. She walked back to her own room, closed the door, slid shut the communication hole door and sat down heavily in her arm chair. Then she began to laugh quietly, so that the clerks would not hear her. Somehow, she had managed to get the better of her horrid boys and it was a very satisfying feeling. Thank you, Ivy, she chuckled. I only hope my husband is as sweet as you when our baby comes, she said, patting her still flat belly. He'd better be, she smiled to herself. He'd better be.

THE FIRST DAY
David Leo

Today is the first day of the rest of your life. Those were the first words on my mind as I jumped out of bed. Hey, I thought, there was still plenty left in this spry body. Six o'clock, and not a minute late. It was the alarm dock in my brain. Not easy to switch it off after thirty-five years. Six o'clock and the sky was still dark, and the air a little nippy. But this morning was different. It had to be the first day of my life.

My wife stirred and asked, "Why do you wake up so early?"

I went about brushing my teeth, shaving and freshening up. The usual routine, but it was with a different kind of expectation. Today was not like any other day.

"What time is it?"

I had to take a look at that poster Jeanine gave me. It was of a little girl running in a field of poppies on a clear morning, and the words ringing in my head: *Today is the first day of the rest of your life*. I had left it in the study without thinking I had need for it. Just another of those pretty things that girls had a weakness for. Especially the sentimental sort. On a day when there was little typing to do, Jeanine would be reading poetry or trying her hand at writing lines. I could see her floating away in her dreams and had to be cruel to bring her feet back on the ground. Other than that, she was an excellent secretary.

"Why don't you go back to sleep? You don't have to go to work. You've retired."

So I had retired, but that was no reason to sleep away my life. Today I had become a free man, free to do anything I wanted. By George, I had waited long enough for this day to arrive. No more pushing a pen behind the desk. No more arguments with the boss. No more agonizing over the demands made by the Union. No more bound by the rules of the office where the first principle had always been that employees were company property. Sure there were good times. On most mornings when I walked into the office, there were greetings of *"Good morning, Mr Tan"*. It made me feel important, the respect and recognition that came with it. And, it made me feel just as good to respond with a, *"Good morning, Stella, I must say you have on a very pretty dress today."* Or, *"Good morning, Hamid, did you enjoy the soccer game on TV last night?"* Or, simply, *"Good morning, everyone, it looks like we're going to have a great day ahead."* And, of course, Jeanine always made sure that nobody stole my morning papers or laced my tea with sugar. I had told her that sugar would kill me before my retirement.

"What... are you thinking about?"

"The poster that Jeanine gave me. I'm going to put it up on the wall."

"There're enough things on the wall."

I opened the curtains a little and the first light of day rushed in. It looked like a fine day outside and it would be foolish not to take advantage of the good weather. Rise and shine had always been one of my obsessions which my colleagues made fun of. When I walked into someone's curtained office, I would suggest that he open the curtains. Why have a window if you don't want to use it? Once, when we were walking down the streets in Tokyo, I had to continually cross the roads each time we turned round the corners, to be in the sun. My pals laughed at me. I was always the one who looked on the bright side of things. Or who tried to, at least. Not that I had not had moments of depression. There were times when I was really down.

"Can you close the curtains, please? The sun's disturbing my eyes."

"What shall we do today?"

"It's too early to decide. Why don't you just sleep a little more?"

I started to dress.

"Where're you going?"

"Out. It looks like a fine day and I'm going out."

"I don't understand you. You have all the time in the world and you're rushing out."

At fifty-five, did I have all the time in time world?

"Why don't you relax and take it easy for once?"

I ran through all the business shirts I used to wear and wondered if I had not had one too many. And the ties to match. What was I going to do with them? There were a couple of them which I was particularly fond of, red stripes or paisley, and these I had reserved for important occasions like a Board Meeting, lunch with the chairman, or some signing ceremony. I had often been complimented for having the guts to wear something so flamboyant and bold, when my contemporaries were complimenting their greying with darker, subdued shades. To me it was a matter of taste rather than courage.

"You don't have to dress like you're going to the office."

I picked a short-sleeved, Balinese batik shirt in various shades of green.

"It's too hot out there. Wear something light."

White jeans would be a pleasant change from the usual dark colours for the office.

"What time will you be back?"

"Probably by noon. For lunch. Cook something nice. It's a special day."

"I know, it's the first day of your retirement."

On the way out, I mused over the poster Jeanine gave me, a message of hope and promises.

Today is the first day of the rest of your life. On the kitchen wall, the second hand of an old-fashioned clock was ticking away. It was no time to be wasting time.

I rode the train to Raffles Place and had breakfast at the MacDonald's. In happy contrast to the tense office faces today I could afford the luxury of time to exult over the aroma of steaming coffee, and bite slowly into a hamburger, gingerly turning my tongue over the different tastes of cheese, onions, tomatoes, and lettuce in my mouth. I sat back on the hard but cool PVC chair and reflected on the pre-retirement programme, which I had attended through the courtesy of my employer.

It was a small class of about twenty would-be retirees. The mood was generally one of dismay and doom, as if the men were about to take a plunge from the plank on a pirate's boat into the deep blue sea.

In their company I was a fish out of water, being about the only confident one, or so it seemed. After all, I liked to believe that optimism was an essential part of my human psyche. Then, even before Jeanine gave me the poster that promised many new adventures ahead, I had psyched myself up for the eventuality of D-day, as those apprehensive greying heads chose to call it, or, to borrow a term from my son's National Service vocabulary, the much anticipated ORD. So, when Professor Winwood said, "There's so much you can look forward to," I followed his beady eyes and gazed beyond the clinical classroom walls, he assuming the vision of a prophet and I expecting to see the colours of a rainbow. Some other attendees just hung their heads.

Professor Winwood was reputed to be a retirement expert, and judging by the aging lines across his face he ought to be! He started on a promising note, proclaiming, "You have a great life ahead!" Of course, few of them believed him, and the conversation during tea-break was caustic and fuming with hostility.

"It's all a lot of bull."

"Why then is he still working?"

Presumably Professor Winwood got paid for the job.

"You can't deny that the money's good."

"Exactly. I need a job too, not retirement."

"It's all for show. You think that the company really cares. Believe me, the day you step out, that's the end. Who cares what happens to you after that?"

I refused to be disheartened, so I listened intently to Professor Winwood as he went on to advise the participants to indulge in activities better known as hobbies. Many suggestions were proffered. *You could keep yourself busy with shovel and hoe.* I was fortunate in that I had a garden. *You could set up an easel and wield a brush.* I could try with the little imagination left in my mind. *You could go fishing.* Nice and leisurely, except that I abhorred the idling, and the infliction of unnecessary pain on God's lesser creatures. *Play more golf.* Why not, if you had the clubs and the friends? *Take a trip.* A cruise on the Queen EII would make a perfect holiday. The message was clear: Do something so that you may continue to find yourself useful.

"What about a job?" someone asked. "I can only be useful if I have a job."

"Uh, huh, that depends on what you mean by a job," said Professor Winwood. "What you really mean, I believe, is gainful employment. Then the answer is no. You can, of course, turn your hobby into gainful self-employment. Jimmy Carter, for example, literally became a carpenter. Now, you may call that a job, but to him it's an interest. He could sell the tables and chairs he made if he chose to. The idea is not to work as you have worked all through your life, but to keep yourself happily occupied with something you have always wanted to do but never found the time for."

There were important words to note, such as *happily occupied*. And the promise of fun. Retirement could be one endless vacation if you knew how. Thanks to Professor Winwood and the company's thoughtfulness.

"That's it," said Professor Winwood, looking at his watch. "I wish all of you many happy years of retirement ahead."

As we left the room, one of the participants remarked that he would become a remisier. Stock-broking was something he had always wanted to do. That way, he would ensure himself of a continuous source of income too. Not exactly something which you could call a hobby, I thought. "What about you?" he asked. I smiled, then said, much to his puzzlement, "I think I'll read the complete works of Shakespeare."

I had always wanted to do something silly like standing on a busy street and watch the world go by. It would be interesting to detach yourself from the familiar 'got-to-rush-no-time-to-stop' routine which you were once caught up in, and see what it was like to be free. So, I strolled along Robinson Road and listened to the discordant sound of the traffic, and watched the people jostle their way through the crowd. There were masses of people, moving in every different direction all at the same time. A faceless throng, always moving, like a roller-coaster without brakes, and the journey one endless scream.

Many of them never got off. I remembered Wu Chi-Min who collapsed on the job and died of a heart attack. The company mourned the loss of an employee who literally worked himself to death, dedicated until his last breath. An obituary was inserted in *The Straits Times* and hordes of colleagues turned up at the funeral. Everyone had a good word for, or about him, and some tears were shed. In only two or three years, Wu would have enjoyed his hard earned retirement, but he had said he would appeal for reemployment. He was not the kind to want to stay home doing nothing. Professor Winwood's tips would have been viewed by him with suspicion as sugarcoated pills to sweeten a bitter end. In a way, he had his wish fulfilled. He died useful.

"Is it worth it?" someone asked.

"Worth what?"

"To work so hard, and before you know it, *kaput.*"

I felt sorry for him then, not that he had not retired, but that he passed on too soon. Any age below eighty was premature.

I stopped at the steps outside Clifford Centre leading up to an overhead pedestrian crossing, and wondered if I should make it over the other side. Lots of people squeezed past me, brushing shoulders, sometimes my body feeling the unfriendly nudge of an elbow or the jerk of strange objects, like a lady's umbrella, or an office file. There I stood, making the Hamlet decision of my life—*to cross or not to cross*—while nameless masses of people continued to edge past me, mindlessly, yet with a purpose, though undefined. *To cross or not to cross:* It sounded so stupid. I had never had to make that kind of decision before in my life. Suddenly I felt foolish and aimless, unsure of where I was going, and a strange sensation of wanting drenched me. Something was missing. I felt alienated. It had to do with the struggle for survival to which I had subjected myself for the past thirty-five years, and by that very struggle I was assured of the liveliness of my flesh and blood. It was by that very struggle too that I found the unquestioned purpose of plodding on, day after day. Without it I was beginning to feel my whole being deteriorate into a flaccid mass of helplessness.

I called upon my defences: Jeanine's poster; Professor Winwood; and my assumed sanguine self. I was determined to re-assert control over my faculties and not retreat into a slow death. There had to be something that I could do. I headed toward a bookstore and picked up a copy of *The Complete Works of Shakespeare*.

Like the faithful husband hat I had been since we got married, I went back home.

"So what did you do in town?" asked my wife.

"Nothing much really."

"I don't see why you should bother to rush with the office crowd and get crushed in the process."

"I bought a copy of *The Complete Works of Shakespeare*."

"Ha, you'll have plenty of time to read it."

Funny... I could almost see a smile on the face of the kitchen clock, its second hand never slipping on the job.

"What's for lunch?"

"Egg noodles. It's your birthday."

Today also happened to be my birthday, the fifty-fifth anniversary of the *actual* first day of my life and it grieved me thinking that she had forgotten. But she remembered, and that sounded promising. There again, what's a birthday anyway? And at fifty-five? It was one of those things that became less important with time. When I was a child, my mother made sure I had a bowl of *mee suah* and two hard-boiled eggs. It was a family tradition. The first year I got married, she called to remind my wife not to forget the thread-like noodles and eggs, much to my wife's annoyance.

And when our children came along, it was the same meal for each of them, on his or her birthday, until they were old enough to protest. Then we switched to French or Szechuan cuisine at a restaurant.

Oh yes, birthdays would be fun with the children around. But like birds that soon grew too big for the nest, they had flown away. Griselde had married abroad and now lived in Vancouver. She would call if she remembered, or send a belated card. I had always been fond of that child, who vowed when she was ten that she would never leave Daddy. She crossed her heart when she said it and we hooked our fingers. She still signed off with love whenever she wrote. Then Chuck came along, the boy that everyone said was a chip of the old block, now pursuing a degree in computer science at UCLA in California. I didn't think he would remember. Even while in Singapore, he had to be reminded. Maybe Marc, mother's little spoilt brat who was determined to assert his independence by living on his own, in a rented apartment in the posh Orchard Road vicinity, would drop by in the evening, if he was not too busy with his girlfriend. Oh yes, they were the joys of my life. Now grown-up and living apart, it was only to be expected that they would have different priorities. Though gone were the days when the children would go everywhere with Daddy, I could not complain, for they had given me fond memories of the good times we had had together. As soon as they grew old enough to make it on their own, I knew the time had come for me to let go. So, I retreated without fuss into the background of their lives, almost disappearing into the far horizon, somewhat sadly at first but never grudgingly.

"What shall we do?" I asked, taking the shell off a hard-boiled egg. "I mean, it's a special day, two in one—my birthday and my retirement, so why don't we do something extraordinary?" No response from my wife, but it gave me time to cook up a proposition. "Your and I can go out together and give ourselves a big treat, like gorging on the biggest ice-cream in town. Oh yes, the 'Earthquake' at Swensen's. Eighteen flavours. Remember the fun we had with the kids when they were here? Or was it the Volcano?" I was desperate for some kind of reaction. "What about high tea or a tea dance?" Any form of acknowledgement would suffice. "Or a movie?" I needed an excuse badly to support my proposal. "And since no one has bought me a present, I will buy myself one with some help from you. What about it? Sounds good, doesn't it?"

"Sounds crazy."

"Even so, does it matter? What do you say?"

"I can't. My friends are coming round for tea. It's our usual Wednesday afternoon programme. You can join us if you want to, but I doubt you'll feel comfortable among so many women. Besides, why don't you do something more sensible?"

I settled for egg noodles: which replaced the *mee suah* of my younger days.

"I can do the dishes," I offered after the meal.

"No, I can manage."

"I'll vacuum the carpet then."

"It was done when you were in town."

"Isn't there something I can do or help?"

"Relax, my dear, enjoy your retirement."

I was beginning to find the word disturbing and exasperating. Almost a harassment. What had Professor Winwood preached that was so different? I read that in Japan, the divorce rate was highest among couples when the men retired and the women faced an adjustment problem. For thirty-five years or so a woman had the freedom of the house when the husband was at work, and when he retired he became an obstacle in her way. Perhaps this was why several old men were seen dozing off in shopping complexes or gazing at an empty runway at Changi Airport, resigned to *que sera sera, whatever will be will be*, returning only when the sun began to sink. How we had grown apart, though living together, without knowing or realizing it. She had a schedule to keep, and mine was wrenched from me the day I retired.

I picked up the voluminous *The Complete Works of Shakespeare* and sank into an easy chair. Ah this had to be the life I'd been waiting for!

I fell into a deep slumber before I was through the first act of *A Winter's Tale*. There were no dreams. It was the waking that was hazy, like a dream, as I emerged like a stranger in an alien land. I felt a certain numbness come over my body and blamed it on the paralyzing heat of the evening sun. Even the furniture around me appeared strangely unfriendly. I looked for some signs of life and caught my wife in the doorway, busy with her chores.

"What time is it? Where are your lady friends?"

"They're long gone. You slept like a log."

I had imagined that they would raise a racket and wake me up.

"They were surprised when I told them you'd retired. Linda said you didn't look that old and they all agreed."

Was I supposed to take that as a compliment and gloat over it?

"You should see some other men your age!"

It didn't matter. Suddenly I was an old man. One day into my fifty-fifth birthday and I had become an old man. So much for Jeanine's poster, with promises of life's first day, and Professor Winwood's sermon on the joys of not working.

"It's all in the mind, really."

Could I go on kidding myself?

"Haven't you heard, you're as young as you feel?"

And with advertising catch-phrases? Like it or not, I was today, classified as an old man. The company told me so when I was struck off the payroll.

"Would you rather collapse on the job? Like Wu Chi-min?"

Wu never lived to collect the goodies that the company gave all retirees in recognition of their years of dedication. Among them was an expensive watch, a Rolex, the type that any progressive young executive would be proud to acquire. "Why don't you use it?" suggested my wife. But what use was a watch to a man when he had retired? Indeed, after thirty-five years, what need had I for a watch? I thought I would give it to Marc. Tomorrow would be another first day of the rest of my life. Thank you, Jeanine, for the poster.

THE BORROWED BOY
Alfian Sa'at

They would borrow the boy for a day. He would be checked out in the morning, after the Aidilfitri prayers, and then sent back in the evening, before his bedtime. During the course of the day he would follow them as they visited their relatives and in all likelihood he would receive some money, just like their other children. People were most generous on the first day of Hari Raya; as the weeks passed the amount placed in those palm-sized paper envelopes would depreciate. Not simply because money is finite but also because the visitors would tend to be more distantly related, people who were encountered once a year. As a matter of fact, the boy would probably receive more than their other children, once it was made known that he was an orphan.

They had already prepared a set of *baju kurung* for him at home. It was made from dark pink satin, and the collar was in fashion that year—the Telok Blangah cut, where instead of a Mandarin collar the neckline was embroidered with a herringbone stitch. The boy might not like the colour, but what was important was that it was the same colour as the *baju kurung* for their other two children. It would make him feel like he was one of the family.

Junaidah walked into the orphanage alone, unaccompanied by her husband and son. They had preferred to wait in the car. The orphans were picked at random, but a week earlier Junaidah had called the person in charge and requested for an eight-year-old boy. The reason, she explained, was that the family had decided to purchase a *baju kurung* for the boy, as a present. Thus it was necessary to know both his gender and age in advance. At the bazaar in Geylang, Junaidah had used her own son as a gauge for the size of the baju kurung; placing it against his back, holding it up with her forefingers and thumbs. For her own son she chose a sky blue *baju kurung*; for the boy, pale orange.

She prided herself on her choice of pastels; it was a sign of good taste. Some of her relatives seemed fond of garish colours: ruby reds and turmeric yellows, which though festive, betrayed an inability to appreciate subtlety. It struck Junaidah that these choices weren't just aesthetic, but also economic: bright colours took a longer time to fade after repeated washings. But most unpalatable to her were those families which had decided to dress their children in identical colours, as if all their clothes had been cut from the same bale of cloth. She had, on occasion, pointed out families attired in such manner. Looking out from their car window, she had once made the remark that they looked like a boria troupe, those performing minstrels from Penang that she had seen on Malaysian television.

After she had picked out the *baju kurung*, her husband had commented that the colours were too muted for children; they were 'old people' hues. Junaidah sighed in disappointment. She had wanted to say that her husband was an engineer; they had a car and did not have to take public transport for their visiting rounds. As such, it was unlikely for the family to cross roads, and thus unnecessary for the children to be costumed like warning flares. Instead, she asked Haikel whether he liked the *baju kurung* she had chosen, in a solicitous voice that guaranteed a fearful, though positive response. When the boy nodded, Junaidah triumphantly walked to the shopkeeper and announced, "I'm buying two sets, can give discount or not?"

There had been an incident in the morning with the *baju kurung*. Haikel had walked into her room as Junaidah laid out the two sets on the Queen-sized bed. The room smelt of the mint shampoo in Junaidah's hair, drying by an electric standing fan, and rose attar, the non-alcoholic perfume that her husband had dabbed on himself before the morning prayers. Because of their new curtains, the light in the room was an underwater turquoise. A brocade jewelry box was opened, its contents twinkling in the dimness of the room.

Haikel was sifting through the box when Junaidah said, "These are women's things. Go and wear your clothes." He then proceeded to reach for the pale orange baju kurung.

"Haikel, that's not yours. Don't you remember?"

"Then whose is it?"

At that moment, Junaidah realised she did not know the boy's name. All this while, she and her husband had referred to him as the 'orphan boy'. Junaidah felt that it was too much trouble to explain what an orphan was to Haikel.

"It's your friend's."

"Who?"

"Don't you remember? Today you're going to have a friend following us around. And that orange one is his *baju kurung*. Yours is the blue one. Remember how you told Mak that you liked it?"

Haikel looked at the two sets of clothes on the bed. The look on his face told Junaidah that her answer was not satisfactory. He knew, with that eight-year-old intuition of his, that she was hiding something from him. And thus he said, his voice suddenly taking on an adult assertiveness, "But I like the orange one."

"You said you liked the blue one, Haikel."

"I never said so. I want the orange one."

Junaidah looked at her husband. He was using a brush to clean the lint off his velvet *songkok*. "Look at Haikel, bang. On the morning of Hari Raya he's making a fuss."

"Haikel," her husband said, without looking up from his task. His voice was stern, but the response was so automatic that Junaidah felt insulted. Even if he had not entirely surrendered all parenting duties to her, sometimes she felt as if he was skimping on his share. And there were times, like this, for example, when Junaidah felt as if she was being treated not so much like a wife but a whiny daughter, petitioning a father weary of the melodramatic antics of little girls.

"That's all you can do," Junaidah said. "You didn't even lift your head to look at him."

"Why do I need to look at him? I know what he looks like."

Junaidah rolled her eyes. In this triangle she was suddenly the petty one, the child. She caught a triumphant smile creeping up on Haikel's face, endorsed by his father's nonchalance. Sometimes Junaidah felt that she would have preferred to have a daughter instead. She was tired of having these two ganging up on her. But weren't daughters supposed to be closer to their fathers, while sons were mummy's boys? Why was it that Haikel rarely took sides with her? She wondered if it might have been better to have asked for a girl from the orphanage instead.

But that would fulfill her own need, instead of the needs of the child. It would have violated a certain spirit of charity. She wondered if there were childless couples who borrowed a child from the orphanage on Hari Raya. No, she decided, it would make too much of a scene, it would highlight the void in their lives, a void to be filled by endless gossip. That poor couple, people would say, playing at being parents for a day, like a bride and groom playing at being king and queen for a day.

Also, she had chosen a boy for Haikel's sake. She knew he was at an age where girls were treated with a mixture of shyness and hostility. And for him to be so ungrateful, to test her with this mischievous amnesia, was unacceptable. They did not know the boy's name yet, but the orange *baju kurung* had been reserved for him. Her son could not ask for it as if nobody else had claimed ownership. Thus Junaidah said, "Don't be naughty ah, Haikel. This one isn't yours."

Suddenly her husband interjected. "But they're the same size, right? They're just different colours. The orphan boy doesn't know which one you picked for him. If Haikel wants to wear the orange one, let him have it."

Junaidah felt as if she had been elected the sole spokesperson for the boy. She had to stand up for him, to assert his presence. She found herself looking at her husband, and articulating silently: *You can have Haikel today. But the boy is mine. I will not start the day by betraying him.* But she suddenly checked herself; she had not even met this boy, and it would not do to become too attached to him.

She let Haikel have the orange baju kurung, and hoped that his victory marked the end, instead of the beginning of what she now uncomfortably realised were the stirrings of jealousy. They had always talked about having another child, but kept on postponing, because her husband had always insisted that Haikel was not ready. It would be traumatic, he reasoned, for the boy to have his parents distribute their affections at so young an age. But Junaidah sometimes wondered if it was already too late for Haikel to learn to share his life—and his parents' lives—with another sibling.

Thus when Junaidah entered the orphanage, she could not help but feel expectant. It was just as well that her husband and Haikel preferred to remain in the car. She would be the first point of contact into the family, and despite the fact that she was not a man, she hoped that he would somehow stick by her side for the rest of the day. A woman in a cream *tudung* was waiting at a counter, which was decorated with *ketupat* woven from shiny light green ribbons. There were children's drawings on the noticeboard, many of them filled with the words 'Selamat Hari Raya'. Junaidah noticed how they were filled mostly with pictures of children, not families. But at least the children were smiling.

After Junaidah had introduced herself, the receptionist checked a list and said, "You're the one who wanted an eight-year-old boy, right?" Junaidah wondered if her request had been exceptional, and immediately felt apologetic. She did not want to come across as someone prone to unreasonable demands. The receptionist smiled and said, "I'll go and bring him down. They're all upstairs right now. They're just had their breakfast. We had *lontong* and *rendang* today. You know *lah*, once a year. Why don't you take a seat first?"

Junaidah sat down on a leather sofa. There was a crater in one of its armrests, exposing the beige sponge padding inside. Someone, probably a child, had been picking at it, fingernails burrowing through the sponge either out of nervousness or boredom. She did not expect the orphanage to look like a school, with two flags at a quadrangle near the façade, and three storeys of what could have been classrooms—except that they were dormitories. It was a good idea to have them sequestered upstairs. Junaidah had feared having to pass through the faces of children, their hopefulness on her way in, their disappointment on her way out. She wondered if she might have asked for another child, and another, just enough to fit into the car.

Was it not somewhat cruel, to choose one over the rest? Except that the orphanage had chosen for her. Perhaps this was a reward for good behaviour, to be hosted by a family for a day. Junaidah felt comforted by the idea that she was merely a host, and that the child was her guest. Her role today was to be defined by hospitality, not the construction of an intricate fantasy. She was not going to pretend that the boy was her son; neither should the boy believe that this family setup was anything more than temporary.

Junaidah had to admit that she had not always been so circumspect. When she had watched that TV magazine programme during the fasting month, the one that showcased the children at the Darul-Ihsan orphanage, it had affected her so much that she could not sleep properly at night. It made her cry just to relate the story to her husband when he later got home from work: all those children without parents, whose Hari Raya would painfully remind them only of what they lacked, no jars overflowing with cookies and biscuits, no filling their pockets with crisp, folded dollar notes, a festival of absence. Her family members didn't know how fortunate they were, it was an obligation to let others partake of their privilege. The next day, she called the orphanage, asked them about the scheme where families could volunteer to provide selected children with a 'real Hari Raya experience', and signed up. When she put down the phone she was flushed with that superior happiness that comes about from making other people happy.

The receptionist returned five minutes later with the boy. His name was Mydeen, and she spelt it out for Junaidah, a unique English spelling for a name otherwise recognised as 'Maidin' or 'Maideen'. He was dark, a Jawi Peranakan child, of Indian Muslim and Malay extraction. Junaidah did not know many Jawi Peranakans, but it sometimes amused her how the 'i's' in their names became 'ee's': Fateema, Jameelah, Lateef.

Mydeen looked at the floor shyly as the receptionist spoke. She told Junaidah that he was in Primary two, a badminton player, and that he was quite reserved. He was wearing his pink satin *baju kurung*, a colour that clashed with his skin tone. Junaidah noticed his thick, well-shaped eyebrows, his high cheekbones, and a sharp, almost hooked nose. He was tall for his age, and while Junaidah believed eight-year-olds were still amorphous, she could already see how this one's features could step out of the haze of youth and solidify; he would turn out to be quite a handsome young man.

"Have you eaten?" Junaidah asked him.

"Yes."

"Was it nice?"

Mydeen nodded. And then he reached out and slipped his hand into Junaidah's. She was shocked by the intimacy of the gesture, and thought to herself: *He must be impatient to get out of here.* Junaidah signed a few forms briskly, thanked the receptionist, and walked out of the building with Mydeen. On her way out, she considered the possibility that the act of taking her hand was something almost reflexive for him, having been fostered out to different Hari Raya families year after year. So she had been mistaken about the automatic hand-holding, a gesture not of animal instinct or need but habit and perhaps even calculation. *I'm not the first,* Junaidah thought to herself. A moment later she found herself beaming in the direction of the family car, a red Honda whose door had swung open to receive her and her dark-skinned guest.

The first place they would visit was the house of Junaidah's mother-in-law. She lived in Teban Gardens, which despite its name was a working-class housing estate. In the car, the two boys were sitting in the back seat. Mydeen had already changed into his light blue *baju kurung*; her husband had helped the boy into it at a toilet in the orphanage. Haikel was playing with his handheld game. On the radio, Sudirman was singing the evergreen 'From Afar I Ask For Forgiveness'.

"Haikel, what are you playing?" Junaidah asked.

"PSP."

"Why don't you ask Mydeen to play along?"

"This game for one player only."

"When you're done, why don't you let him try?"

Haikel did not reply. And Junaidah thought there was little point in forcing him to share his toy. Did she even imagine that the two boys would be able to get along? Junaidah suddenly thought of all the other children who would be present at Teban Gardens. Could Haikel somehow rally his cousins together to exclude the boy from their activities? Was her son capable of such a thing? Suddenly Junaidah felt a certain protectiveness rise within her, a feeling that caught her by surprise. On the radio, Sudirman was winding up his song with the final lines: "I hope for perpetual blessings from Mum and Dad, for your son who is far away."

When they arrived at the house, there were already about a dozen pairs of shoes at the door. While taking the lift up to the eleventh floor, Mydeen had asked to press the floor button. It was the first statement he had made, actively, which was not a response to a question. Junaidah felt a certain sense of reassurance: the boy would know how to conduct himself later. He had just made a desire known, and she would not have to attend to him all the time. Wasn't that what children were essentially, the exhausting mystery they presented to her, as she tried to meet their needs: are you hungry, cold, sleepy, in pain? It was the one thing all mothers said to their children, patting a crying child, or rocking one in her arms, not 'I love you' but 'what do you want… what do you want?'

It was her mother-in-law who greeted them at the door. She was a widow, who had raised four sons on her own. Her husband had passed away at a British shipyard accident when the youngest was still an infant. She had married young, and a popular story they liked to tell was how her late husband had come home one day to find his wife playing hopscotch with her friends outside their *kampung* house. Junaidah's husband was the eldest and the only one with a degree, and it was no secret that he was his mother's favourite.

"You're finally here," she said. "Why are you late?"

"We had some business to attend to in the morning," her son replied.

"Haikel," she said. "You haven't visited grandma for so long! And who's your friend?"

"He's a boy from Darul-Ihsan," Junaidah replied.

"Oh, Ihsan. Come in, Ihsan."

"His name's not Ihsan. His name is Mydeen."

Haikel's grandmother was hard of hearing, and Junaidah sometimes found conversation with her a draining affair. The old lady, however, always had a smile on her face, and even if she had misheard something, was likely to have heard it in a completely benign way. Mydeen, without any prompting, began to salam her, and then went around the living room, seeking out the hands of all the adults.

"Go and salam everyone, Haikel."

Haikel would usually resist, backing up indulgently against his father, but this time, he readily complied. He retraced the path that Mydeen had taken, grabbing hands and holding them up to his nose, bowing perfunctorily, but at such speed that he managed to overtake Mydeen. After he was done, he started to seek out the rest of the children. It was not difficult to find them; shrieking and laughter were spilling out from one of the bedrooms.

"Who's the boy?" one of Junaidah's brothers-in-law asked.

"He's from the orphanage," Junaidah replied. "He's following us for the day."

"Just for today? He's such a well-mannered boy. Why don't you keep him for one week?"

Junaidah had not considered it. But why not? Already she was observing the effect the boy's presence had on Haikel—arousing in him a competitive nature, an eagerness to please. She recalled Haikel's demands for the orange *baju kurung* in the morning, and suddenly the exchange of the clothes between the boys assumed a significance for her. Maybe siblings had a mutually tempering effect on each other: Haikel would learn to be more generous, and Mydeen would be drawn out of his shell. The receptionist had supplied Junaidah very little information about Mydeen. Was he a real orphan, abandoned after birth? Or was he sent to live there because of a broken family? Were his parents in jail? What was life like in the orphanage?

She thought about the routine that they had conducted just before leaving the house—did they have such a thing at the orphanage too? Every Hari Raya, Junaidah's husband would set up a self-timed camera in the living room to take the family portrait. But before that, they would participate in a ritual of forgiveness. Even though Hari Raya did not mark the Muslim New Year, it had always felt that way to Junaidah. In the morning, those who went for the *Aidilfitri* prayers in the mosques sought clemency from Allah. And then later, the members of her family would solemnly seek the forgiveness from their seniors. Time moves in a single direction. How else could one start anew, other than through absolution by another, an annual clearing of accounts? Hari Raya helped to formalize a necessary moment which might have otherwise been too difficult, too awkward. That remorseful sobbing while clasping another's hand was rescued from theatrics by the fact that it was a scene that happened in every living room across the island on that one morning.

Junaidah looked around her. There were six Tupperware jars on the table, each one placed on a white doily. They were filled with the usual Hari Raya fare: pineapple tarts, layered cake, cashew cookies, almond biscuits, glazed cornflakes, shrimp rolls. She wondered when Mydeen would come out of the room to sample them. The living room was sparsely decorated; two vases of plastic flowers provided some cheer, the curtains, cushions and carpet were new. A wall was painted lime green, which provided Junaidah with yet another example of how some Malay families were colour-blind. They were kampung colours, she thought, their brashness perhaps suitable to mask the drabness of wooden walls, but entirely inappropriate for a HDB flat.

She gazed at the television. Every year, after a few conversations, everybody's eyes would converge on the screen. The Hari Raya Variety Show was something everyone could agree upon; men preferred the news, the women preferred dramas. A new singer, someone probably unearthed during an idol-style competition, would sing a Hari Raya standard. There were cutaways to well-wishes from local personalities, like that singer who started covering up when her age advanced, but in her own flamboyant way: no *tudung* and long-sleeved *baju* for her. Instead, she wore a turban, and elbow-length gloves, which made her look like an exotic fortune-teller. There would be comedy sketches, and everyone would agree that

P. Ramlee's comedies were better, more unforced, his formidable deadpan leaving these mug-faced exertions in the dust.

Her mother-in-law started serving lunch. She had cooked her specialty: *sambal goreng*, a Javanese beef and vegetable sauté, in coconut-based gravy. The children were summoned to wash their hands. Haikel was panting when he got out of the room.

"What have you been doing, Haikel?"

"Playing monster-monster."

Junaidah had seen a version of this game played once—one of the older children would adopt a fearful character, while the rest would huddle in a corner, sometimes shielding themselves with pillows or the edge of a mattress. They might sometimes launch futile guerilla attacks, throwing useless projectiles like balls of paper at their tormentor. Junaidah remembered one of the adults scolding Haikel for playing the game because it would give her child 'nightmares' later on—a euphemism, as Junaidah had later realised, for bedwetting.

"Where's Mydeen?" she asked.

"I don't know."

"Isn't he with you?"

"No."

Junaidah looked into the room. There were five children inside, two girls and three boys. Mydeen was nowhere to be seen. Junaidah asked her husband if he had seen Mydeen. He answered no, too. She looked into the remaining bedroom and the toilet. He wasn't under the bed, behind the curtains. The storeroom? Nothing but boxes, a vacuum cleaner. She walked to the front door. The gates had been left open—but to receive visitors, not eject strangers. She looked at the swarm of footwear at the threshold. What was Mydeen wearing on his feet? She put her fingers at her temple and tried to recall. She picked up a small pair of black sandals and shouted into the living room.

"Whose sandals are these?"

"Those are mine," one of the boys answered.

Junaidah asked Haikel again, "When was the last time you saw him?"

"He was inside the room with us just now."

"Were you playing with him?"

"No."

"So what was he doing inside?"

"He was just watching us."

"Why didn't you play together?"

"He's not our friend."

Junaidah was stunned. She grabbed Haikel by the shoulders and shook him.

"Do you know whose *baju kurung* you're wearing?" she asked, bitterly. "I asked you to take care of him, didn't I? What's wrong with you, Haikel? Why are you like this?"

Haikel was starting to cry. Her husband said, "What are you doing? Don't blame the boy."

"He's somebody's child. He was put in our care. What will they say now?"

"Who?"

Junaidah wanted to answer, his parents, you fool, but that answer would make her the foolish one, not him. For whatever reason, Mydeen had lost his parents. They were the void in his life. But what void in whose life does the missing orphan make? Emptiness upon emptiness, one void seeking union with another. The boy who had held Junaidah's hand would forever be beyond her reach.

"Let's go look for him," Junaidah's husband said. "I don't think he could have gone very far."

A search party was formed. The grandmother would look after the children, and the adults would comb the block. Junaidah and her husband decided to scour the void deck. The rest would sweep across the corridors, knocking from door to door, asking if they had seen a Jawi Peranakan boy in a sky blue *baju kurung*.

While taking the lift down, Junaidah found herself sobbing uncontrollably. All she wanted was to bring the boy into the fold of a family, a typical Malay family. But now it seemed as if her family wasn't typical at all. It was too self-absorbed in its own image to pay attention to the boy. What Junaidah did not anticipate was that it was through the boy's eyes that the real image of their family was formed. They had been judged and now, deserted.

They walked around the void deck, with Junaidah calling out Mydeen's name. She did not want to sound angry at all in case it frightened him; neither did she want to sound too pleading either, because she had to cut her voice off from the panicked hope that was its source. She understood then the double vowels in his name, of how her voice had to reach across its length; built into its spelling was the sound of a wail.

There was a group of people at a Senior Citizens' corner who stared at her. Junaidah's husband had a word with them. They shook their heads, and Junaidah took a deep breath. If Mydeen appeared, it was not because he had heard her summons. It would be because the sound of her voice had congealed in the air to become him. Now all she needed to do was to find the right tone, the right volume, the right…

Her husband pointed him out to Junaidah. At the car park, a family, uniformly attired in shiny grey, was walking across to the main road. In their midst, in his sky blue *baju kurung*, was Mydeen. Junaidah and her husband chased after them.

"Mydeen, where did you go?" Junaidah asked.

The men from both families exchanged greetings. As it turned out, the family in grey had found Mydeen taking the lift alone.

"He followed our family last year," the father said. "Such a coincidence. We asked him where he came from, but he said he couldn't remember which house you were at."

"He was with you last year?" Junaidah's husband asked.

"Yes. The children remember him. You remember *abang* Mydeen right? All of you, wearing pink colour?"

The two children nodded. They were younger than Mydeen, probably still in kindergarten. Junaidah looked at them. The boy had a little tail of hair sticking out from the back of his head. The girl, despite her young age, had red lipstick on. The father reeked of strong, unfiltered cigarettes. You did not choose your families. But Mydeen had chosen.

The mother said, "You know boys his age, they like to play with the lift. We were just about to take him back to the orphanage." Unlike

Junaidah, she wasn't wearing a tudung, her henna-dyed hair blazing under the sun.

"What do you mean send him back? We'll take him visiting again, just like last year!" said the father. "You're so lucky you found him. Don't stray again *ah*, Mydeen?"

Not as lucky as you, Junaidah thought to herself. "I think we'll go up now," she said. "Everyone is so worried."

Junaidah took Mydeen's hand and led him back towards her mother-in-law's block. She promised herself that she would not let him out of her sight for the rest of the day. While walking back, Mydeen had turned around and waved at the family in grey. "Bye bye!" he said to them. "Selamat Hari Raya!" The two children echoed him back.

It was already night when they finally got home. They had made two visits for the day: first, to Teban Gardens, and then later to Yishun, where Junaidah's parents lived. When Mydeen was brought back to the house at Teban Gardens, everyone had fussed over him. Junaidah wondered if Mydeen was used to being the centre of attention at these gatherings. She had thought that it was better for him to blend into the background, among the children, indistinguishable; did she not, at times, also enquire whose child belonged to whom? She did not want the boy to turn out as an exhibit. But evidently Mydeen knew his place.

They made him try all the *kuih*, and asked him which one was his favourite. One of Haikel's uncles taught him a hand-illusion, involving a thumb that seemed to be severed from the hand. When it was time to leave, some of the relatives gave him two paper envelopes of money, instead of one. Before leaving, everyone queued in front of the grandmother, and took turns to kneel in front of her, asking that their sins for the past year be reset to zero. When it came to Mydeen's turn, the grandmother patted his head and waved him away, saying, "You've done no wrong, child. We just met you. But you must come back next year."

At Yishun, it was a similar affair, the relatives doting on Mydeen, but never to the point of smothering him with needless curiosity. They played a cartoon on the DVD player, and the children crowded in front of the television set. Sometimes Junaidah allowed herself to observe the proceedings just like she had seen it on television, the orphan boy surrounded by his surrogate family, the Hari Raya diorama of crystal glasses filled with Coke, little girls dressed like dolls in mini *kebayas*, the gold and silver threads on the *songket* worn by the men, and in the evening, the fairy lights turned on at the window, bathing the balcony with alternating waves of jeweled colours. But she would snap out of it, suddenly reminded that the boy was on loan, and that all this would vanish for him by the next day—the money in his pocket and his *baju kurung* being the only mementoes smuggled out from a dream.

They decided not to return the boy to the orphanage that very evening. Junaidah made the necessary call to the orphanage, and then brought out an extra towel and toothbrush for the boy. By the end of the night, Mydeen was playing the PSP, with Haikel peering over his shoulder and coaching him. Junaidah wondered if Haikel would ask for Mydeen after the latter had gone back. They had spent so little time together. But what if they had spent more? What was his place in their lives, and their place in his? And what if he ran away from them again?

Junaidah thought about Hari Raya next year. Haikel would be one year older. And so would the boy. But she knew she would not go to the orphanage to ask for him. She thought about the other family they had met, blessed by their unexpected reunion with Mydeen. She wistfully wondered whether such a thing could happen to her family too. For a lift door to open and reveal him, as if he was the answer to some unanswerable longing. Junaidah decided that she would return Mydeen the next day, and with this decision came the knowledge that she would think of him every Hari Raya for the rest of her life. Later that night, she rose from her bed, unable to sleep, her head filled with images of a lift, black sandals, a *baju kurung* like a shred of blue among grey clouds. She entered Haikel's room, where Mydeen was sleeping on a spare mattress. A fan was humming drowsily. The time was 11 P.M.; Hari Raya was not over yet. Junaidah knelt down and rested her hand at the edge of Mydeen's foot. She was asking for his forgiveness but no words came out of her mouth.

BARD BY NUMBERS: THE FUNDAMENTALS
Jeffery Lim

Bard's Digest presents
BARD BY NUMBERS: THE FUNDAMENTALS
by Mr. Penglipur Pertama of Singapura, Contributor to the *Sejarah Melayu* (The Malay Annals)
NOT TO BE SOLD TO A NON-BARD

This Week's serialised instalment—No.7: "Gloss, Detail and You."

I was lecturing a class of aspiring bards when one of my more avid students accused me of meddling with facts, of doctoring my histories. He said he couldn't stomach the blatant use of 'creative liberties'. It made him feel cheap, made him feel like a liar.

Apparently, his father had actually lived through the events described in my bestseller. His father, a sailor on the ship which had brought my master and I to Singapore so many years ago, recalled that the events I described in my story were very different from the truth.

"My father says the Prince was a bungling idiot."

"Wen," I said, "That bungling idiot is now King so I'd be careful about what I say about him."

He didn't get the hint. "And this animal they caught. It *wasn't* a lion. I've *seen* lions. They don't have white heads, black chests and red manes. My father says it was really some kind of baboon."

There was a nervous laugh in the classroom. I thought it best to get him to the point I knew was coming.

"So what are you saying?"

"I'm saying you made up the fact that it was a lion and so that the Prince had an excuse to call this island the Lion City. That you've made everything up just for show."

"And you don't like that?" I asked.

You see, every class has them. An apprentice who wants to compile the most *accurate* and *comprehensive* account of a signature event. Someone who honestly believes that by being complete, future generations will thank and honour them and lay offerings on their altars when they are gone.

My advice: *"Be a philosopher, not a bard."*

For bards, detail is to be manipulated, not documented. History is about evoking feelings and memories, not compiling them.

Now in *this* week's serialised installment, I'll discuss the fundamentals of making detail work to your advantage and how *you* as the struggling bard can make a name for yourself by being good at this. I shall, of course, be referring to my own experiences for illustration.

Why manage detail?

We answer this by referring to some fundamentals raised in previous issues. There's Fundamental #3: "Perception is limited and memory is flawed." Only a fraction of what happened is seen and only a fraction of *that* fraction is retained.[1]

It's easy to forget this when you're composing. And don't forget Fundamental #1: "Opinion is necessary for feeling; feeling is necessary for good writing; opinion makes bias inevitable and so bias is important for good writing." Something that no bard can afford to ignore.[2]

Now putting both these principles together, it's obvious: the complete and exhaustive account *doesn't exist*.

---

1 See *Bard's Digest #317* - pg 22; Bard By Numbers: Fundamental #3 "Make flawed memory work for and not against you."
2 See *Bard's Digest #315* - pg 1; Bard By Numbers: Fundamental #1 "Take a Stand."

It's a fiction. There's another reason for managing detail and it springs from another fundamental already discussed: Fundamental #2: "Know What Your Client Wants."

After all, every bard works for a client. If not the hero you follow, then the audience you are addressing. Every good bard knows that too much detail can offend your client or bore the audience.

Tip #1: Using your knowledge of what your Client wants.

Although we've discussed this in issue #316,[3] it's worth mentioning it here again because knowing what your client wants is the first step in learning how to select detail.

Every bard serves a master. It's our job. This is how we make a living. If you want to live well, and you want to live long, give your client *exactly* what he wants.

In my case, my client (and subject) was Prince (now King) Sang Nila Utama, also known as Sri Tri Buana, the founder of Singapore, the Lion City. He was the Prince of Palembang, the son of an incompetent military king, Raja Chulan, whose most famous exploit was to bungle a purported invasion of China (but more on that later).

Like most noblemen, Utama wanted to look heroic. You'll find that when you're working for a noble ruler, they need all the credibility they can get to govern. For some reason, it's always an uphill struggle. Royal families have a way of becoming complete and utter disgraces to the nation, not to mention a waste of taxpayers' money.

Well, all the raw material I had was the story of his life.

And just to give you an idea about how difficult that made things, let me show you what I had to work with:

Fact #1—Utama's father, Raja Chulan, was the world's biggest idiot. Believing himself to be a descendant of Alexander the Great, he decided to invade China without quite knowing where it was. The Emperor of China sent some ships manned by toothless old men, rusted iron ingots,

---

[3] See *Bard's Digest #315* - pg 16; Bard By Numbers: Fundamental #2 "Your Client & You."

orange trees and a message. The old men told Raja Chulan that China was so far away, they'd actually grown old. Their iron had rusted and their orange saplings grown into trees on their voyage back. And the Raja, rather than trusting his fellow sailors who knew better, decided that he'd believe these suspicious old men who would ordinarily have struck someone as being senile or suffering from sunstroke.

Fact #2—Utama's escape. Where do I begin? If I were Alexander the Great, I'd be *spinning* in my grave. This Utama, he appoints his three best friends as general, chamberlain and admiral. They lose every battle they fight and soon his hometown of Palembang is besieged. They escape by crawling out of a sewage tunnel and get into a ship.

Fact #3—The storm. And then Utama's not blessed with heroic luck either. While at sea, a ferocious storm rises and threatens to sink the ship. Our hero starts throwing gold, weapons, things of value into the sea. Even injured men, women and children are kicked off into the surf in his frenzy to stay afloat. Not that it was working, mind you. We were still sinking like a rock. And then, unexpectedly, he drops his crown into the water. Only self-preservation keeps him from diving after it. And then, miraculously, the moment the crown sinks, the freak storm suddenly stops.

Fact #4 - The Lion. Once, we're on the island, our hero's moping. He's thinking about what a failure he is. His thoughts are interrupted by this strange looking animal that suddenly appears. It's the size of a goat, it's got a black body, a white head and a red mane of some kind. It's not really scary but he screams all the same. One of his men catches it and we think is good eating so we keep it in a cage. What do we call it? To be honest, I was thinking along the lines of "deformed dog" but one of the generals says it's a lion. Why? Because he'd heard someone somewhere that lions were "big pussycats". So Utama's mighty pleased with himself and thinks this is a good omen. He calls the island 'Singa' (Lion) and then decides to build a city (Pura). So now, we've found the lion city—Singapore. And while everybody's celebrating, the creature escapes from its cage.

That's the raw material. A natural farce. No one could have blamed me for a few creative liberties. Especially in the light of how I was called in to 'set the record straight', with the young Prince turning to me and saying:

"I want to be a hero. And if I'm not impressed by your story, I'm going to relocate your testicles."

Generally, if your subject is a hopeless incompetent and his enemies are smarter, more eloquent, then you must cast your subject in a tragedy. The loser you follow is always a tragic hero. In my case, the hero survives against all odds. He lucks out in a bad situation.

So I suppose I had to cast him as a favourite of the gods. I had to go for a tale where the hero rebuilds his life against all odds. I had to stretch for themes of heroic resilience.

Bearing in mind the oaths of silence that all bards take, let's look at how I touched the story up:

Tip #2—You don't have to do too much.
The good bard knows when there's been too much doctoring of detail. Only use the brushwork for the really important bits.

Illustration 1: the father's story. You'll notice that I left the father's story of his bungled invasion in. Why on earth, you ask, would you want our hero associated with such an incompetent?

Well firstly, Raja Chulan is not my client. He doesn't relocate my testicles if I leave something true in. The less you have to fudge, the better. Secondly, it's always good to show the son as being a radical improvement on the father. Given the way his son turned out, I think the prince would appreciate *any* favourable contrast.

On the other hand, I've dressed up the story of Rajah Chulan and his wife because that concerns the Prince's birth. So I have called his mother a daughter of the sea (a mermaid), to give my client some mystique. Also, I've left in his father's assertion that he was a descendant of Alexander the Great. Emphasising the prince's genealogy is good press.

Tip #3—Ask yourself what detail can you lose/play up?
You can't drop details if losing them means you lose the flow of your story. If you need a scene or a detail to explain why something important in the

story happens later on, then you're stuck with that detail. You might lose details that leave the story sounding *incredible,* but NEVER lose anything that make the story *illogical.*

Illustration 2a: a detail I couldn't lose and why. Utama meets the Lion. That's an important detail. After all, the island is called Singa Pura, 'Lion City' and so it will seem illogical to call it that if you don't say that there was a lion around on the island when we landed after the storm.

On the other hand, you *should* lose events which, even with blatant fudging, would be disastrous to the prince's credibility. This is material you've got to lose in order to stay true to your client's wishes.

Illustration 2b: the gaps I could live with, I could lose the Prince's bungling of his campaigns and his ignominious flight from Palembang through a sewage hole. I should also forget about the incompetence of his advisors—since the Prince was responsible for appointing them.

Now the fact that he lost his Crown *by falling over* in the storm is embarrassing. Not only that, it's an ill omen. So I had to come up with an alternative explanation (see Tip #4). And of course, never mention that you were there, all good bards try to keep themselves of the story—otherwise it gives the audience the suspicion that you are biased.

Tip #4 — Filling in any gaps you can't avoid with gloss: creative liberties. Once you take out the undesirable details, you'll be immediately aware of some omissions. Glaring gaps. For example, the Prince's loss of his crown. The question that a listener might have is why didn't he have it when he came to the island?

My job was simple. Make the loss of the crown a remarkable feat of heroism. Also, don't be afraid of the gaps, use them to your advantage. Just bear in mind that every bit of gloss must serve your client's purpose. And be colourful. The audience *is* listening.

Illustration 3: the loss of the Crown. In my record, Utama doesn't trip over and drop his crown into the ocean. Instead, he *sacrifices* his crown to save everyone on the ship — you know, as an *offering,* to the gods. And just to add a little more magnanimity, I avoided any mention of him throwing over helpless women and children to save the ship.

Illustration 4: the Lion. If Utama wanted a lion, I say we give him a lion. Here of course, I was stretching the imagination. I'd never seen a lion in my life so all I could do was to describe the animal the way I saw it and hope I wasn't misinformed when the general said that he remembered that lions were a big pussycats.

I do admit however that it felt better to call the island Singapore instead of 'Baboon City'.

Let's recall issue #316 and Fundamental #5: believability not veracity — attractiveness, not truth. The story that's attractive, if not contradicted, becomes the truth.

Use attractive details as part of your gloss over things.

The Fundamental of the Instalment: Okay, we've reviewed our four tips for this issue: know what your client wants; don't do too much; lose some details and play up others; fill in any gaps with reasonable gloss. Now let's look at the fundamental of this installment which should now be apparent:

Detail is everything.

DON'T let any detail escape into the story if you can't explain it away. It's because of this I decided that it'd be better not to try and describe the capture and escape of the lion. After all, anyone who'd seen a real lion might smell a rat and I figure the less he knows about the lion, the better.

TURNING A BLIND EYE
O Thiam Chin

Aunt Mei Ying lost her right eye to the blunt end of a rice ladle wielded by her husband during a violent argument eleven years ago. She claimed she did more damage to him when she kicked him in the groin and called him a weakling. My uncle hated to be thought of as less than a man, which was exactly why she went for the kill. Yet Aunt Mei Ying didn't leave my uncle; they continued to love hard, and madly, until he died of testicular cancer three years ago.

"He had many good qualities," Aunt Mei Ying said at his wake, tears flowing freely from her one good eye.

I have always admired my Aunt Mei Ying for her ability to see more with her one eye than most of us in the family can see with two. To my third uncle, who gambled too much, she admonished: "Why do you do this to your wife and daughters? Stop before it's too late. Otherwise, you will have nothing left but regret. Think. Think carefully." To a recently widowed younger aunt, she put a hand on her shoulder and spoke softly: "Cry now. Cry hard. Know that you will be stronger, later. You are a woman. You will make it through." To me, at a family gathering to celebrate our grandma's seventy-fifth birthday, Aunt Mei Ying said: "Leave him. Leave him now. He is bad for you. Open your eyes. See him for who he is."

She had led me to a corner of the packed living room, away from all the noise, the loud chatter, held my arm, her one eye piercing both of mine. I tried to draw back; the scooped-out hollow of her missing eye was relieved only by a mish-mash of flesh that was at once fascinating and frightening. Her grip on me tightened. "You cannot pretend everything is okay. I can see what is happening and it is bad. Do you understand? You have to leave him. You must leave."

Aunt Mei Ying loosened her grip as I struggled to respond, searching for words, a plausible story, meanings, but nothing came out. In the end, I sighed and stepped away from her. "I'm okay. Everything's okay."

The first time Teck hit me, he punched me in the face and knocked me out cold. I woke up a few hours later, bones stiff, my head throbbing in pain. Teck had passed out beside me, lying in a pool of vomit that was congealing on the floor. His fists were clenched, the knuckles on his right hand already bruising.

He claimed he didn't know what he was doing, that he was drunk, too drunk to know what was going on. Then he was pleading, calling himself an asshole. He broke down in front of me, dropped his face into his open hands, and cried. He reached out, throwing his arms blindly around me, holding me like his whole life depended on it. He begged for forgiveness, tears streaming down his face, his voice dry and hoarse. As I looked into his eyes, I saw something new, something raw, like an exposed nerve, bloodied, pulsating, and it terrified me.

He tried his best to stay sober, and for a while, maybe a week or so, he didn't touch a drop. It made him irritable and restless. He found it hard to sleep. I could hear him in the living room, prowling about, switching the television on and off, the loud blare of discordant music, voices and mechanical laughter reaching me in the darkness of the bedroom. I could hear the glass—vodka? gin? whisky?—striking heavily on the glass side table. Pulling the bed covers close, I listened cautiously for any movement or sound coming from the living room.

In the morning, exhausted, I took the scissors from under my pillow and put it back in the sewing basket in the dresser drawer before going into the living room to clean up the mess, trying not to disturb Teck, who was slumped unconscious on the sofa. It was heartbreaking to see him so helpless, so lost.

"If you ever hit me again, I will kill you," I said. It was a lie, and he knew it, and soon he would hit me again, and I'd let him.

When Teck broke my arm after he slammed me against the wall, Aunt Mei Ying came and took me away. She didn't even give me time to pack anything I needed. Like Lot's wife, I looked back at the apartment and felt forlorn, a crumbling pillar of salt.

"No. You will not go back." She dragged me away as if rescuing me from a raging fire.

"But..."

"No. You will not see him again. He is no good for you. He is a bastard! Can you not see?"

For two months, I stayed with Aunt Mei Ying in her sparse two-bedroom flat in the ageing neighbourhood of Ang Mo Kio. Time passed slowly and gradually my fears began to fade.

Aunt Mei Ying fed me well, made sure I had everything I needed, and gave me space and privacy to think, to recover, though I could feel that her eye never really left me, as if waiting for me to falter or fall.

Finally, and I knew he would, Teck turned up, hammering on the door, screaming, ferocious, like an angry bear ripping apart a tree. I put my hand on the cool surface of the spare bedroom door and held my body still, the air in the room charged with a suffocating tension. Aunt Mei Ying's voice was firm, even, in control. "She is not going back with you."

"You fucking bitch! Let me see her. I need to see her."

I could feel the front door shaking with another round of kicks.

"No! Go away! She will never see you again. I will not allow it."

Teck raged like a tempest. Aunt Mei Ying did not yield. I opened the bedroom door a crack and could see her facing the dead-bolted door, a stout defender. Then, just as suddenly as it began, the storm died away. Teck's delirious shouting ceased; silence enveloped the house.

Aunt Mei Ying tapped on the bedroom door a few minutes later. I was still standing behind the door, immobilised with fear.

"I'll cook dinner now. Will you help me, please?"

"Why didn't you leave Uncle Seng when he poked out your eye?"

I asked Aunt Mei Ying as we sat at the dining table breaking the long leafy Stalks of *caixin* into smaller pieces in preparation for dinner.

"He was a good man, that's why," she said, as if she were simply stating a well-known fact, before putting the leafy greens into a big ceramic bowl. I could see she was thinking, maybe trying to recall something from the past.

"But how did you know he was good?"

"He was very sad over what he did, taking out my eye. He didn't mean to do it. He didn't want to see me afterwards. He didn't know what to say."

"I didn't know that."

"He locked himself in the house and wouldn't come out. He wouldn't see anyone. I was in the hospital, but someone told me what was happening. He stopped eating, wouldn't eat for two whole weeks. Two weeks. Such a long time to go without food. When I got out of the hospital and went home, what I saw pained my heart. He was so skinny, nothing but bones. I think he lost almost thirteen kilos. When he saw me, he tried to stand, but fell down. Then I knew he was a good man. Then I knew it in my heart."

Aunt Mei Ying sighed, looking out the kitchen window as if she could peer across the wide expanse of time to see the past. "He was so weak. He couldn't even stand. I held him up, I held him so he wouldn't fall."

She broke a stalk of *cai xin* with a crisp crunch, put it into the ceramic bowl, got up and took the bowl to the kitchen. I listened to the rush of tap water as she washed the vegetables and clattered around the wok.

I found many ways to justify Teck's violent behaviour. He had an emotionally distant father who disciplined first with his fists, and then with the stinging whip of silence. His work as a coffee-shop helper meant he was subjected, day in, day out, to the humiliation of often rude and hostile customers who looked down on him and his menial job. After a while, I didn't bother with the reasons anymore. It could have been anything.

If he had a bad day at work, I'd stay out of his way, slipping out of the house to buy something I didn't need at the mini-mart or just hang around under our block of flats.

Sometimes I'd just wander around the housing estate, walking from street to street, waiting for the hours to pass, waiting for him to pass out.

My timing was never perfect and I'd come back and find him at the height of his drunken craze, and things would become unavoidable. The best I could do was to try to contain the damage. A few slaps on the face could be easily camouflaged with thick foundation or make-up. Likewise for the cuts and bruises on the arms, thighs or legs. Punches to my chest and stomach were still okay because they were not visible. At times, I found myself subconsciously directing Teck's attention, and punches, to these parts of my body. After exhausting his anger, he would totter into our bedroom and slump on the bed, dead to the world. Then I'd begin my night work of repairs, with copious application of ointments and rubs to my body and face.

It is funny how one can slowly get used to anything; sooner or later, I think, indifference does set in, like a stranger taking over a house.

Sometimes I have dreams that get stuck in my head long after I'm awakened by them. In these dreams, I become a different woman, a woman of many parts that pull in every direction, each crying for dominance, significance, each offering ability or strength beyond the usual means.

Courage normally takes centre stage. I remember drawing out a long knife, plunging it deep into the massive beast-like body of Teck, gushing Niles of blood.

We fight, we rage; our sweat-glistening bodies entangle like a *coil* of tightly-wound rope, snapping, releasing, grinding, my feet struggling to stand firm on slippery ground, my heart thumping like crazy, fuelling my veins with new blood.

As my strength grows, Teck's wanes. I push on, *seizing* every opportunity to overcome, to subdue. When he blinks, wiping away the blood from a deep cut on his forehead, I plunge my knife into his eye and gouge it out. Then I swing around and, with a clean slice, remove his head. He crashes to the floor like a mighty tower.

I hold his head above me, blood pouring from *it,* baptizing me. I lick my lips, savouring the sweet victory, the goodness of It.

In other dreams, Teck holds up my severed head, which swings from the hair bunched in his closed fist. I gnash my teeth, filling the air with livid growls. I look down at him, my thoughts draining away fast, and meet his eyes, daring him, taunting him. He laughs, his eyes closed in deep merriment, and his laughter washes away all other sounds, like a flood sweeping everything before *it*.

More and more, when I wake up from these dreams, I can feel every muscle in my body stretched achingly taut, and my fingers still tingling from the grip of an invisible knife in one hand, the weight of an imaginary head in the other.

"You must decide," Aunt Mei Ying said. "If you decide to go back, I won't stop you. You're an adult, old enough to decide."

She stood in the doorway of my bedroom, watching me pack my things. Three months had passed.

"Maybe he has changed," I said.

"You don't know that."

"I just know," I replied, finally meeting her eye. We stood facing each other in complete silence, in mutual frustration.

"Go then. Go now. But you don't know what you're doing. You think he has changed, but he will never change. You are blind, but I can see. I see you hopeless, hurt by him, but you don't want to learn from your mistakes. I won't stop you. Go."

"Aunt Mei Ying, please understand…"

"I can't understand. You are a smart girl. Why do you want to go back?" She was exasperated; I could hear *it* in the strain of her voice.

"He's my husband, I know him; he will change. I know he will…"

Aunt Mei Ying opened her mouth, but restrained herself, biting back the words. Her forehead was creased with deep furrows. The fluorescent light overhead cast a deep shadow in the hollow of her missing eye; I saw a mysterious void and felt my whole being drawn towards it.

I finished packing my bag. She stepped aside. I slipped past her and left the house.

Looping in my mind *is* a succession of images, a horrifying dream-like mirage.

I enter the flat and see Teck lying on the sofa, looking listlessly out the window. His attention shifts to me, but he doesn't seem to register my presence. I could have been just a passing shadow in the room. He brings his cigarette to his mouth, takes a deep drag, puffing out a cloud of smoke that obscures his face.

I walk up, stand in front of him, throw the bunch of house keys on his chest and say: "So now what?"

Teck jerks up from the sofa, brings his hand to my neck, his fingers closing around it. He tightens his grip, choking the air out of me. I try to pull his hand away but his hold is too strong.

He rams me against the wall and puts his face close to mine hissing, "If you ever leave again, I will kill you!"

I spit at him. My spittle is strung across his eyes. With his free hand, he wipes it away and strikes me hard across the face. Once, twice, three times. I taste blood as it fills my mouth, the sting spreading across my face like wildfire. I spit a ball of blood in his face, and try to dig my fingers into the whites of his eyes. He flinches and drops me to the floor.

On all fours, I crawl to the kitchen, escaping, breathless, my vision blurring.

I feel a sharp rug on my scalp as he pulls my hair, then a rain of punches land across my head and back. I fall flat and hard on the floor. He drags me by the hair to the kitchen windows, throws them open and hoists me to my feet. He tries to push me out the window.

"No, please, Teck… no"

I grab hold of his body and lock my arms around his chest.

His muscles are tense-hard, as if cut from marble. He tries to pry open my arms, but I hold even tighter, whispering, "Teck, no… no… no, Teck…"

He puts up a fierce struggle, but slowly his body begins to surrender to mine.

I desperately seek out his eyes, and for a very brief moment, I glimpse the old Teck, the one that I had loved and lost, many years ago, recalling our first night in the flat and his embrace and kiss, such a long, honest kiss. "This is it. Our own home. Ours. Finally."

I drop my arms and Teck stumbles away from me.

He leans against the side wall, his face a mess of tears and blood; it is a face I know by heart. I look into his eyes, so blank and sorrowful, and can't find anything but a consuming emptiness, a dark lake, impenetrable. He looks straight at me and I know he doesn't see me at all; he's gone, his mind has slipped away.

I struggle to my feet, hobble to the sink and find half a bottle of turpentine under it. I take it, pick up a box of matches lying next to the stove, and limp towards Teck. I pour the turpentine down his legs. Teck wears a look of incomprehension, an almost-childlike curiosity, and cocks his head to one side. The viscous liquid glistens like a fine layer of molten gold on his powerful calves and thighs. I strike a match and toss it into the turpentine pooling around his bare feet. Orange-blue licks of flames jump with agitation, like a net of trapped fish.

Teck's face registers, slowly, what is happening and he leaps up, pushing his body away as if trying to escape his burning legs. I step aside and watch his dancing, gyrating figure, the flames flapping like flowing incandescent robes around him.

The air fills with the gelatinous smell of burning flesh, not unlike pork left too long on the barbeque, thick, sticky, savoury. I wet my lips in reflex.

Teck gives up and collapses. I go up to him now and take off my T-shirt, beating out the flames. Tiny bits of wet flesh come off with each stroke, spattering all over the kitchen floor.

By the time I'm done, the lower half of Teck's body resembles an amateurish watercolour painting with garish dips, smears and swirls overlapping, melting into one another, a frightening, ravishing flesh-scape. It looks soft, raw, pliable, a torment, and I sit staring at it, unable to break away.

My hands are splotched a numbing red, my skin prickling with a rude burning sensation. I can see Teck's chest rising and falling, and I place my hand over his heart. He is still alive.

Maybe this time it'll work. Maybe we can start over again.

IT'S A WONDERFUL LIE
Felix Cheong

I

Tonight, everything looks brighter, sweeter, clearer. When nothing matters and nothing distracts, you can part the crowd like a scalpel sensing bone and skin.

You pass the shopping centre's redemption counter, where a snake of people awaits that one shot at luck, that one chance to be redeemed. And for what, a keychain, a purse, maybe dinner for two?

With a sneer, you notice how the redemption counter resides beside a complacent Christmas tree reaching for the sky. "Humbug!" you almost snarl, but you know better than to invite irony.

These are moments of hyper-clarity, as though you are on ice, like seeing things for the first time without meaning to, without knowing why. And suddenly, you remember who you are.

You are the boy who went to church seven times a week, flowering a prayer to St. Jude for every exam question too tough to answer.

You are the teenager who pored three weeks over a 1,000-piece jigsaw of *The Last Supper*, seeking the face of Christ in the browns and blacks.

You are the young man who majored in philosophy and knew God was nothing but a man-made charm. You are a child of the world, chasing paper and living it up, obvious as money, transparent as wine.

You are flotsam. You are a grain of sand in eternity. You are a sleepwalker's hesitant steps. You are Macbeth gone too far who cannot turn back.

This is your confession. You have done nothing to counter the nothingness. Nothing will redeem nothing.

II

I flinch as my coffin feeds the fire. So, this is cremation, the tail end of creation. But I can barely feel the heat as it eats its way through my skin.

Afterwards, there'll be coffee and tearing tales, gathered like so many starry eyes, so many sunset remembrances about me. There'll be time to eavesdrop on versions and revisions of stories.

For now, I watch these flames mulling over flesh and wood, hungry and generous to a fault.

III

It's been two minutes since my body broke down as my death broke through. On the eve of Christmas too. What ass luck. What arse timing.

Timing has always been my problem. Never knew when to cut more slack, or cut the thread. Dead thirty years too soon.

I guess you die the death you deserve, for nothing else will be as equal.

That's my body, if you still haven't noticed it, slumped over the steering wheel, cracked head over heels. Mortally brought to rest—remember Newton's First Law of Motion?—by a lamppost dressed as a Christmas tree, can you beat it? I beat one light, only to be beaten by another.

Reader, meet the late James. James, meet your reader, alive and still smoking like a misfired gun.

IV

I was on my way to work. *The Grateful Dead* were playing on the radio like there was no tomorrow. I was recalling my life, wife, strife—they rhymed and somehow met at the back of my mind.

Shall I tell you the same old story, in so many words?

"James, why can't you for once...?"

"Jannie, why must you be so...?"

"James, are you listening to me? You're not the same person I married!"

"Jannie, get the hell out of my life!"

Yes, hell broke loose that day. And what remains of love are three quick flash cards staring back at me blankly—'glows', 'goes' and 'ghosts'. What is marriage but a pair of handcuffs?

V

They've all arrived here, relatively friends and friendly relatives, decked out in various combinations of black, white and grey. It's not that the Christmas spirit has come too late but that Ash Wednesday has sprung too early.

Isn't that Celine on whom I had a crush a long while ago? What, only two classmates from my secondary school days? It won't be too long for them too, for I can see a pair of dark wings hovering over them. And where are my golfing buddies, Shaun and Lee? Surely a funeral can't take up that much of their time?

Someone has turned the volume off. I can't hear the eulogy by my good friend, David, holding back between the lines. I can't hear the priest sending me off with his watery blessing of peace. I can't hear the howls of Jannie and my mother, hugged as one in grief.

I can see you, Jannie. I'm not dead yet. I'm driftwood between worlds. I didn't mean what I said. I couldn't say what I meant.

VI

I remember what my father told me once. "Be careful what you say because when you're dead, not even God's lovely angels can retrieve it." That must have been when I was six or seven, shortly before his heart failed.

I don't remember much of the wake and funeral, the way my four-year-old son will probably not remember mine. What mourners mistook for a thoughtful little boy meditating over his father's body, stiff and starched, was merely me imagining fairies fluttering over it, trying to mine from his mouth the many tongue lashings he had unleashed on me.

And so my last words to Jannie would remain, such dead knots twisted into her memories.

VII

I remember bringing my son to the Cathedral of the Good Shepherd once. We knelt at the altar but Bryan started praying loudly, his voice echoing through the quiet afternoon.

"Shh... Not so loud. God can hear you in the silence of your heart."

"Dada, then God's hearing must be very sharp!"

VIII

There must have been a moment when I wished I could be undone like a child, vanished a week or two and be the spectator of my divided life. Watch from the sidelines how the pieces fall into place as the place falls to pieces.

There must have been a Faustian moment when it was easy to relieve my hands of control, step on the gas and wipe the tears away. Let it all spin beyond me—memories, names, places, hearts, things that take more than blood to sign off and express.

But here I am, awake now and still not returning, a ghost walking the length and breadth of my days.

This is where it has ended and will continue to end. A man—perhaps he sees himself as a moth—smashed and humbled, at the foot of a lamppost, his Christmas tree.

ABOUT THE AUTHORS AND THEIR STORIES*

Gopal Baratham (1935–2002) His fiction is distinguished by a distinctive style that is satiric and ironic, directed at issues like political dissent that pushes boundaries in Singapore writing. "The Leg Glance" is taken from *The City of Forgetting*, published in 2001. A few of his novels are also published in London.

Don Bosco Loves reading and writing, and reading about writing, and writing about reading. The story included here first appeared in a short story collection and has been featured in *Mining for Meaning*, published in 2009. His latest project is *The Secret of Monk's Hill*, an urban fantasy for young readers.

Colin Cheong (born 1965) He has published short stories and novels. His short stories, especially those in the collection *Life Cycle of Homo Sapiens, Male*, first published in 1992, contain sharp observations of male-female relationships from which the story included here is taken. They are well-made stories. His most recent books are *Polite Fiction* and *The Colin Cheong Collection*, both published in 2011.

---

* Except for one author, information about the rest represented in this anthology can be found in Google, Wikipedia or Infopedia. Readers are directed to these sources for more information.

Felix Cheong (born 1965) He has published three books of poems and novels for young readers. This story, "It's a Wonderful Lie", is taken from his first collection of short stories *Vanishing Point*, to be published in 2012. There is a poetic quality in his stories apparent in this story.

Goh Sin Tub (1927–2007) Like Lim Thean Soo, he lived through the same period and also wrote about the Japanese occupation of Singapore, of which "The Shoes of My Sensei" is an excellent example. He was a prolific author who mixed fact and fiction in his stories and anecdotes. The story included here is taken from *One Singapore*, published in 1998.

Ho Minfong (born 1951) She has written many novels set in Southeast Asia. What distinguishes them is their ability to appeal to both young and mature readers. Her writing are mostly realistic and the story included here, "Birds of Paradise", stands out because it is allegorical in its use of the Aesopian fable. It is taken from *Journeys*, published in 2008.

Philip Jeyaretnam (born 1964) He was written short stories and novels. His first book, *First Loves*, published in 1987, made literary history by staying on the Times Bookshop bestseller lists for months. The story in this selection works on a subtle, symbolic level that is rare in Singaporean short fiction, and is taken from his collected works, *Tigers in Paradise*, published in 2004.

David Leo He has published short stories, poems and novels. The story included here is taken from the short story collection *Ah… The Fragrance of Durians*, published in 1993.

Catherine Lim (born 1942) A prolific writer of fiction and certainly the best known of Singaporean authors internationally. She is also known for her trenchant commentary on Singapore politics. Most of her novels were first published in London. This story comes from a collection of ghost stories *They Do Return… But Gently Lead Them Back*, first published in 1983. Not many readers are aware of this foray of Catherine Lim into the popular genre.

Suchen Christine Lim (born 1948) One of Singapore's leading novelists, her novel *Fistful of Colours*, published in 1992, won the first Singapore Literature Prize Award. Her late entry into the short story category came with her first collection *The Lies that Build a Marriage*, published in 2007. "Gloria", included here, was first published in Malaysia in 2009, anthologised in a book in Indonesia and translated into Spanish in 2011.

Jeffery Lim He has two collections of short stories, *Faith and Lies* published in 1999 and *The Coffin That Wouldn't Bury* published in 2008. Some of his stories are experimental, including the one included here, which is taken from his first book.

Lim Thean Soo (1924–1991) He was an eyewitness to the process of colonisation, decolonisation and the Japanese Occupation of Singapore, and about these he wrote with much insight and compassion. "The Expatriate" in this collection is a good example.

O Thiam Chin He has published two books of short stories, *Free-Falling Man* in 2006 and *Never been Better* in 2009. His stories have been widely anthologised in Singapore, Malaysia and Hong Kong.

S. Rajaratnam (1915–2006) Born in Ceylon (present day Sri Lanka) and raised in Seremban, Malaysia. He was in London during World War II, where he published short stories in international journals and wrote radio plays. He returned to Singapore in 1947, co-founded the People's Action Party (PAP), was the first Minister of Culture in self-governing Singapore in 1959 and the first Foreign Minister of independent Singapore in 1965. The story included here "The Terrorist" is taken from *The Short Stories and Radio Plays of S. Rajaratnam*, edited by Irene Ng and published in 2011.

Alfian Sa'at (born 1977) Undoubtedly one of Singapore's most versatile authors with a repute as an enfant terrible, he writes in both English and Malay. Best known for his controversial plays, he has also published two books of poetry and a collection of stories called *Corridor*. His poems and plays have won many awards.

Kirpal Singh (born 1949)   He has published poems, short stories and edited many books and is one of the best promoters of Singapore writing internationally. He is also an expert in creative thinking. The story included here is taken from an international collection of pieces about the Hollywood actress Ava Gardner.

Tan Mei Ching   Her latest book is a travel narrative, *Towards the Blue: Adventures of a City Wimp*, published in 2007. The story included here is taken from a book of short stories, *Crossing Distance*, published in 1996.

Claire Tham (born 1967)   She has published short stories and a novel. Her stories are relatively long, unique in that they do not observe the conventions of the traditional short story and have the occasional difficult diction. The story included here is taken from her second book *Saving the Rainforest and Other Stories*, first published in 1993. Her works are collected in *The Claire Tham Collection*, published in 2011.

Simon Tay (born 1961)   He has written poems, short stories, a book of travel with political/cultural commentary, and a novel. *Stand Alone*, his book of short stories published in 1991, contains experimental stories. His novel, *City of Small Blessings*, won the Singapore Literature Prize in 2010. I have included "The Phenwick Phenomenon" as an interesting example of a 'campus' tale.

Arthur Yap (1943–2004)   One of the most original poets to write, not only in Singapore, but internationally. His poetry is influenced by his linguistic studies and this shows in the story selected here. He is also a noted painted who has held several one-man shows.

Robert Yeo Cheng Chuan (born 1940)   Like Baratham, he also writes about political dissent in his plays, *The Singapore Trilogy*, published in 2001. He has also written poems, a novel, libretti and his memoir, *Routes 1940–75*, published in 2011. He came late to the genre of short story writing.